The
Shattering

Karen Healey

LITTLE, BROWN AND COMPANY
New York   Boston

Copyright © 2011 by Karen Healey
Reading Group Guide adapted from *The Shattering* Educator's Guide copyright © 2011 by Hachette Book Group, Inc.

Little, Brown and Company

Hachette Book Group
237 Park Avenue, New York, NY 10017
Visit our website at www.lb-teens.com

Little, Brown and Company is a division of Hachette Book Group, Inc.
The Little, Brown name and logo are trademarks of Hachette Book Group, Inc.

The publisher is not responsible for websites (or their content) that are not owned by the publisher.

First Paperback Edition: February 2013
First published in hardcover in September 2011 by Little, Brown and Company

The Shattering Educator's Guide prepared by Anne Quirk

Library of Congress Cataloging-in-Publication Data

Healey, Karen.
The shattering / by Karen Healey. — 1st ed.
p. cm.
Summary: When a rash of suicides disturbs Summerton, an oddly perfect tourist town on the west coast of New Zealand, the younger siblings of the dead boys become suspicious and begin an investigation that reveals dark secrets and puts them in grave danger.
ISBN 978-0-316-12572-7 (hc) / ISBN 978-0-316-12573-4 (pb)
[1. Suicide — Fiction. 2. Murder — Fiction. 3. Supernatural — Fiction. 4. New Zealand — Fiction. 5. Mystery and detective stories.] I. Title.
PZ7.H3438Sh 2011 [Fic] — dc22
2010047996

10 9 8 7 6 5 4 3 2 1

RRD-C

Printed in the United States of America

For my younger siblings, Scott, Ben, and
Gina, the first players in my first stories

And for Carla, who knows all about families,
born and chosen

CHAPTER ONE
Keri

$\frac{7}{}$

THE FIRST TIME I BROKE MY ARM, I WAS READY for it.

I was seven years old, and Janna van der Zaag and I were playing in her backyard. Janna's backyard was a fantastic place for kids—a big dollhouse and a lot of bush out back for playing hide-and-seek in and a brand-new zip line her dad had made, sloping from a tall platform built into the sturdiest tree down to a brace attached to the next sturdiest.

Janna had been using the zip line for days, and she flew

down with style, blond hair like a banner, the T-bar gripped tightly in her hands. I climbed the ladder and clung there as she ran the T-bar back up to me on its long rope. The zip line hadn't seemed so high up from the ground.

What if I fell off and broke my arm? I thought. And I mean I really thought. I pictured it in my mind, working out the way it could happen and what I should do if it did. I decided that a bone would go *crunch* or *crack*, and I would sit up and cradle my arm and yell, "Janna, get your mum!" and then go to the doctor in the family's big blue van that fit all the van der Zaag kids for Sunday Mass.

Then I opened my eyes, grabbed the T-bar, and took off flying all the way down the wire, screaming laughter at the rush of flight. My landing was perfect, and I ran the T-bar back up to Janna for her turn, heart jumping with joy and terror.

My body was so free.

On the fourth time down the line, my palms were too sweaty. They slipped, I fell, my left arm went *crack*, and I yelled, "Janna, get your mum!" before her big blue eyes could even fill with tears.

Everyone praised me for being so brave, but I had still been scared. I had only known what to do if the worst happened.

After that, it just seemed a good idea to be prepared. I hung a go-bag on my door in case of a fire or an earthquake and put a mini first-aid kit in my backpack, and I rehearsed possible disasters in my head, over and over, until I was sure I knew how to react.

I knew it sounded a little bit crazy, and I stopped telling

anyone about it when Hemi Koroheke called me creepy and, with smug emphasis, neurotic, which was our Year Eight Word of the Day.

But I did it anyway. I had plans for what eulogy to give if both my parents were hit by a car, how to escape or attract help if I were kidnapped, and how to survive if I were lost in the bush. It wasn't as if I thought all these things were likely to happen. But I knew they could, and if they did, I wanted to be ready.

In the end, it didn't do me any good. Because I didn't have a plan for what to do if my older brother put Dad's shotgun in his mouth and pulled the trigger with his toes.

My mistake.

I found Jake—I mean, I found the body—but I don't remember that. A couple of weeks later I couldn't find my favorite pair of jeans, and Mum said she threw them out because of the blood, and I suddenly remembered the feeling of something heavy in my lap. I might have imagined it—I don't know. But I think it was real, that memory of wet weight across my thighs.

That's it, though.

Jake killed himself and he didn't leave a note, and I lost bits of my memory and my favorite pair of jeans. I'll never get a pair like those again—they don't make that style anymore. They were scuffed in all the right places and cut to fit my short legs and big bum, and they were comfortable and a choice faded dark blue that looked good with everything.

That's not a metaphor. I loved those jeans.

I loved my brother more. Jake was my favorite person—my

3

best friend, my first supporter, the last one to get angry with me when I said something that was just too sarcastic. At nineteen, he was two years older than me, but we weren't one of those sibling pairs who hated each other as kids and then hit adolescence and got along. We'd always been that close. My first word was *Chay*.

There had been no warning. He didn't give away his possessions or say things like "It'll all be over soon." His girlfriend, Sandra-Claire, swore up and down that he didn't act depressed or fight with her, and even though she is a heinous bleached and bony bitch who told me that if I kept cutting my hair short everyone would think I was a lesbian (and she didn't say *lesbian*), I believed that Jake hadn't done any of that stuff, because I knew he would have told me first.

I knew what to do if someone you love showed signs of suicide, because we'd studied it in Health. It's a myth that people who talk about it aren't going to do it; 74 percent of suicides give a warning sign of some kind, and if Jake had ever mentioned it, I would have had a plan. A plan for what to say, how to tell Mum and Dad, what to do if he did it and failed, what to do if he did it and succeeded, what to do if he did it and succeeded and I found the body. But he didn't and I didn't, and it happened anyway. It made no sense at all.

It was a lot easier to think about how irrational Jake's killing himself was than to think about how my insides had been ripped out.

Because Jake's death was a suicide, we nearly didn't get to hold a proper *tangi*, in case all the celebration and ceremony for the dead encouraged other kids to copy him. But I think

Nanny Hinekura put her foot down, and all the family on Dad's side turned up at the *marae* farther down the coast. It was three days of people crowding around us and talking about Jake. All the stories: how he'd bagged his first deer; how he'd gotten his first swimming medal by crashing into the end of the pool; how one Christmas he'd played PlayStation for twenty-one hours against any cousin who'd take him on, and he'd fallen asleep in front of the TV, thumbs still twitching. I liked the stories a lot better than the formal speeches, which were mostly in Māori. I'm all for valuing our cultural heritage and that, and I'd taken Māori for two years to make Nanny Hinekura happy, but it turned out I was just no good at languages.

Jake was much better. He would have translated for me.

The mourners cried and laughed and talked—so much noise, everyone saying "Jake, Jake, Jake," echoing the way my heart beat out his name. When everyone slept, on the mattresses spread out under the high carved rafters of the *wharenui* roof, I could feel the thick emotion leeching out of them, sticking to my skin like steam. I was surrounded by love, but it felt like I was smothered by it. I'd been at tangi before and watched grieving families take comfort. But I couldn't. Not with Jake in the closed coffin beside us instead of sitting with me, adding his own stories to this mix.

I gripped Mum's hand, very pale in mine, and didn't let go.

Once we went back to Summerton, I didn't go to school for the last bit of the year—there was no point with the Christmas holidays coming so soon, and I got compassionate consideration on all my final assessments anyway. Mum cleaned the house as if she would die if she didn't, and Dad had to go back to work. I walked a lot, trying to avoid people who would say useless, comforting things, like "Well, I'm sure he's in a better place."

I couldn't believe any of that crap. The room he'd died in had been blessed and a farewell *karakia* chanted, but Jake wasn't going to take the long trip to Cape Reinga to find the home of Dad's ancestors. He wasn't in heaven with some white-bearded God. He wasn't hanging around, keeping an eye on me. And he sure couldn't do all three, which was what Nanny Hinekura seemed to believe. Those were just stories, things people made up to make the world nicer. How did they know? Where was the proof?

No, Jake was dead. He wasn't in a better place. Everything left of him was in the ground, where it would rot.

Two weeks after the burial, I was in Summerton's only department store, trying to find a replacement pair of jeans. Janna van der Zaag walked up to me and said, "If you want to find out who murdered your brother, follow me."

So I did.

Janna was cute and short when she was seven. Now she was tall and skinny and gorgeous in a perky blond-and-milky-complexion way, which was probably one of the reasons why she put on eye makeup like she was painting the house and dyed her hair every two weeks (right now it was shiny purple-black) and wore black velvet blazers and plaid skirts.

The other reason was that she was in a band.

She looked right at home in the alley between Lauer's Department Store and Mimi's Muffins, leaning up against the redbrick wall behind the trash-filled Dumpster, wanting to talk to me about murder.

"Hi, Stardust," I said. "I thought you only came out at night, with the other vampires." Ever since primary school, everyone had called Janna Stardust: van der Zaag → Zigzag → Ziggy Stardust → Stardust. So it's not actually a cool nickname, but she acts like it is.

Normally this is the sort of thing that gets me a reputation for being a bitch, but Janna didn't seem to care that I'd just called her a bloodsucking creature of the night. She probably thought it was a compliment.

"Do you believe me?" she said. "About the murder?"

I looked at my fingernails, all bitten down to raw nubs. "Not yet. But it makes sense."

She nodded. "No note, right? No warning?"

My interest sharpened. "Right."

"I knew it. Exactly the same thing happened to Schuyler."

I very nearly said, "Who's Schuyler?" but then my brain got in the way. Schuyler was Janna's older brother. He'd killed himself ten years ago by hanging himself in the garage. It happened about three weeks after I broke my arm on the zip line.

"Someone murdered your brother?" I said instead, and Janna nodded again, tugging at her collar with black-painted fingernails. Hers weren't bitten at all.

"And yours."

I leaned my head to one side. "Huh."

"You're weirdly calm about this," she said.

"I'll cry later," I told her. She rolled her eyes, so she might have thought I was being sarcastic, but I was telling the truth. I felt like a girl-shaped open sore, walking through a world made up of salt and lemon juice. But there was a limit to how much anyone could cry in public, and I'd reached that limit at the tangi, tears rolling down my face while the aunties clustered around me.

I refocused. "If you think they were murdered, shouldn't you go to the police?"

She laughed. "In this town? I don't know who the murderer is, but he'd know I'd been talking in about ten minutes. Twenty, tops." She made a gesture at her throat. "And then I might 'suicide.'"

She had a point, even if she was being typically melodramatic about it. It didn't take long for gossip to get around Summerton.

"I want you to meet someone," she said.

"Who?"

"This guy I know. He gets here from Auckland tomorrow."

I choked on a laugh. "Wait, he's a tourist?"

"Sione's a good guy!" she said, really defensively, as if being a tourist and being a good guy were normally mutually exclusive. As far as I could tell, they were. Summerton is a tourist town. People got worried a while ago when an earthquake destroyed the famous limestone Steps to Heaven, which stood just off the coast, but the tourists keep coming every summer, and the money keeps rolling in. In fact, there are more tourists now than ever before. Other towns on the coast have lost young people to the cities and old people to retirement. Thanks to the tourists, Summerton's still going strong.

But no one actually likes the tourists, though people like Janna are happy to party with them. In my experience, most of the tourists are rich snobs, and the ones our age are only interested in surfing, snogging people of the opposite gender (mostly other tourists), and leaving puddles of vomit drying on the streets for me to dodge when I did my paper route.

"He lost someone, too," Janna said.

"Has he looked under the couch?" I asked.

Janna gave me a look that said I wasn't following the script and then proved she had a sense of humor by giggling. But she looked guilty afterward. "Are you doing okay?" she asked, and her voice was soft and kind.

Up until then, I had been just about enjoying the conversation. Sure, Jake had been a big part of it, like every other conversation I'd had for the past few weeks. But Janna hadn't bothered to keep her voice low and her gestures gentle, or even, right up to that point, ask me how I was.

"How do you think I feel?" I said.

"How I felt," she said. "How Sione feels."

I rocked back on my heels and considered it.

"We'll meet tomorrow at the Kahawai to show you something," she said. "Eight PM. Okay?"

"Okay."

"Well," she said, and made a sort of uncertain gesture. "And…I can't believe I didn't start by telling you that I'm really sorry. Because I am."

"It's okay. We're not exactly friends."

"Well, we used to be. And Jake was always nice to me."

Jake was always nice to everyone. I took a deep, deep breath against the hurt and the tears. "See you tomorrow."

Other people might have tried to hug me, but Janna just nodded and walked away, the thick soles of her red platform shoes making no sound on the asphalt. I sniffled for a while, then took more deep breaths of leftover-food stink. How could anyone wear black velvet in this weather? She must have been sweating like a pig under all that makeup.

I wondered if she was pulling some kind of joke. I didn't really know much about her now, and people change a lot from when they were seven. We didn't play pretend anymore; I played rugby, and she played bass. Not that you couldn't do both, but we didn't. We were in the same English class (I was okay; she sucked), and we knew each other enough to say "Hi" and "Good game" and "Good gig."

That was about it.

But I was pretty sure she wouldn't do this to me, not after Schuyler. Her intense face had said she believed every word coming out of her mouth. So she was delusional or had been fooled by this Sione guy—or she was right. Jake had been murdered.

I scrubbed my eyes with my T-shirt hem. I didn't have what I'd come for, but I didn't want to go back to Lauer's and buy inferior jeans from Candace Green or let anyone in Summerton see me and think, *That poor Keri, she's been crying again.*

I had to get through the holidays. The holidays and then one more year of school and the holidays again. Then I could get out of here. Go to uni in Dunedin, or head to London for a working holiday, or anything to get away from Summerton and the room I couldn't go into and the memory of Jake laughing all over town and heavy and wet in my lap.

I rode home with the sun on my back, warm through my T-shirt. It rains a lot on the West Coast—outsiders joke that it should be called the Wet Coast—but Summerton has the kind of summers you read about in books. Long, warm, dry days, perfect for swimming or lazing around with a book or doing a bit of a hike in the green and shady bush. But maybe not so good for biking along Iron Road, up the hill, past the fancy hotels and time-share apartments, to the places where real people actually lived. There was sweat pooling unpleasantly at the base of my spine.

I coasted down the concrete driveway, leaned the bike against the garage, and slammed my way into the kitchen. I needed a shower, a cold drink, and some quiet to think about what Janna had said.

Mum was waiting for me, still in her clean white blouse and black trousers, but her sleek, blond hair was falling out of its French knot, and her eyes had that red pinched look.

"Where have you been?" she snapped.

"I went to buy jeans."

"You didn't tell me you were going out!"

"You were at work."

"You could have dropped in. You have to tell me when you go places, Keri!"

"No, I don't," I said, and she reached across the kitchen island and slapped me. I stared at her for a moment, then slapped her back.

"Oh, *God*," she said, and spun away to lean over the counter.

"I won't do it, Mum," I said. "Not ever." *Damn Jake anyway*, I thought, and then felt guilty for the rage. My hand was stinging, and pain and anger and guilt went around and around in my brain. Grief was so exhausting.

"I know." She gulped and wiped her eyes. "I'm sorry. I had a tough day at work, and then you weren't here and I worried. I shouldn't have slapped you."

"I'm sorry, too," I said. I was wondering about evidence. Maybe there'd been something peculiar about Jake's body—a dropped cigarette butt or something, anything to point to a murder and not a suicide, something to prove that Janna wasn't being weird and crazy. The police had investigated, of course, with officers coming across from district headquarters in Nelson to assist the locals and everything, but they'd mostly seemed concerned with making sure that Dad had his firearms license and had followed the safety rules.

Which he had. The shotgun and the two rifles were always unloaded and locked up when they weren't in use, and the ammunition was stored separately. But Jake had his own license, and he knew where the keys were.

The cops had seemed satisfied with that, though there had to be an inquest anyway after the holidays.

Mum might have seen something more. I found the body,

but she found me holding it, and there were no gaps in her memory.

But I wasn't going to ask her now, when she was slapping me and home early from her first day back at work.

"I saw Janna van der Zaag today," I said instead.

Mum was pouring herself a glass of water. "How's she?" she said, and then turned, face crinkling. "Didn't her brother—"

"Yes," I said. "She said she knows how I feel."

Like no one else did. No one in Summerton had died so young or so violently for years and years. No one else knew what to say.

"You two used to be such good friends."

"I'm meeting her for dinner tomorrow. To meet a friend of hers. If that's okay?"

"Of course, Keri," she said. "Here, let me—where are you going?" I let her reach for her handbag on the table, even though I had my own money from the paper route and I knew Mum and Dad were running short. The funeral and burial had been expensive. The family had given us *koha* to help, of course, crisp notes in clean envelopes, but the costs added up.

But this was Mum's way of apologizing for hitting me. So I stood there and waited for the cash.

"Janna said the Kahawai."

Mum hesitated and then pulled out a purple note instead of a green. I blinked at the fifty-dollar note but tucked it into my pocket.

"Try the snapper," she suggested, as friendly and detached as if I were one of the hotel guests. Then her face stopped being Ms. Lillian Pedersen-Doherty, concierge extraordinaire, and went back to being Mum. "No drinking, home by ten thirty."

"Yes, ma'am," I said, hoping to make her smile.

She was looking at my empty hands. "Didn't you find any?"

"Huh?"

"Jeans."

"Oh. No. Nothing that really fit the same."

She nodded again, rubbing her eyes. I had a sudden vision of what she would look like when she was old. "I'm going to lie down. Can you scrub some potatoes?"

"Sure," I said.

I could scrub spuds and tell her where I was going when I left the house and take her apology money, and none of it would do anything to really help. Mum needed Jake back; she needed him to have never done it. I couldn't do anything about that.

Unless he hadn't.

Right then, in the kitchen, I decided that Janna had to be right. Jake had been murdered.

I felt the world click into place again. I had a plan for what to do if a member of my family was murdered.

It went (1) find the killer, (2) make sure he was guilty, (3) destroy him.

Completely.

14

CHAPTER TWO
Sione

✝

SIONE INCHED CLOSER TO THE BUS WINDOW and wished, for about the 912th time, that he'd had the guts to say no to Janna.

"So you're traveling alone?" the elderly white woman sitting next to him persisted. "It's a real family vacation spot, I thought."

Sione nodded. She'd been talking since the bus left Nelson, and he had managed not to say much, which was almost as good as not having to speak at all. She probably thought she was being nice, but conversation with strangers was hard and small talk was torture.

"You kids are all so independent these days," she said. "I'm always surprised by what your parents let you do."

Me, too, he thought, but managed to come up with, "I'm meeting friends."

"Ahhhh. A group of you, is it? Are you going early or late?"

"Friends who live in Summerton." Well, Janna was his friend, sort of. This Keri girl was an unknown quantity. If Janna was wrong, and Keri thought they were nutcases and started talking, it could ruin everything. Mum would be on the next flight back from Samoa.

But when Janna suggested bringing Keri in, he hadn't said no.

"This is beautiful, isn't it?" the woman said, and leaned over Sione to stare out the window at the intricate shades of green that made up the view. "Is this your first time, too?"

"No. I've come with family before." Mum and Dad in front, and he and Matthew in the back, up and down the road that wound through the Karamea peninsula, over the hill to its tip, where Summerton, the most beautiful place in the world, was nestled in the bay. Matthew would have been able to talk to this lady. He'd have charmed her and flirted a little, but not too much, and by the time she got off the bus, she'd be eager to tell all her friends about the nice Pacific Islander boy who'd been so polite.

Instead of the sullen P.I. boy who kept staring at his fingernails.

"Are you going for a holiday?" Sione said, and then wanted to put his head through the window's glass. Of course she was going for a holiday. Retired old ladies didn't go to vacation spots for business.

Stupid, stupid, stupid. Sione Felise, total spaz.

But she gave him a kind look and nodded. "Yes, dear. With the lawn bowls club. I'm heading down a little early to make sure everything's prepared."

Sione nodded, aware that his cheeks were hot with embarrassment. She was probably being nice because he looked so awkward. Which meant that she would have to be nice to him until the end of time, because he was *always* awkward. He could try to make it up to her, though. "Would you like to swap seats? The view's best as you come in."

"Oh, no, I'm fine, dear."

But she leaned over him anyway as the bus rose and then dropped over the last big hill, the bay spread out before them. The entire bus held its collective breath, staring down at heaven.

By the time he could blink, his eyes were stinging, and nearly everyone on the bus was wiping away tears. The Summerton magic, the tourism videos called it, though it never looked that good on TV. In person, it was nearly impossible to look away.

He felt wrong about it, though. It should have been less beautiful now that Matthew was dead.

He got to the meeting spot far too early. The restaurant was already busy. Besides him and two Asian couples by the big windows overlooking the balcony, everyone else was white. The only person in the restaurant who looked anything like him was the guy behind the bar, waiting in his black apron with his big brown arms folded over his barrel chest.

The bartender saw Sione looking and winked as he went past.

Matthew would have gone over and said hi, and they'd have been lifelong mates after five minutes. Sione nodded, jerky, and let the blond waitress show him to the private room Janna had reserved.

It was a little alcove beside the balcony with a view of the sea, probably meant for honeymooners, and maybe too small for three people. But it had its own door that closed, and that was important. Sione didn't like strangers listening to him at the best of times, but especially not when it was this kind of information.

He tugged on his pressed cuffs. He was worried about the shirt, which was an Elusiv design, olive with subtle black stitching picking out a pattern on the back and at the side. Would it impress Janna, or would she think he was showing off? He hadn't really brought anything cheaper. Maybe he should have gone full out in the other direction and worn a tie.

He checked his watch and tapped his fingers on the table.

The waitress knocked and opened the door. "Drink while you wait?" she asked.

"Orange juice. Please."

"Sure thing. What's your name? You look familiar."

"Sione Felise."

Her eyes went a little wide. No way people had heard of his

18

dad down here. No *way.* Maybe she just recognized him because they'd been coming here for so long for the holidays. Or maybe she'd hooked up with Matthew sometime.

She didn't say anything, though, just, "I'll get your juice."

He told himself he was imagining the look she gave him as she left, leaving the door open. "Van der Zaag party?" he heard her say outside. "This way."

Sione looked up, hoping for Janna. It wasn't, of course.

This Keri looked a little bit Islander herself. She was short and sturdy, with short, dark hair lying shaggily around the small features of her snub-nosed face and skin a few shades lighter than his medium golden-brown. Green eyes, taking him in, his fancy shirt and black trousers.

He tried not to steel himself too obviously to the task of greeting her and stood up, holding out his hand. "Hi, Keri? I'm Sione."

Keri's little fingers squeezed around his in a firm, warm grip. She looked at her rumpled cargo shorts and baggy, dusty-green T-shirt. "I should have dressed up."

"Uh, it's okay."

"I knew that I should have dressed up. I just didn't think of it." Her voice was nice, soft and sort of furry. "It's hard to think sometimes. Since it happened. Does that sound crazy?"

So she wasn't much for small talk, either. "Not really," he heard himself say. "Right after Matthew... died, I thought I could hear him talking to me in my dreams. Whenever the phone rang and stopped ringing before I could pick up, I thought it was him checking in. That's crazy." Oh, Jesus. He had told a girl he'd just met that he was a head case.

But she didn't run screaming from the room or shoot him down with the loser look. Instead she gave him a half smile and said, "My nanny believes things like that. But you don't think that now?"

"No," he said, which was mostly true. "It's been ... how long for you? Since?"

"Nineteen days." She said it automatically, without having to count, and he recognized that, too.

"Oh, man. You're allowed to still be crazy."

Keri grinned at him properly then, and her green eyes lit right up, crinkling at the edges. "What's your surname? Janna didn't say."

"Felise. It's Samoan," he added, and then felt like a dick. "I mean ... I'm Samoan."

She only nodded. "My dad's *Kāi Tahu*, my mum's *Pākehā*. How long for you?"

"Six months, and"—he paused, thinking—"four days."

"Hey!" Janna said, walking in. Something thumped hard into the pit of Sione's stomach. The room was suddenly close and hot. *She'd* dressed up, a black strapless dress that hugged her—well, her chest—and then flared out over a stiff net petticoat and ended at her knees. She was wearing stompy black boots that laced up to her knees and shiny red gloves that fit over her elbow.

Sione knew instantly that he should have worn a tie.

"You look like an evil debutante," Keri said.

"That was the idea," Janna said, and stripped off her gloves. "God, these are hot. Hey, Sione! Looking good! Have you gotten taller since last summer?"

He had. But he still wasn't as tall as Matthew. "Little bit."

Keri leaned in, clearly not caring at all about his height. "Janna, you said Sione had something to show me."

Sione reached for his laptop, but Janna put her hand over his, and he froze, trying not to move into her touch.

"Drinks, then talk, then dinner," she decreed, and while Keri's eyebrows rose, she seemed okay with letting Janna call the waitress back.

"So how do you two know each other?" Keri asked when the drinks arrived.

Sione felt the flush start under his collarbone. "Uh, well," he began. "We met at the gelato place last year —"

"We hooked up on New Year's Eve at the Beach Bash," Janna said.

"Weren't you going out with Patrick Tan?" Keri said.

"No, we broke up before Christmas. And then he rebounded with Serena White. But then she got together with Christian Gough at New Year's, and then Patrick wanted to get back with me, and I said no chance, and then Serena changed her mind, and they hooked up again anyway." Janna shrugged. "Whatever, right? Anyway, I don't cheat." She picked up her glass.

"Oh, yes, you do," Keri said. "You married me behind the bike sheds when we were seven. We exchanged gummy rings. Does that mean nothing to you? You're a cheating whore, Stardust, and I want a divorce."

Janna snorted into her drink and flapped her hands wildly. "No fair," she protested when she got her breath back. "You're not allowed to be funny when I've got something in my mouth."

"That's what you say to all the boys." Keri sighed and turned to Sione before Janna could respond with more than stutters. "So, now talk. I guess you brought the laptop for a reason?"

He nodded and opened it without speaking. It was better to be careful with girls like Keri, all fast brain and sharp tongue; they could turn you inside out in double time. Some of his girl cousins were like that; they made a game out of it.

"Don't the black ones cost more?" Janna said enviously, staring at his laptop, and when he shrugged, she leaned over and nudged Keri. "Sione's parents are loaded."

"Not loaded," he protested. "Just...we do okay."

"Felise Finance," Janna said. "For all your investment needs."

He pulled up the spreadsheet, spun the laptop around so it faced the girls, and glared at the back of it. There was nothing to say to people about the money. He didn't have money; his dad did. And he couldn't exactly choose for his dad *not* to have it, could he?

Keri's green eyes focused on the spreadsheet. "Okay," she said. "What am I looking at?"

Now that was something he could talk about. Sione shifted his chair closer to hers. "They're arranged by year." He pointed at the columns. "That's the name. That's the date they did it. That's the location. That's the...uh, method."

"Strangulation," Keri read. "Poison. Exsanguination?"

Janna made a slashing gesture down the inside of one wrist and grimaced.

Keri's mouth twisted. "Strangulation...that's popular,

three entries. I guess that's hanging? Poison again. Carbon monoxide. Gunshot." Her voice was as flat on that as on the others, but the table rattled as her hands pressed convulsively against the edge.

"Do you see the patterns?" Sione asked.

"These all look like guys' names. The locations are all over the place, but the dates are pretty close together. One most years—you've got a few gaps here—and two this year."

"We're pretty sure there's at least one every year, around the middle of winter," Sione told her. "But I wasn't able to confirm for these three. I didn't want to add unconfirmed data." He pointed at the entry above the last one. "That's Matthew."

"And that's Jake. And Schuyler up here at the top." Keri looked up. "So these are all supposed to be suicides, I get it. But it doesn't say anything about murder."

"No," Sione agreed. "But in the year they killed themselves, every one of those guys was in Summerton for New Year's Eve. And not one of them left a note."

Keri's gaze jerked up from the screen to meet his. There was a noise outside, and they all went still, but the waitress's voice said, "It's just me. I can't open the door, could you—"

Keri got the door and took her own plate from the waitress, freeing one of her hands. "Thanks, Emily," Keri said.

The waitress leaned over Sione's shoulder to put down his plate and then paused, blinking at the laptop screen. Sione swung it closed, feeling an uncertain smile tug at his mouth. Even a fast reader couldn't have seen much, he told himself. Just a spreadsheet with some boys' names.

At any rate, the waitress didn't say anything, just wished

them happy eating. The door closed behind her with a soft click, and they all looked at one another. Sione was dying for one of the girls to break the silence.

"So what I think you're saying," Keri said at last, "is that there's a serial killer in town."

Keri didn't seem to be a very trusting person. She had questions. Lots of them. As they picked at their food, Sione and Janna tried to answer them to her satisfaction.

"He e-mailed me," Janna said. "When Matthew..." She made a waving gesture. "And I said, that's awful, Schuyler, too."

Sione nodded. That e-mail had been so stupid—a sort of long, heartsore wail to a girl he'd kissed once and thought about ever since and talked to only a couple of times on IM.

But after that e-mail, Janna had been kind.

Sione tried to ignore the mixed guilt and triumph in that thought and spoke again. "It was only a coincidence until I met Tarquin."

"*Tarquin?*" Keri said. "Did his parents hate him?"

"From what he said, pretty much. We met at a grief support group for teenagers." Keri's eyebrow flickered, and he figured she was one of those people, the tough-it-out-yourself kind. "My mum's a psychotherapist," he said, trying not to sound either defensive or preachy. "The group helped a lot. Anyway, he talked about the last family holiday he had with his brother, before he killed himself last year."

"It was in Summerton," Keri said flatly.

"And I said, hey, me, too, what a coincidence. And he got really freaked out." Sione remembered Tarquin's sudden interest interrupting his perpetual stoner haze. It had been about the only emotion Tarquin had ever shown in the group sessions. He had been a really good example of how not to deal. "Because it turned out —"

"He knew someone else whose brother had killed himself, who'd spent New Year's in Summerton."

Janna grinned. "I told you she was smart."

One of those girls. "Yes. Five years ago."

"So you asked around," Keri continued, "and you found the others."

"Well, it wasn't as easy as that." Sione rubbed his lip. Months of checking obituaries in the library, of calling families, claiming that he was doing a project or posing as someone from the Ministry of Health — whichever lie had fit the situation. Months of lying to strangers and keeping secrets from his parents. He'd hated it; he hadn't even known if he could do it. If Matthew hadn't died, he might never have known.

"But that's how it turned out," Janna said, grimacing. She'd done even more of that work than he had, listening to strangers cry on the phone.

"There are other patterns," Sione said. "Matthew was the only one who lived in Auckland. Tarquin had moved to Auckland from Blenheim when his folks split up after his brother died; the guy he knew was from Wellington. Schuyler and Jake are the only Summerton residents. All the other victims lived in separate places, scattered all over the country."

"How's that a pattern?"

"It's too neat. A quarter of New Zealand's residents live in Auckland, and almost a fifth of Summerton's yearly visitors are from the Auckland region. But only one victim—Matthew. Three-quarters of the population are in the North Island, and well over half of Summerton visitors are from there, but the victims are spread almost evenly between North and South Islanders."

"Deliberately spread out. Got it." Keri tapped the screen, leaving a greasy fingerprint. Sione winced. "What's this number?"

"Number of younger siblings."

Keri's eyebrows twitched. "They *all* had siblings?"

"They were all brothers and all the oldest. No girls, no middle or youngest children, no only children."

"Why?"

"We have no idea. But working out the motive might help us work out who the murderer is, and how he did it," Sione said. "And looking at patterns, seeing why these guys were picked, might help us with motive."

"Why don't you take this pattern to the police? They could do who and how."

Sione looked into Keri's eyes. She had brown flecks around the pupil of the left one, he noticed, even as he made his voice calm and quiet, willing her to believe. "They'll laugh at us. Or they'll be very nice and very concerned and call our parents, who will be very nice and very concerned. And then I don't know what will happen to you guys, but my mum will slap me back into therapy so fast my head will spin. They'll say it's just a weird coincidence. A lot of people come to Summerton for New Year's, and a lot of New Zealand teenagers kill themselves. New Zealand males between fifteen and twenty-five, especially."

"You can't tell anyone," Janna said. "Some of what we did to find this out—Keri, we can't tell *anyone* yet, especially not the police. We'll call them in when we find real proof and cope with whatever punishment we get then."

"It *could* be a coincidence," Keri said.

"You don't believe that," Janna told her, with more confidence than Sione felt.

"No. I know he was killed. Jake wouldn't go without saying good-bye."

Sione finally relaxed back into the chair, only realizing then that there was a thick line of sweat right up his back. *Real cool, Felise.* "Do you know if there was anything unusual about the murder scene?"

Keri shook her head. "I don't remember."

So she'd found her brother, too. Sione did remember, but he made himself think about Janna's strapless dress instead. He'd put everything he knew into Matthew's file; it was there, he could look at it when he needed to, but he didn't have to think about it right now.

"My eyes are up here," Janna said, but not like she was offended. He blushed anyway. She'd grown a bit over the year, too.

"When we find the killer," Keri said abruptly, her soft, furry voice intense with purpose, "we are going to destroy him. Completely."

Janna didn't even blink. "You bet."

When Sione was honest with himself, in the dark hours of the night, he had to admit that he hadn't liked Matthew very much. He'd loved him, but that was just a family thing — biology and proximity and shared memories mostly. If they hadn't been related, they wouldn't have gone anywhere near each other. Matthew's friends were either morons or too cool to bother with Sione, and Sione didn't exactly have any friends. But that could have changed; Matthew might have stopped being a homophobic dick who thought caring about clothes made Sione a fa—a gay person, and maybe Sione would have developed an interest in sports or cars, and they could have been mates as well as brothers.

Sione hadn't gotten a chance to like him, and now he never would.

"Yeah," he said, and stood up. "Whoever murdered them will pay." He shoved the chair away a bit harder than he'd meant to and looked out the window as he righted it.

The Kahawai was set into one of the three hills, high enough to look down on the town and the bay. It was getting late, but it was the high days of summer, and the sun was just setting over the water.

Sione went dead still. "Wow," he whispered, knowing what was happening but unable to drag his eyes away. It was the same gut-wrenching awe that had grabbed him when the bus had gone over the hill. "It's so beautiful."

The girls exchanged looks. "I guess, yeah?" Janna said. "It's a nice evening."

It was the kind of thing she'd said last summer, the same

uncaring incomprehension whenever he'd tried to talk about Summerton. Other visitors seemed to understand, but the locals walked around in this paradise every day without paying any attention. His mum said they were just used to it, but how could anyone get used to this?

He tried again. "You don't get it. I've been back to Samoa with my folks and to the Twelve Apostles off the Australian coast, and they're really great. But this..." He waved at the view: the green curve of the bay; the neat lines of the white buildings all aglow in the dying light, in sharp contrast with the soft gray-white sand of the beach; and beyond, the shimmering, red-gold sea. "Summerton is the most beautiful place in the world."

There was a brief pause.

"My parents say the Steps to Heaven were a little bit like the Apostles," Keri offered at last.

Janna laughed. "Remember how, just after they came down, the council was like, 'Let's rebuild them in plastic'?"

Keri snorted. "Some tourist attraction that would have been. The idea was to get people to keep coming, not scare them off."

"Why were they worried?" Sione asked. "This is just...it's enough by itself. For anyone." And he breathed deeply, trying to inhale all the beauty and calm of the sun-drenched bay.

CHAPTER THREE
Janna

★

JANNA CONSIDERED TELLING SIONE THAT taking deep, patient breaths was distracting and not very attractive, but that might have given him the wrong idea. It was summer, and there were tourists—new guys, *different* guys—who could appreciate a girl with a sense of style and a mean knack for bass. Not that Sione didn't appreciate her—he was just kind of like, well, not a puppy, because she didn't like dogs, and she liked Sione. A kitten. That needed to stop shedding on her clothes.

Of course the *main* priority was getting even for Schuyler, and Jake, and Matthew, and the others she hadn't even known. But she couldn't be focused on that all the time, because it would look suspicious and also because she would go completely mental.

Emily Rackard rang up their bill. Emily had been a few years ahead of them at school, and she'd gotten some crap there. She wasn't pretty, she wasn't smart, she wasn't sporty, and she was a teacher's daughter. Janna liked Mrs. Rackard okay, but she wasn't everyone's favorite teacher. Janna wondered if it was weird for Emily to carry drinks and clear plates for kids who were younger than she was or maybe even for the people her own age who had bullied her and gone on to better-paying jobs in the town. It would be super weird for Janna, which was yet another reason for her to get out of Summerton.

"Did you enjoy your meal?" Emily asked, red lipstick flashing on her crooked teeth. Janna felt even more sorry for her. Janna had a Grape Dracula shade of lipstick that she'd worn only once. Awesome color, but it had rubbed off on her teeth and smeared around her mouth like a big clown smile.

"Very nice, thank you," Sione said automatically, in his richest, politest voice. He reached for the bill and then looked nervously at the two girls. "Uh, I'll get this?"

Keri frowned, but Janna said, "Sure. Next one's on us," and Keri looked away. Janna was a feminist, too, but if someone could afford to pay more than the other two could and wanted to, it only made sense to let him do it. Anyway, she was nearly out of babysitting money after buying her new amp, and Keri's paper route couldn't be bringing in much.

Sione paid with a credit card, as if he'd done it lots of times before, and for a moment Janna wished so hard for rich parents that it hurt. Then she got over it.

Emily pointed at Sione's laptop, which he was hugging like a baby, except he would probably have been a lot more awkward with a baby. The laptop fit him. "You seemed pretty busy."

"Business meeting," Janna said at the same time Keri said, "Special project."

Sione smiled at Emily. "Working out Janna's big break," he said, which was pretty smart, but did he have to go revealing the innermost secrets of her heart? In *this* town?

"I'm going pro!" Janna said, posing with her hand on her hip. "Not until after I finish school," she added hastily because she didn't want Mrs. Rackard calling her mum. "But you know, long-term plan."

"Wouldn't you have to leave Summerton?" Emily said, pale blue eyes puzzled.

"Well, *yeah*," Janna said.

Her high school career was massively more successful than Emily's had been, but there was a whole world out there, and New Zealand was all lonely at the edge of the map, and Summerton was the loneliest place in New Zealand. Westport and Greymouth were down the coast and close-ish, but they didn't count, and tiny little Karamea was up the coast and closer, but it counted even less. Summerton was a three-and-a-half-hour drive to Nelson and nearly *six* to Christchurch and decent shopping.

She, Janna van der Zaag, could be a star. She wasn't good at the study part of school, but she was *great* at bass, and she knew she looked right (which shouldn't matter, but totally did). Most important, she wanted success really, really badly and would work her ass off to get it.

Everyone else could choose to stay in Summerton and work in the restaurants and hotels and cute boutique stores, and then they could get married and have kids and settle down and *die*, but she was going to take care of Schuyler's murderer and then skip the hell out of town. No more bratty sisters and fighting parents and small-town snoops knowing everything about anything she'd ever done from the day she was born. She could be *anyone* in a real city, and she wanted to find out who.

In fact, she couldn't work out why *Emily* hadn't left.

Some of this must have shown on Janna's face because Emily was frowning at her with deep wrinkles that were flaking her makeup all over her forehead.

"Say hi to your mum for us," Keri said, and Emily relaxed and smiled.

"I will. Have a nice night."

Keri led them outside, which, after being in the air-conditioned restaurant, was kind of like walking into an oven. Janna grimaced in the heat, but Keri just started walking to the parking lot, where her bike was chained to the cast-iron fence. "What's the plan?" she asked.

"First we try to find out if someone left town during the times people died," Sione told her.

"You're sure he's a local? Some tourists come every year."

"That's what I said," Janna said, brightening.

Keri looked thoughtful, then blinked. "No, but he has to be a local. Because of Schuyler and Jake."

"Jake is anomalous," Sione said in his I'm-a-big-math-brain voice. "He was the second murder in a year and the second murder in one place. It could be a copycat —"

"Copying *what*?" Janna cried. "No one but us knows it's murder!"

"— or an escalation, or something we can't account for yet," Sione continued, much quieter. "However, all the victims overlap over one time period — New Year's Eve — and at least a couple of days before. And we shouldn't assume the murderer's a he."

"Most serial killers are men," Keri said, which was just the sort of creepy fact Keri had liked to pull out when they were kids.

"Statistical likelihood isn't statistical certainty," Sione told her. "I agree the killer's more *likely* to be a man, and a local, but we shouldn't rule out women or visitors. At any rate, the murderer probably chooses the victims during that time, so it makes sense to look for people who were here at that point and away when each victim was killed."

Keri's eyes narrowed. "It's the twenty-second today. You're saying that we've got less than ten days to find out who it is and stop them?"

"No, only to find them," Janna said. "We have plenty of time to gather evidence and take it to the police after we work out who he — who *it* is. The murderer didn't kill the boys until winter."

"Except Jake," Sione said quietly.

"Well, we'll work fast," Janna decided. "We did lots of it already. I checked the electoral roll at the library and ruled out

34

everyone in town under twenty-six, 'cause they would have been too young when the murders started, and everyone who I definitely remember was here when Matthew died, like the teachers and the guys at Books 'n' Tunes. We can probably narrow it down a bit more tomorrow. But Sione figures the best thing is to look for suspicious people watching potential victims — guys who are fifteen to twenty-five with younger siblings."

Keri almost smiled. "So your plan is to go undercover... to hang around with guys."

"It's a sacrifice," Janna said. "But I will totally make it."

Keri counted off on her fingers. "Okay. So between now and New Year's Eve, we identify as many boys as possible who fit the pattern and are potential victims. We watch adults around them carefully for any suspicious activity. At the same time, we work it from the other end and identify as many adults as possible who were out of Summerton on the dates of the murders." She looked thoughtful. "We need information, which you've got, and a base of operations."

Base of operations, Janna thought, and remembered that Keri was a planner. It had freaked her out when they were kids, how detailed Keri got about terrible things that were never going to happen, but it was kind of comforting to have her doing it now about terrible things that really existed.

"Sione, where are you staying?" Keri asked.

"Uh... the Chancellor."

"That's my mum's hotel," Keri said.

"Your mum owns it?"

"Ha! No. My mum's an assistant manager."

"So we'll make that headquarters?" Janna asked.

Keri nodded. "Meet you both there at nine tomorrow morning?"

"Yeah," Janna said.

Keri pushed the button on the side of her watch and squinted at the glowing numbers. "Shit, I've got to go. Night, Stardust. Good to meet you, Sione. Thanks for dinner."

She hauled her massive bike into place and began pedaling down the hill. She could have just coasted, especially down the steep bit, Janna thought, but then she realized that this was Keri, who had won, like, four school awards for captaining the girls' rugby team to second place in the South Island champs, and probably not for coasting through anything, ever.

Sione was fiddling with his cuffs, looking as if he was working his way up to saying something embarrassing.

"Want a ride back to the hotel?" Janna said, just to fill the space, and then regretted it when he gave her the world's most wide-eyed, grateful smile.

Luckily, all he said was, "Uh, thanks," and then, "You've got your full license?"

"In two weeks. It'll be okay, though. I carry passengers all the time. We'll keep an eye out for the cops."

"Wow. Dangerous living."

And that was very nearly a joke. He was actually managing to talk. Good, maybe things weren't going to be awkward.

Janna had thought about cleaning the Corolla that afternoon, but working out the riff on Patrick's latest composition had been so much more appealing. Sione carefully inserted his feet between the crumpled takeout packets, some empty and crushed cans of Fanta, and an issue of *Remix*, which Janna had bought in August because it had an interview with Lani Purkis, badass bass goddess.

"Why does she call you Stardust?"

Janna jiggled the key into the ignition, flicking it over the sticky spot just right. "Because I'm vital to the existence of the universe."

Sione's laugh got lost in the engine as it coughed to life, and Janna swung them into the sparse traffic heading down the hill and along the main road. Noticing that Sione was clutching the handle above the door, Janna rolled her eyes. She was really a pretty good driver, but everyone just assumed that her driving would match the dusty, rusty car and never paid any attention to the smooth, careful way she actually handled it.

Which was why, when the black SUV at the intersection leaped out in front of her, she had the comfort of knowing the accident wasn't her fault.

That was her first thought as she stamped on the brake and clutched the wheel tightly with her bass-calloused fingers, yanking hard to the right—*I didn't do it*—and then sanity came back in a stomach-dropping howl. The Corolla screeched and spun ninety degrees in a turn tighter than anything she'd have thought the beautiful little rust bucket could manage, slamming into the side of the black car with a force that rattled every one of her teeth and smashed the left back window into a thousand glittering cubes.

She hadn't seen the car at all. She'd had right-of-way, but she hadn't even *seen* it.

"Mary the blessed mother of *God*!" Sione yelped.

"Fuck me!" Janna said, and turned off the ignition before she scrabbled for the seat-belt release. "Sione, you good?"

"I'm good," he panted. "I'm okay. Thank you, Jesus."

Her door didn't open right away—even though it was on the other side of the impact zone, which meant the crash had buckled the frame—but she shoved it hard and stumbled out, reaching over the hand brake to help Sione. Her legs weren't working right, all trembly and weak like the new foals on her cousin's farm.

"Adrenaline," Sione said, taking her gloved hand without any fuss and letting her help slide him over to the driver's side and then out. His window was a haze of greenish cracks.

"What?"

"My hands are shaking. See?"

"My poor baby," Janna said, feeling her voice hitch. She touched the Corolla's side lightly, as if the weight of her own trembling fingers might damage it more. All that babysitting, saving for *years*, and now some idiot tourist had *killed* the thing that made her most free.

"The other car!" she said, remembering, and they both staggered around the hood of the Corolla, clutching at each other to make up for the jelly in their legs.

The SUV had fared a lot better, but the back left side of the Corolla had come to rest against its middle in a biggish dent. A fair-haired, red-faced man was wobbling toward them, looking just as shell-shocked as Janna felt.

"Are you all right?" he yelled.

"We're okay!" Janna shouted. "Are you?"

"All fine!" he assured her, and then put his head back and laughed. "Jesus! Jesus H Christ! You just appeared out of nowhere!"

Janna could see a red-haired woman sitting in the passenger's seat, pushing down the air bags and staring at them with wide, horrified eyes. "We're okay!" Janna repeated, and waved at the woman. "It's all right." It wasn't, it *really* wasn't, but Janna could see that yelling at people who looked this shaken up wouldn't get her anywhere.

The woman gave her a quick nod and then leaned over the dashboard to take long, deep breaths.

Janna heard a siren start. There was a problem with that, but she couldn't remember what it was. A few other cars were dotted around the intersection, people rushing toward them.

"It was our fault," the guy said. "You had right-of-way. Shit, I'm so glad you're okay." There was a speck of something green down the middle of his short-sleeved button-up shirt. *Lettuce, maybe,* Janna thought, and then thumped the side of her head hard twice with the heel of her hand. *Enough!* Her brain had to work.

"I'm on a restricted license," she remembered, and stared at Sione in horror. But the other driver understood right away about insurance and police reports and lost licenses and winked at her. "No worries. We never saw him."

"Right," Sione said. "Right, I'll just walk."

"Don't be a dumbass," Janna said. "Just…sit over there. Pretend you're rubbernecking."

"Like a tourist," he said, and grinned dizzily at her, in such

39

obvious relief at not being abandoned that she couldn't help but grin back as he made his way over to the curb.

Janna was just thinking that the SUV was really far too big a car for only two people when the door on the undamaged side opened and two kids about her own age clambered out. The girl was a bit younger than Janna, maybe, all long, messy curls and long, freckly legs in a floaty orange sundress. It clashed with her reddish hair, which she'd obviously inherited from her mum.

The boy...

Janna sucked in a breath and then tried to make it look like the same kind of deep breathing the red-haired woman was doing.

"I'm Steve Fisher," the man was saying. "And that's Deborah, my wife, and that's Aroha, and this is—"

"My name is Takeshi Hoshino," the boy said. His front teeth were kind of crooked, which Janna instantly decided was *totally* cute, especially on a guy who had careful spikes of black hair folding over dark brown eyes that turned up at the corners, like they were permanently smiling. And really impressive shoulders poking out of his black sleeveless shirt.

"Is that a Japanese name?" she said. That was not the best line in the history of ever, but she figured that you had to expect your flirting to be less than ideal right after a brush with death that destroyed your four-wheeled baby.

"Yes. I am an exchange student from Japan."

Janna swept her hair out of her face with one hand and offered him the other, grateful that she'd put on the booby dress. "Hi, Takeshi. I'm Janna."

He bowed slightly when he shook her hand. "It's nice to meet you, Janna."

Janna gave him her most dazzling smile and felt a thrill go right up her spine as he smiled back, crooked teeth flashing. She could feel Sione staring from his seat on the curb, legs stretched out over the gutter, but she didn't turn to look. The hot guy was in the right age range to be a victim, so it was really vital that she make successful first contact. At that thought, she felt her smile fade a little.

There were blue lights flashing off Takeshi's shiny, shiny hair, and Janna turned around as the cop car pulled up, ready to lie her ass off and to cry if things seemed to be going badly.

But when she touched her face, the fingertips of her gloves came away already wet and smeared black, too. She wasn't really *crying*, she decided. Just sort of leaking, all the delayed stress of the moment spilling down her cheeks.

And what a crappy mascara.

Waterproof, her exceptional ass.

CHAPTER FOUR
Keri

$\bf{\it{f}}$

I USUALLY LIKE MY PAPER ROUTE. CYCLING'S good cardio training, in-season and off. Even on the frigid days of ice rain, when my fingers go numb to the knuckles and cold track pants flap wetly about my calves, I know that I can get back to the house for a hot shower and breakfast before school. There's a rhythm to it, clutch and flick, brake and glide. It switches off my brain, and when you've got a brain that's always calculating the worst possibilities of any situation, that can be good.

But I also like sleep. And when I don't get enough, getting up at six to do the route is torture.

I stared at my ceiling for most of that night. Sione didn't seem like someone playing mind games—just a nervous boy with expensive clothes and a crush on Janna so obvious that it was hard not to feel a bit sorry for him. I trusted him and, more important, trusted his spreadsheet.

And what the spreadsheet implied was very clear. Someone had murdered my brother. Very possibly someone I knew.

So it wasn't a restful night, and when I made myself get out of bed and onto my bike, I discovered that some morons had crashed on the main road. All the safety glass had been pushed to the side, where I had to cycle through it.

I got home just as Mum was leaving for work. "Morning, Keri. How was dinner?"

"Good," I said. "The snapper was great."

"Oh, lovely. Is Janna's friend nice?"

"Yeah. Bit flash, maybe. He's staying at the Chancellor."

Mum nodded, a gesture that might have meant she wasn't paying attention but could equally have meant she was taking it all in for use at some later date. "Your dad called while you were out. He sends his love."

Dad was at a major roadwork site three hours into the center of the island, on one of the mountain passes. It was too far away for easy commuting, so he and his mate Hone were staying in Hone's RV.

"Oh. Good."

"And I said hello from you."

"Won't you be late?" I said, making motions toward the

door. All this conversation was starting to wake me up, and I had plans to sleep for another hour. I sure didn't want to do any more lying on my back and looking up. I'd already memorized the position of every glow-in-the-dark star.

Mum patted her French roll and gave me a professional smile. I didn't like the face she put on for work: smooth foundation, pale pink lipstick, and carefully arranged dyed hair. With her laugh lines and crow's-feet neatly concealed, she seemed much less my mum and more a construct of some sort—a champagne-blond Chancellor cyborg.

"Keri, love…are you sure you don't mind about Christmas?"

No Christmas this year, she'd said when Nanny Hinekura asked us about it after the burial. *No, I can't do it, no.*

"I don't mind." This was sort of a lie. I understood what it was to want everything to stop, but even if we didn't have a tree in our own house, we couldn't avoid Christmas, because it was everywhere else. The streetlights had their tinsel decorations, and the hotel lobbies all had massive displays, and all the trees along the waterfront were strung up with lights. Christmas came up every time we turned on the TV or the radio or stepped into a shop. We'd even gotten two days into our own home Advent calendar, opening the little cardboard doors for the chocolates inside.

One for me. One for Jake.

After we got back from the tangi, I took the calendar into my room and ate every piece, including the big chocolate manger behind the door for Christmas Day. It made me sick, which felt right. The crumpled calendar was the only piece of

Christmas left in the house, and it was lying under my bed like a piece of trash.

"I hadn't gotten around to getting presents anyway," I added, and that was completely the truth.

"Me, neither," she said, which I knew for a fact wasn't true at all. "But I mean...you can still go down to your grandmother's, if you like. It's not too late. All the cousins would be happy to see you." Mum and Nanny Hinekura did not see eye to eye, so this offer was a big deal.

But now I had to stay to find out who'd murdered Jake. Even before, I hadn't wanted to go. I couldn't think of anything worse than being surrounded by all those family members, so conscious of the one who was missing.

"Nah, it's okay," I said.

"Well...I'm working on the twenty-fifth."

"But you had the day off."

She checked the fold at the back of her collar. "It's triple time. We could use the money." She didn't meet my eyes, and I thought, *Whoever did this to my mother is going to pay.*

So when she left, I didn't crawl back into bed. I took a shower and put on my inferior jeans and the blue T-shirt Jake had given me last Christmas and got back on my bike.

Iron Road is the main road into town—it's State Highway 100 until it passes the SUMMERTON WELCOMES YOU!! sign. Because the road's steep all the way down, the hotels crowd around it, each promising bay views. I raced down to the esplanade, happy about the breeze off the sea tugging at my shirt. In the brief time since I'd finished the paper route, the traffic had thickened. It was mostly tourists: big cars with tinted windows and cute, bright-colored hippie cars. Every now and then some idiot would look at the bay and get caught in the Summerton Effect, freezing instead of going at a green light.

And that pile of broken glass was still there.

I should have gone by the back roads, but since I was there, I moved my feet in slow, lazy circles, looking at the manne-quins in the windows of Lauer's and the crystal display at Inner Light and the Beach Bash posters that plastered the library's and art gallery's outer walls. The air was loud with seagulls and little kids chattering and people honking at the green-light gazers. The traffic cleared as I headed south, where the bay curved out again, and I sped up, standing on the ped-als as I turned inland to go up the hill to Janna's house.

Both of Janna's younger sisters were in the front yard, play-ing some complicated game that involved digging around the roots of trees with pointed sticks. They looked up when I sailed into the driveway, and Petra bent over her stick without meet-ing my eyes. Fifteen. Not too old for pretend games but old enough to know she was supposed to be too old, especially in front of the team captain. She'd be a good forward, if she grew into those wide shoulders.

I braked. "Is Janna home?"

Mariel rolled her eyes. "She's still in *bed*. You should go wake her up." She wasn't much like Janna—little and dark, and I'd seen her reading at lunchtime.

"Sorry about your brother," Petra said, and Mariel lost her smile.

"Me, too," I said, and did that one-legged flamingo hop over the bar of my bike, which was a boys' one. Girls' bikes didn't have that bar, which was just more evidence of how badly organized the world was. The last thing guys needed was to land hard on a bar if they missed the seat, and yet there it was. "This okay here?" I asked, and waited for Petra's nod before I kicked the stand down and walked around the house to the back door.

I hadn't been to Janna's house since I was ten or eleven, when we'd drifted from each other, and I was surprised by how much of the house was still the same. The kitchen had a dishwasher now, rumbling beside the sink, but the peeling pink Formica was the same shade I remembered, and the dark paneling in the hallway was still there. So were the pictures of the Virgin Mary holding a baby and Jesus with a bleeding heart, and the crucifix above the mirror at the end of the hall.

I knocked on the door of the room that had been Janna's and, when I got no answer, pushed it open. It had a crumpled, empty bed with pink covers, and Petra's MOST IMPROVED PLAYER trophy on the dresser.

I pulled back, disoriented, and knocked on the door of the next room. It had still been forbidden to everyone the last time I'd come over.

Inside, someone groaned.

It must have been okay now, if Janna was in there, but I still took a deep breath before I pushed open the door to Schuyler's room.

Everything had changed. I remembered faded yellow wallpaper with a pale green rose pattern, almost covered with meticulous star maps and posters of the planets. Schuyler had wanted to be the first New Zealander on the moon.

Janna had painted the walls—not black, I saw, as my eyes adjusted to the light filtering in around her curtains, but a very dark purple—and stuck up posters of Hole and Bikini Kill and Mindless Self Indulgence and Elemeno P. Her cherry-red bass was on a stand in the corner, on the only piece of floor clear of magazines and clothes and scraps of paper. One bookshelf leaned into the other, and the air was thick with the burnt flower smell of cheap incense.

Janna lay facedown on the bed, which was jammed under the window, with her head buried in the white pillow. She was naked. I blinked at the dust motes dancing in the shaft of sunlight that fell on one long leg and decided not to be embarrassed.

"You better get up," I said, closing the door behind me and turning on the light. "We've got work to do."

She hunched away from the light and then jerked awake, scrabbling for the sheet, which had fallen off the bed during the night. "Jesus, Keri!" she hissed, and wrapped dark blue cotton around her like a towel. "We were going to meet at the hotel at nine!"

"I knocked."

"Did the brats let you in? I swear, I'm getting a guard dog."

I snorted. "Liar. You hate dogs." It was surprising how easy it was to fall back into being friends with Janna. She was good at friendliness, and I was too bloody-minded to care what I said, and somehow the combination worked out okay. "You know that if we'd waited for you there, you'd be late."

She groaned but shuffled off the bed and yanked the

wardrobe door open. "You could have more pity on an accident victim."

"What?"

"You didn't hear?" she said, as if everything she did should be on the front page. To be fair, during the holidays I would normally hear all the town news through Mum, but her gossip-relaying abilities had taken a whack recently. "The poor Corolla is *totaled*."

I sat on the edge of Janna's bed and let her tell the story while she put together her costume for the day. This involved a lot of taking things off hangers and out of drawers and throwing them on the floor, but eventually Janna settled on a white T-shirt decorated with a sparkly unicorn (I was informed it was an *ironic* unicorn) and a black-and-gray pleated skirt.

"Sergeant Rafferty asked about nine million questions. He was pretty nice, though. I think we got away with it." She sighed. "My darling car. I'm totally gutted."

I had stopped paying much attention to her tale of woe after she'd mentioned this Takeshi Hoshino.

"He's the right age?"

"Yep. *And* he's an oldest brother, with a younger brother and a baby sister."

"You two compared family details at a car crash?"

She fished out a pair of purple underwear from the top drawer, frowned, threw them back in, and grabbed a red pair instead. "No. Sergeant Rafferty asked him."

My head came up, and the thought must have hit her at the same time because she swiveled, smudged eyeliner making her wide eyes look even bigger.

"Not Rafferty," she said.

"It could be anyone."

"He was just asking. Like, oh, welcome to New Zealand, do you like it, does your family miss you. He asked us all questions. Normal questions. He was checking we were okay."

"Did Rafferty ask how long the family was staying?"

She nodded.

"We'll put him on the list," I said, and ignored the face she made as she grabbed clothes and the towel lying over her desk chair and left for the bathroom. I understood: Sergeant Rafferty was the *good* cop, who inched up to parties with the siren blaring so that underage drinkers had time to get into the bushes. He wasn't exactly soft, though. He did the DARE program at school with an expression that said he knew some people smoked weed and he wasn't that happy about it. Also, tourists who tried to bring in meth or cocaine or anything harder got arrested if the police could prove it, and got the hard-ass treatment if they couldn't. And the hard-ass treatment was pretty intimidating from a guy taller than six feet four with hands like legs of mutton.

Janna was singing loud enough to be heard over the clanking pipes. I listened for a minute, hoping for a Vikings to the Left scoop, but it was that Shihad song about coming home again. I poked around her bedroom instead. The shelves were mostly full of CDs. The few books seemed to share a theme: dusty paperbacks on the Goddess Within and the pagan tradition. It was a shame Janna and I hadn't been mates during her witchy stage. Her fights with her Catholic mother must have been legendary.

I pulled out a book called *The Green Man and the Great Lady* and flipped through it. Janna had scribbled things in the margins — some badly spelled notes on magic, but mostly song lyrics or phone numbers or random doodles. A big black heart in one corner went around PATRICK + JANNA: 2GETHA 4EVA.

Well, they hadn't been together forever. But even just wanting to be was a sign: I could eventually get over this raw aching. Claim a life without Jake in it.

I didn't want to right now, but it was reassuring that it was an option.

"You should be a spy," Janna said, banging back into the room, skirt skimming her thighs. She brushed past me to stand in front of the dresser.

"Spies don't get caught red-handed," I said, watching her pull her hair into two braided pigtails and make pouty faces in the mirror. "Do you believe this stuff?"

"Wicca?" She leaned over and brushed a plum-colored mouth over her natural pinkish one.

"Magic."

"Yeah, I do. It works."

She really seemed to believe it, and it was hard not to be mean about it. Witchcraft. Like having a birthday in early September meant that I could predict my future by reading what the daily horoscopes had to say about Virgo.

Even though I managed to keep my mouth shut, she must have seen my skepticism in the mirror, because she turned around, lip brush poised in her sturdy fingers. "*You* don't have to believe it," she said. "I'm just saying. It worked for me."

"Willpower and symbols," I said, putting the book back. "It makes as much sense as anything."

I meant that nothing seemed to make much sense, but Janna took it as a peace offering and gave me one of those shiny smiles she did so well. "I stopped, though."

"Why?"

"Well, if you want to get serious, you have to study, which" — she floated her hand in the air and scrunched up her nose — "is not really my thing. I couldn't do it by myself. It was even worse than learning stuff for my confirmation. So I talked to Daisy at Inner Light, but she said I was much too young to join her coven, especially without Mum's permission. I tried a few spells on my own before I stopped." She looked self-satisfied for a moment. "Like a love spell."

"And it definitely worked?"

"Depends on what you mean by *worked*." She swept mascara over her lashes. "I wasn't trying to make anyone in particular like me; that's left-hand path. Black magic. You don't want to get started down that road; it's really hard to stop yourself from doing worse and worse things. So it was just a spell to open my eyes to love. But before the spell, Patrick was just this guy in the band, and the day after, I couldn't stop looking at him. He's a very good kisser, by the way. Highly recommended."

"I'll keep that in mind," I said. The chances of my kissing Patrick Tan approached nil, but Janna didn't need to know that. "But how often do guys say no to you, anyway?"

"Oh, you'd be surprised," she said, and put the mascara down, looking at my reflection in her mirror. "Matthew did."

"Sione's brother?" I said.

"Yeah. I made kind of a dick of myself, actually. But he said no, girlfriend at home."

Aha. That explained something I'd been wondering about. "And *then* you hooked up with Sione."

"Yeah. Just once. I'm not proud of myself."

"Because substitute kissing is gross, or because it was Sione?"

Janna spun around. "Sione's a good guy!"

"I know."

"I mean…I don't want to go out with him, but he's a really good guy. He's nice. I don't want to be mean to him, either."

"That's always hard for me," I said mournfully, and surprised a tiny smile out of her. But a change of subject was probably best. "So, this witchcraft thing, I guess it wasn't your typical teenage rebellion?"

"Ha, maybe. I think it was the only way I could leave the Church. Do something really spectacular, you know, so Mum knew I was serious." She shrugged. "But I do believe. I'll do more with Wicca later, when I get out of here. Right now I go to Mass at Christmas and Easter because it makes Mum and Dad happy, and sleep in every Sunday morning."

The mention of Christmas made me stagger. It was so weird, how stuff could slam me out of nowhere. "Mum's canceling Christmas," I blurted out. "Jake and me went through the present-hiding place in her wardrobe six weeks ago. He was getting a Wii. But now she's working Christmas Day, and she lied and said she hadn't bought any presents."

"Oh, shit," Janna said. "That's messed up. I'm sorry."

Once again, her matter-of-fact approach made me feel better. She didn't make any fuss, just laced up knee-high black leather boots—in *this* weather—and grabbed a yellow backpack covered in appliqué butterflies (probably ironic butterflies). Whatever was in the bag looked heavy, but I didn't offer to carry it, concentrating instead on pushing the hurt back down to something I could manage.

"Good to go?"

I nodded, and she led the way back through the hall, the dusty light gleaming on her tiny blond roots.

She grabbed one of the two bikes in the garage, slinging the helmet over the handlebars, and began pushing it up the drive. It was a sleek, slim-wheeled thing in dark blue. I'd seen Petra riding it home after practice sessions. Janna didn't handle it with the same grace, cursing as the spinning pedal caught her booted calf. When we reached the end of the driveway, I grabbed my own bike.

But Janna had stopped. "Mariel! Stop digging around that damn tree! You'll kill it."

Mariel's cheeks blew out in annoyance. "Mum didn't say anything."

"Mum won't have to live in a world where vast deforestation has further devastated oxygen levels and reduced the planet's capacity to handle carbon dioxide, will she?"

Petra shook her hair out of her eyes. "It's just one tree, Janna," she said.

"They're *all* just one tree," Janna muttered, but her heart didn't seem to be in it. Then, getting permission clearly as an afterthought: "Can I take your bike?"

Petra thought about this. "Get it back by four. I'm going to the pool before tea."

"You're my favorite little sister—"

"Hey!"

"Who isn't my *youngest* sister, okay? Jesus, Mariel, you're such a drama queen."

"Takes one to know one, blasphemer."

"Brat."

"Heathen."

"Can we get going?" I said. "You guys are making me feel better about being an only child."

Petra's jaw dropped. Mariel looked intrigued.

"*Nice*," Janna said, grinning, and flung her leg over the seat.

"Helmet," I reminded her, doing up my own.

"Ugh," she said, but obeyed. "God, I miss the Corolla. That was some *terrible* luck."

"Bad things come in threes," I said automatically, and then shook my head at my own superstition. "But not that bad. I hope."

"That's why I like you, Keri," Janna said, standing on the pedals to throw more weight into her cycling. Her pleated skirt blew up with the motion, showing glimpses of the red underwear. She didn't seem to mind. "You're always so *optimistic*."

CHAPTER FIVE
Sione

†

AFTER THE CRASH, SIONE COULDN'T STOP shaking. Even in the elevator back to his room, he could feel his hands trembling.

Matthew had died in a car.

Not the way Sione almost had, all fast tearing and blood. Matthew had just sat there, vomiting and turning bright red while his body tried to breathe the stinking exhaust fumes.

He'd been in his old car, the clunker he was so proud of

because he'd earned every cent for it himself, with no help from Dad. Dad had offered—nearly insisted: *No son of mine needs to*—but Mum had said, *He needs to establish his independence, Elijah.* And when Mum decided something was going to happen, especially when she decided it in Samoan, it happened. After a while, Dad had decided it was his own idea, teaching Matthew the value of a dollar.

Newer cars had catalytic converters that reduced the carbon monoxide output. It would have taken Matthew much longer to die in a newer car.

Sione might have even made it home in time.

After dinner with the girls, he'd planned to spend the evening unpacking and organizing his clothes—really exciting plans, a typical Sione Saturday night—but the shaking moved down his body, and he couldn't make it stop. Knees wobbling, he staggered down the blue-carpeted hall to his room, peeled off his shirt, shoes, and pants, and fell facedown into the pillows.

He meant to only rest for a while.

When someone knocked on the door, he woke up some of the way and groaned. Light was pouring in through the windows. He hadn't even closed the curtains last night.

The knocking came again. *It must be housekeeping*, he thought. Staggering out of bed, he tried to think about throwing on more clothes, but his brain was too foggy. He'd just poke his head out and tell them not to worry about cleaning this morning.

It wasn't housekeeping. It was the girls. And Janna had sweated a deep vee into her white T-shirt with a unicorn on it.

The fabric clung to her breasts and was nearly transparent over her cleavage, just above the unicorn's glittery horn.

Sione woke the rest of the way up.

"Rise and shine," Janna said, and pushed the door wider. The hem of her skirt brushed his thighs as she breezed past him, and he had a balls-clenching vision of what would happen if he let himself think about that in nothing but his boxer briefs.

"I'll get dressed," he said, and grabbed clothes from the suitcase at random, clutched them at waist level, and crab-walked to the bathroom.

Ten minutes later he was in dark jeans and a pale yellow polo shirt, so at least he'd lucked out on the clothes. His hair gel was still in the suitcase, and he tried to slick back his springy curls with water. Wisps flew out immediately. He gave up and went back to join the girls.

Janna had pulled a pile of papers with close rows of small type from her backpack—which was *amazing* and completely her, all yellow silky stuff and crazy butterflies—and was dividing it into thirds. Keri was pulling hotel stationery out of the big wooden desk.

Neither of them, he was relieved to see, had touched the laptop. They still needed him for something, then.

"We have a name for the possibles list," Keri said. She wrote the name in graceful, loopy handwriting under the Chancellor letterhead. "Sergeant Rafferty."

"He was there last night," Sione said slowly.

"Yep. Did you notice how he asked Takeshi all those questions?"

Not exactly. He'd been busy trying to convince himself that

Janna wasn't staring at the Japanese bloke the way she'd once stared at Matthew—the way she'd never looked at Sione. She'd kissed him, but she'd never looked.

"There were a lot of questions," he said.

"Exactly." Janna slapped the mattress. "He asked whether Takeshi had brothers or sisters and whether they were older or younger."

"Oh."

"And I checked the dates," she said, and waved her pile of papers at him. "Rafferty moved here three years before Schuyler died."

"What's that?"

"The electoral roll. I photocopied it at the library last week."

Sione stared at her. "You can't photocopy the electoral roll!"

Janna rolled her eyes and shook the sheaf of papers. "Oh yeah?"

"A good argument," Keri said. She winked at Sione. He decided she could be really pretty if she tried. "So we should keep an eye on Rafferty. But we shouldn't concentrate on him exclusively. Okay. Let's get on with the plan."

The plan was to go through the roll. Janna had already put a pink highlighter through everyone who'd had a Summerton address before Schuyler's death and had been old enough to kill him. The girls had to go through that list and work out who they were sure had been in town on the dates of the more recent deaths and so could be crossed off. Sione thought he wouldn't be able to help, but Keri put him on computer correlation duty, putting all the possibles into a spreadsheet.

Considering what they were doing, it should have been creepy, or even boring, but it wasn't. The girls talked as they worked, comparing notes about whether their English teacher had been in Summerton when Matthew died (she had) and what the minimum age for the murderer had to be at the time the murders started (they decided on fifteen because the killer probably needed a driver's license for the second murder, which was in a little town near Wanaka). As long as Sione didn't think about what the list was for, it was calm and cozy, sitting there while the air-conditioning hummed, listening to the girls talk, and inputting name after name.

There were way too many names, way too many possibilities. *We're working the problem*, he thought, and tried not to worry about it too much.

Every now and then he lost himself, looking out over the beautiful bay, but the girls made allowances for his being a tourist and didn't give him too much shit for it.

It was getting pretty close to eleven, and Sione was wondering how to bring up the subject of the breakfast he hadn't had, when Keri sat straight up and said, "Wait. This is weird."

Janna drew a line through each of the Maukis brothers— "We were playing at an art show opening that day, and they were both there, the slimes"—and then looked up.

Keri was frowning at the roll, as if she couldn't quite believe whatever it was she'd found. "No one's moved here since Schuyler died."

"Sure they have. There was that Ekaterin Ivanova bitch in our class in Year Nine, and the Afghan family who lived down the street from us—"

60

"No one has moved here and stayed. They come, and they go." Keri's eyes widened. "And I think...no one who moved here before Schuyler died has ever *left*."

"We do school trips all the time! I go to Christchurch for—"

"No. I mean, no one's left for good."

Janna sucked on the end of her pen, turning her cheeks hollow. Sione twitched and then consciously halted the motion. "That's weird," Janna said judiciously. "But they must, right? I just can't think of anyone right now. People go to uni. *I'm* going to leave. I can't be a rock goddess from Summerton."

"I'm leaving, too," Keri said, but she was still frowning. "Seriously, though. People go to uni or polytech or teachers college, but they come back. They do hospitality courses, or vet science, or hair and beauty. But they come back, and they keep Summerton going."

"Huh," Sione said.

Janna was chewing her lip. "I guess it's a pattern," she said. "And we're looking for patterns."

"Not all patterns are relevant," Sione heard himself say. Again, it felt strange to be arguing with Janna, even a little bit. "There is such a thing as coincidence."

"I want to check it out anyway," Janna said. "See if Keri's right."

"I'm right," Keri said, looking fierce.

"We can't afford to waste time on diversions," Sione said, but the girls were both looking at him, and he could feel his shoulders caving over his chest. "Okay. Okay, look, I'll check the census data. That won't tell us about individual people moving in and out, but it'll give us overall population movement."

Sione accessed the hotel's wireless and started grabbing data from the government websites, moving as fast as he could. This was something he was secure in, diving into data and bringing back numbers solidified into facts, implications, projections. "Okay, if we look at other West Coast data for a comparison point and track motion over, let's see...There is a census every five years, so if we take from two censuses before Schuyler was killed up until today, we can see that..." He blinked at the screen.

"We can see that what?" Keri demanded. Janna was looking at him, and he thought she might have been just faintly impressed.

"Well, okay, accounting for births and deaths, the population stays steady," he said. "So you're probably right, it's a pattern. But Summerton is a really nice place. I can see why people would want to stay here. And it's still got nothing to do with the murders."

"The important thing is that we were right and you were wrong," Janna informed him breezily. "Remember that we have the hometown advantage."

"But you're not too bad," Keri conceded. "For a tourist."

Sione wasn't sure whether he'd just been complimented or insulted. Janna's backpack started singing, and she dived for it. Her skirt flipped up as she landed on her belly on the bed, and Sione jerked his head around as she fished the cell phone out.

Keri gave him a sideways look. It could have been a pitying one.

To keep his mind off the flash of red over Janna's curvy bum, Sione concentrated on the art on the hotel wall. It was a landscape of Summerton, looking from a point in the ocean up the beach and toward the town. But it was like the TV ads—not a good reflection of the real thing. The colors weren't quite right; the ocean blues were too subdued, the bush greens not deep enough. And there was a thick cloud bank weighing down the sky, even though the crowds on the beach were clustered around a stage, clearly gathered for the annual Beach Bash. It never rained on New Year's Eve; that was one of the things Summerton was famous for. So maybe it was an imaginary landscape. The tourists looked almost unreal in it—brightly colored little figures dancing in the muted world, ignoring the massing clouds.

In the bottom left-hand corner were square letters that read OCTAVIAN AND TIBERIUS MAUKIS. He remembered the names; Janna had crossed them off the possibles list.

"...you think, Sione?"

Sione jerked. "What?" The girls had been talking while he dreamed about crappy hotel art. More than talking—Keri's jaws were clenched, and Janna's fingers were flashing in and out of fists. "I wasn't listening," he added, which was true, but not very diplomatic.

Both girls snorted, then glared at each other as if they suspected the other was making fun of them.

Sione reminded himself that they weren't mad at *him*. "What's going on?" he asked.

"That phone call was from Patrick Tan, our lead guitarist. One of the New Year's Eve Beach Bash bands canceled, and

Vikings to the Left has been given a once-in-a-year opportunity—
no, once-in-a-*lifetime*—"

"Which Janna will have to turn down," Keri said firmly.

Janna's hands made fists again. "Like hell she will!"

"You can't play at the Beach Bash! New Year's Eve is the
one night we know for sure that all the boys were here. They
probably all went to the Bash. I know Jake did—"

"Matthew, too," Sione added.

"Right. So we have to be on the lookout, not—"

"Exactly," Janna said. "*Exactly*. We have to be on the lookout, and do you know the best vantage point? The stage! What
do you think, Sione?"

Sione had the dizzy feeling of going around in circles. He
cleared his throat. "Uh, you both have good points. But I think
Janna might be right."

"Of course you do," Keri said, and then waved her hand in
the air before he could get annoyed or, worse, start blushing.
"Okay, why?"

"Well," he said, working it out as he went, "Janna will get
privileged access, right? Behind the main stage, that sort of
thing. And she probably can get a pretty good view from the
stage. But you and I, we'll still be undercover, hanging out in
the crowd."

Keri cocked her head, looking less like a dog about to take a
bite out of his leg and more like one considering whether it was
worth the trouble of barking.

"I can signal to you!" Janna said. "And come to think of it,
Rafferty will be there. He always is. We can watch to see if he
talks to any of the boys or looks weird or something."

"And that's only if we don't work out who it is before then," Sione added.

Keri sighed. "Okay. I guess Janna can have her fifteen minutes."

Janna squealed and threw her arms around Keri's neck. "You are the best *ever*," she said. Keri's eyes went wide, rings of white all around the green irises. After a moment, her hands rose to rest on Janna's shoulders. She squeezed once, briefly, and stepped away.

Janna was too happy to notice, but Sione saw the way Keri's shoulders hunched and her arms crossed over her chest, warding off further touch, and thought he understood. After Matthew, everything had felt raw and numb at the same time, and any touch or word could hurt without intention.

It wasn't like that now, but he remembered the feeling really well—like a story he'd read too often for too long.

"Let's get some lunch," he suggested.

"Mmm," Keri said. "I dunno. I really want to finish this."

Someone knocked on the door, and they all went still for a second before Keri grabbed the list and shoved it into Janna's bag. Sione went to the door, peering cautiously through the peephole.

Sione saw a tall, broad-shouldered man in a dark suit, thick blond hair brushed back into careful waves above a square forehead and muddy blue eyes, and instantly knew why the man was there.

Sione slapped on his politest smile and opened the door. "Mr. Davidson," he said. "How are you, sir?"

"Very well, thank you, Sione," Kirk Davidson said, shaking Sione's hand. His gaze flickered over Sione's shoulder toward the two girls, then returned. "I heard you were in a car accident last night. Are you well?"

"Yes, thank you," Sione said, fighting the urge to grind his teeth. No wonder his parents had insisted he stay at the Chancellor instead of one of the cheaper options. They'd asked the hotel manager to keep an eye on him. "I was just a bystander, really."

"Glad to hear it," Mr. Davidson said affably. "Now, your mother asked me to make sure that you got out in the fresh air sometimes."

She'd probably phrased it that way, too. Like he was ten.

"We were just going to lunch," Sione told him.

"Good! Good! Well, don't let me stop you. Nice to see you, Keri. I'm so sorry for your loss."

Keri mumbled something that could have been thanks, reluctantly getting to her feet. Janna casually picked up her bag, list hidden inside, and moved into the hall. Sione didn't bother to take his own bag, instead grabbing his wallet from the table. The thought of getting ready to leave under Mr. Davidson's supervision made him feel like a preschooler.

Mr. Davidson stood aside as Sione pulled the door closed behind them, then smiled at them all. "I'll look in on you later," he promised Sione.

"Aren't you lucky," Janna whispered as they went down the hall toward the elevator. "Your own personal spy."

"Lucky, lucky me," Sione agreed, trying not to react to the laughter in her voice. *Parents.*

CHAPTER SIX

Janna

★

JANNA WAS IN LOVE WITH THE ENTIRE *WORLD*.

The Beach Bash! Vikings to the Left were going to play at the Beach Bash!

She skipped down the hallway ahead of Sione and Keri. The Bash was televised and webcast, and if the right person saw Vikings to the Left, they were *made*. That was how Caramel Fudge from Christchurch had gotten their deal, and now they were living in LA with a single that had placed on Billboard. And that country-singing girl from Gore, Terry something, who'd gone all the way to the Grand Ole Opry with songs about *cows* or whatever.

"You guys, you guys!" she half sang, smacking the elevator button in time to the riff from "Elephant in the Bath." "Do you know what this could *mean*?"

"Does it mean you're going to be like this all day?" Keri wondered.

The elevator dinged. "Maybe!" Janna said, and whirled as the doors opened. "But it also means..."

Takeshi Hoshino stood back from the door, looking surprised and then pleased.

"That this is the best day *ever*," Janna decided, and pranced into the elevator, feeling her smile stretch her face even wider. "Hi!"

Skinny, ginger-headed Aroha was there, too. "Wow," she said. "I like your T-shirt."

"Thanks! Oh, Keri, this is Aroha, whose dad kinda totaled the Corolla, but he's really nice and didn't argue about the blame or anything, and *this* is Takeshi. Takeshi's from Hiroshima!" Keri nodded at both of them. Janna hoped she wouldn't say anything too bitchy. "And you guys remember Sione?" she added. Sione's expression was closed off, and she didn't really feel like interpreting it.

"Yes," Aroha said, smiling shyly. "Wasn't that awful? Is your car okay, Janna?"

Janna shrugged. "I'll find out after Christmas. The mechanic is kinda busy right now, and I'm low-priority. So! Are you heading out for lunch?"

"Yes," Takeshi said, doing this completely adorable thing with his eyelashes sweeping up and down. "We could eat lunch together, maybe."

"That is an *excellent* idea," Janna told him. "We know all the best places, don't we, Keri?"

"Sure," said Keri, looking amused. Amused with Janna, probably.

But Janna had never minded being obvious. What was the point in playing games? If she liked someone—or the opposite—better to make it clear so everyone knew where they stood. Okay, so she'd kind of made a fool of herself with Matthew, and hooking up with Sione instead was something she still felt a bit ashamed about, but that had been a year ago, and everyone made mistakes.

The elevator door opened again.

"I think sandwiches," she said, linking arms with Aroha on one side and Takeshi on the other. "Do you like sandwiches?" Takeshi was wearing a black jacket, surprisingly soft against her bare arm.

"My favorite food is sandwiches," he told Janna, and stepped closer to her to make the linking easier.

Good sign.

◢

Lunch was at Mimi's Muffins, where the tiny, curvy booth was free, its red vinyl bench sticking to Janna's bare legs while they ate sandwiches and cake. It turned out that Takeshi had chosen to come to New Zealand because he was a rugby player, which made Keri straighten up and start talking. And Aroha played drums and sang. She wasn't actually in a group, but her taste wasn't totally lacking, and she was suitably impressed by Janna's new Beach Bash credentials. Janna would have preferred if Aroha and Takeshi had swapped interests, but she could cope. The four of them discussed training schedules and the rugby sevens team selections (Takeshi and Keri), whether the kinderwhore look was making a comeback and if that was a good thing (Janna and Aroha), and the awesomeness of Summerton as a holiday destination (Aroha and Takeshi, with Janna chiming in to be polite and also to demonstrate compatible ideals).

Sione barely spoke at all, and Janna remembered how quiet he'd been last year, always hanging on the edges of Matthew's group. Since June, they'd chatted so much online that she'd almost forgotten that he didn't really talk in person. She pushed that out of her mind and stole another of Takeshi's chips. She'd been taking one every time he turned to answer one of Keri's questions about the Japanese training system. Takeshi finally caught her stealing when she jogged his arm, mostly by accident. She popped the chip in her mouth and smiled at him, close-lipped, while she crunched.

He laughed. "You are..." he began, and then said something in Japanese, tilting his head at Aroha.

She swallowed a bite of her carrot muffin. "Um, not sure."

Takeshi nodded and poked at a little electronic dictionary until he found a definition that suited him. "You are a thief," he told Janna, the *th* sound soft and *outrageously* adorable.

Keri shook her head. "Stardust, you shouldn't be allowed out."

Takeshi squinted at that. Janna felt proud of herself for recognizing the gesture as one reserved for when people spoke too fast or didn't use proper English. "Janna is a star?" Takeshi asked.

"It's my nickname," Janna explained. "Stardust. Um...dust from the stars. Star dirt?" *Oops, that wasn't very sexy.*

"I'm a star, too!" he said. "*Hoshino* means 'field of stars.' That's awesome!"

"It is awesome!" Janna said, gazing into his eyes and watching his pupils dilate. Okay. He definitely liked her, too. She could smell his shampoo, something herby and cool. A green, classy smell.

"My name means 'love,'" Aroha offered.

"Uh-huh," Keri said, looking amused. "In Māori."

"Well, my mum picked it," Aroha said, going pink. "Sione, what about your name?"

Sione looked up from where he was pushing crumbs around his plate with his finger. "Mmm? We should get back to that project...." He gave Janna and Keri a significant look.

"I have to see the Maukis brothers to pick up the Beach Bash contracts," Janna explained, surreptitiously passing her backpack under the table to Keri. Keri raised her eyebrows, but she took it.

"Maybe you could give Takeshi and Aroha the Summerton tour?" Keri suggested, which sounded like a really good way to get them out of Keri and Sione's way, and an even *better* way for Janna to get to know Takeshi.

Aroha stood up. "Actually, I'll go back to the hotel. I've still got to unpack."

Janna loved Aroha so much, she *tingled*. Maybe Janna could do something nice for her, like dye her hair. Chocolate-brown would look good with those freckles.

"So, meet us at seven," Keri said, looking at Janna.

"I'll walk back with you guys?" Aroha asked, and gave Sione a smile that Janna easily recognized as significant.

Excellent! she thought. That would work out nicely for everyone.

Janna linked her arm with Takeshi's as they walked, wondering if she should go all out to snag him before any other girls noticed how ridiculously amazing he was or wait until tonight, when she could consider other options at the beach.

The Maukises' gallery was a heritage building whose entrance was down an alleyway between the town library and the gallery. Tiberius was waiting by the entrance as they went in, eyes flickering over Janna's legs.

Ugh. The Maukis brothers were creeps extraordinaire. Every time they looked at her, Janna always felt the desire to scoop their eyeballs out of her cleavage and stomp on them.

But the brothers were on the New Year's Eve committee, in charge of the Beach Bash bookings. "Thanks for thinking of Vikings for the Beach Bash," she said.

Tiberius's eyes twinkled like a lecherous Santa Claus. "Our pleasure. You know we like to support young up-and-comers."

His gaze drifted downward—*Ugh, ugh, ugh*—then, surprisingly, sideways and up again to Takeshi's face. "Why don't you come up to the office? Sign the contract, get the paperwork out of the way now."

She was supposed to be just picking up the papers because technically Patrick was the front man. But it surely didn't matter whose signature went on the forms, and it couldn't hurt to show Takeshi how professional she was. "Sure."

Janna was prepared to admit that the gallery itself was okay, all high white walls and pretty wooden floors, but the Maukis brothers' idea of art always left her cold. Landscapes of the view she could see every day were not exciting, though the tourists just ate them up—including, she was sad to see, Takeshi, who praised the artwork as they went through the little rooms downstairs and then up the staircase, which opened onto a corner of the big upstairs space. This was the best room of all, one huge, light-filled gallery that, except for the office at the other end, took up the whole second floor. The paintings up here weren't Maukis ones, but a visiting exhibition, with lots of vivid, abstract slashes and splatters. Janna kind of liked them.

Unfortunately, the center of the room was reserved for a big limestone block that had been part of the Steps to Heaven until they crumbled. Only pompous artists would drag a huge chunk of stone out of the bay when there was plenty in the hills, and only *bad* artists would have made the thing that sat on top of the block.

Takeshi blinked at it.

"Ah, yes," Tiberius said. "The Pride of Summerton."

Janna's effort to not roll her eyes was *heroic*.

The Pride of Summerton was a crown made out of glass, thick and blobby with uneven spiky bits at the top and a bumpy base that wasn't quite level, so that it leaned drunkenly to the left. The sign proclaimed it WEARABLE ART, but only a Maukis could claim the crown was either. Tiberius had designed it, and Octavian had blown it and then stuck bits of blue and red and green sea glass all over it. The pieces were probably meant to look like jewels, but the crown had come out looking like her little sister's art projects. From when Mariel was *four*.

But the Maukis brothers didn't care that no one else liked The Pride. They kept it in the middle of the gallery, stuck it on all the brochures, had designed their logo around it, and, grossing Janna out the most, put it on all the posters for the Beach Bash as the symbol of Summerton.

Takeshi looked slightly stunned. Janna didn't blame him.

"Contracts are in here, Janna," Tiberius said, and ushered her into the office. She half expected him to use the excuse of close quarters to brush against her, but he seemed distracted, looking back at Takeshi and the crown. "So read it carefully, then sign here and initial here." He went back out into the gallery, pulling the door nearly closed behind him.

Janna bit her lip and glared at the two pages of small type. Reading wasn't really her thing—she got by okay; she wasn't *illiterate*—but this wasn't a magazine, where it didn't matter if she skipped a word or two, or even one of the school texts Mrs. Rackard quietly helped her with. The contract had things like *consideration of services rendered* and *represent and warrant that* and *hereby acknowledged by each party hereto.*

I'll have to learn about this stuff, Janna thought. *Get Patrick to go through a contract and explain it.* Or on second thought, not Patrick. She could ask Mrs. Rackard when school started again.

But she couldn't sign now, not when she didn't know exactly what she'd be signing. The Maukis brothers were fully capable of ripping people off.

Janna picked up the contract and pulled the door open, meaning to tell Tiberius that she'd have to discuss it with the others after all, and stopped before the first word passed her lips.

Takeshi was still standing in the middle of the gallery, and Tiberius, smiling, was lowering The Pride of Summerton onto Takeshi's head.

Maybe the Maukis brothers knew more about art than she gave them credit for. On its stone plinth, the crown looked stupid. But up high like that, the crown caught the afternoon light through the windows, the colored glass casting weird lights on Takeshi's glossy black hair. It looked—well, not beautiful. But kind of ugly-pretty. It made him fascinating in a way that left her feeling a little shy and awkward, which were feelings she didn't have that often, and didn't like.

"How does it feel?" Tiberius asked.

"It is…*omoi*," Takeshi said, his voice thick. "Sorry, my English. I forget." He turned and blinked across the room at Janna, very slowly. Through some trick of the light, the crown ringed the dark brown of his eyes with gold. The air seemed warm and fragrant, and her fingers ached to touch him, like they sometimes ached with the need to touch her bass. A possessive, tender longing.

Tiberius's smile grew wider, until he followed Takeshi's line of sight and saw Janna, frozen in the doorway.

"Is there a problem?" he asked, swiftly taking the crown from Takeshi's head and putting it back on the plinth.

Janna shook her head straight and remembered. "Um...I just want to get the others to look over the contract, if that's okay?"

He nodded brusquely. "That's fine."

She moved toward them. Takeshi was still staring at the crown. "Could I try it on?"

"Oh, I don't think so. It's a delicate piece. I don't want to stress it with too much use. Your boyfriend seemed so interested, though."

Janna thought about saying "He's not my boyfriend," but she really just wanted to get the hell out of there. That golden, warm feeling was gone, and Tiberius was creeping her out more than usual. Too bad he and his brother were both confirmed noncandidates for the killer list; they would have made perfect suspects.

"Well, it was nice to meet you, Takeshi," Tiberius said. "I'm sure I'll see you around."

"Good-bye," Janna said, wrapping her hand around Takeshi's and tugging gently. He blinked at her again, looking less dazed, and walked down the stairs with her. Janna hoped Tiberius wasn't going to hit on boys now. It was bad enough that he leered at all the girls.

"Do you want to get coffee?" she asked.

"Heavy!" he said. "*Omoi* means 'heavy.' Yes, I would like to drink coffee with you."

"Or" — she checked her watch — "crap. I have a rehearsal. A band practice."

"I see," he said peaceably, but there was a glint of curiosity.

"Would you like to watch?" she asked on impulse, and when he grinned and nodded at her, she knew it had been the right thing to say.

This one, she thought, grateful for the rushing in her blood, the certainty of another summer high note. *I want this one to like me.*

He was leaving in just over a week, and she'd have to work fast. He'd seen her flirting over lunch, and awkward in the art gallery, and crying and shaky after a car accident.

Now let him see her at her very best.

Introducing her new hopefully-fling to her once-upon-a-time boyfriend was probably supposed to be awkward. But Patrick raised a bushy eyebrow, nodded at Takeshi, tapped his fingers on his guitar's neck, and gave Janna a look that she easily interpreted as "Make sure he stays on the couch and doesn't get in the way." Visitors were tolerated at Vikings rehearsals but only if they were seen and not heard.

Janna settled Takeshi on the couch and brought him a Coke from the mini fridge. "I hope you won't be bored."

"No," he said. "This is interesting."

While she checked the settings on her pedals, Hemi Koroheke leaned down from his drum set and whispered, "Chewing up another one, eh, Janna?"

"Jealous, Hemi?"

"Don't you wish. What's with the yellow fever, anyway?"

"Don't be gross," Janna snapped.

Takeshi hadn't heard, but Patrick straightened. "For the record, Chinese New Zealander and Japanese are *not* the same thing," he said.

Hemi held up his hands. "Just a joke, my man. You're all invaders to me, eh?"

Janna knew from experience that this could easily turn into hours of passionate debate over colonialism, racism, and land rights, which was fair enough, but not what she'd brought Takeshi to see. "I can't believe we're going to be on TV!" she said quickly.

"And paid," Kyle Hamilton said, calmly tuning his guitar. "I'm going to buy a new Fender."

Hemi grinned. "I need the *World of Warcraft* expansion."

Janna sighed. "I have to pay the insurance deductible to fix the Corolla."

Patrick looked disgusted, but then again, that was his basic state. "Don't spend the money before we've earned it," he ordered. "I don't know if you've thought about this, but we have eight days to prepare for the most important gig of our lives. We need to be focused!"

"We need a set list," Janna said, and slung Cherry Bomb over her shoulder. "Let's start with 'Elephant in the Bath'; it's jumpy, and everyone loves it."

That, as she had predicted, started an argument about what to play in which order. Patrick won, because he was picky and stubborn and also because he had an annoying habit of being right. Takeshi watched them shout at one another for a while, but his eyes began to wander, inspecting the equipment and the egg cartons nailed to the garage walls.

Janna was wondering if this had been a bad idea. She picked out a B-flat scale, held the final chord, and stepped on the chorus pedal. The sound reverberated around the room. The boys stopped talking. And Takeshi's eyes snapped back to her.

"Could we, I don't know, *rehearse*?" she asked.

Patrick tilted his head, and the twist of his smile said that he knew exactly what she was doing. But he was a good ex-boyfriend.

"'Elephant in the Bath,'" he said, stepping up to the mic. "One, two, three."

And Janna felt Stardust come up through the soles of her boots and take over. The work was all Janna's, learning the song, getting the timing, playing alone and with the boys over and over and endlessly over until it clicked at last into what they needed. But once that part was done, and the song was muscle memory in her strong hands, it was sexy, powerful Stardust who took the stage, the backbone of the band, the rhythm that drove them all on and up to new heights. She could *feel* Takeshi's attention, warm sun on her skin, as her calloused fingers spider-walked through the opening notes.

And the boys, as always, felt her shining and went for it.

They finished, note and beat perfect, with Patrick breathing out the final words, energy crackling among them.

"We're going to kick ass," Hemi said, grinning. And Janna

thought that was true, but it was Takeshi she looked at, for the first time since Patrick's countdown. He was staring directly at her.

"What did you think?" Patrick asked.

"Good," Takeshi said. "Very, very good."

But he said it to her.

CHAPTER SEVEN
Keri

⚡

THE SHOCKING THING ABOUT SANDRA-CLAIRE, who was my brother's girlfriend before he died, was that she's a witch. Not as in *bitch*, although she's definitely that, too, but as in someone who practices ritual magic. There were quite a few neo-pagan types around Summerton, I guess because beautiful isolated country communities with nice weather attract hippie types. Apart from the hippieness, they were mostly normal.

I suppose it might have seemed a little bit weird. But I

mean, Janna's mum gets up in Mass every Sunday and thinks she's eating a chunk of Jesus, and my nanny believes that she saw Grandad Wiremu three weeks after he died. When you think about it, believing in magic and tossing sage and rosemary and whatever around to cleanse the air of evil influences wasn't any stranger than all those other things that weren't true. Anyway, my point is, Wicca isn't like *Macbeth* when we studied it in Year Eleven, with "When shall we three meet again" and boiling up babies and deals with demons. Most of the Wiccans I've met were pretty nice.

So I was shocked when Sandra-Claire first told us that she was a Wiccan witch, because she was a horrible person.

An example: When I got home from the Chancellor, brain still ferreting out the reasons why people might stay in Summerton, I opened the door to find her rooting through the kitchen cupboards. In our kitchen. Without looking up, she snapped, "Have you seen my roasting dish?"

No hello or anything.

"What?" I said to her bony ass, most of which was sticking out of her low-cut jeans.

"My roasting dish! I brought it over for Jake's birthday dinner, and your mother never gave it back to me."

I let the door slam behind me. "What are *you* doing here?"

She pulled her head out of the cupboard to glare at me from behind her fried blond bangs. Her nose looked even more than usual like the prow of an upside-down ship, sticking straight out and angular. Sandra-Claire wasn't pretty, but she was polished, like a cold, shiny stone, so careful with hair and clothes that she fooled a lot of people. She fooled Jake, and my big brother wasn't stupid about anything but her. She was two years older than he was, and now he was dead at nineteen and she was going to keep getting older.

There's no justice.

"I'm sorting out my things," she said. "Taking some mementos." She must have seen my outrage because she added, lip twisting, "I called yesterday. Lillian said it was all right."

Mum hadn't told *me*, leaving me to walk in on her instead of buggering off to go for a run or something instead. It probably served me right for not checking in with Mum, but damned if I was going to waste all this resentment on myself.

"You shouldn't wear baggy shirts," she said. "You look like a pregnant dwarf."

"You look like a plumber," I said, pointing at her jeans. "What's the matter, couldn't afford a whole pair?"

She sneered. "You couldn't afford that other X chromosome?"

I stepped forward, fists clenching. I had kept off her back at Jake's request, and at Mum's, but neither of them were here. There was no reason not to hit Sandra-Claire in the middle of her bleached teeth and yank out her overprocessed hair. That had been one of my plans for a very long time. Of course, I'd been planning on Jake's coming to his senses and dumping her beforehand, not getting shot in the head, but a breakup was a breakup. To give her some credit, she didn't flinch for a second, her eyes hard on my own.

"Sandra-Claire, did you really want all these T-shirts?" a voice asked. A woman rounded the corner from the hall, box first. She set it down on the table and smiled at me. "Hello, Keri. How're you holding up?"

"Fine, thanks," I mumbled, resenting the lost opportunity. But it was hard to dislike Daisy Hepwood for long. She was Sandra-Claire's boss at Inner Light, and one of the *nice* witches.

"Your aura's a bit dark, dear," Daisy said. "But that's certainly understandable. I'm so sorry for your loss."

"It's hit us all hard," Sandra-Claire snapped. She acted as if Jake's death had been an attack on her. I despised her for it, not least because I sometimes felt like that, too. I'd seen her on my walks around town, looking as lost as I felt, and it made me furious. She didn't have the *right*. She'd only gone out with him for one year. He'd been my brother my entire life.

"What T-shirts?" I said, peeking into the box. Jake loved those shirts with the sayings on them; weird, or cool, or funny, or stupid: If he could order it online, and get it shipped at huge prices, he wanted it.

The contents of the box looked like most of his collection.

I pulled out the olive-green one that said +3 CHARISMA, recoiling at the softness of the cotton against my fingers. "You can't take all his stuff!"

"Lillian said it was all right," Sandra-Claire repeated, and put the T-shirt back in the box. "Besides, I gave him most of these."

I yanked out the one that read MARRIAGE: GAME OVER. "Not this one! I gave him this one for his birthday!"

"Yeah, I remember," she said, and raised her already-poisonous glare a notch or two on the toxicity scale.

84

"Oh, dear," Daisy said, wringing her ringed hands. "I'm sorry, I didn't realize." Her curly salt-and-pepper hair swung around her skinny face as she backed away.

There was being mean, and then there was being mean to Daisy. "It's okay," I said. "I'll just keep it."

"You want to go through the rest of them?" Sandra-Claire asked.

This was a trick question. If I said yes, she'd roll her eyes and say something sarcastic. If I said no, she'd walk out of here with all of Jake's things. I stared at her for a second.

"I have a New Year's Eve committee meeting," Daisy said, looking sorry. "I do have to get going rather soon."

"Look," Sandra-Claire said, opening her wallet. "Why don't you, I don't know, go get an ice cream or something? Daisy and I will get this done, and then I'll be out of your hair."

"Oh, happy day," I snarled, making no move to take the money she offered me. *Ice cream.* Like a little kid. "This is my house, and you want *me* to leave? Why don't you get out? You've been talking about leaving Summerton forever anyway."

She stiffened. "Believe me, I plan to."

"Good," I said, and stomped off to my bedroom, backpack hanging heavily on my shoulder. Daisy shied away from me as I went past, looking appalled at this unsisterly aggression. Once this hit the grapevine, I was going to catch hell from Mum. Assuming she had the energy to deal with me.

Well, if I was going to have a tantrum, I might as well go all the way.

I slammed the door and flung myself onto my bed, still clutching Jake's last gift from me, twisting my hands in the T-shirt's fabric. My heart was hammering, and my vision narrowed as the what-ifs began to take over. What if we never found the killer? What if he found us poking around and decided to take care of us himself? What if Jake had been tortured before he died; what if he'd been hurt and crying? What if he'd been waiting for me to come home and help him, and died, hopeless, when I never came?

It was going to be okay, I told myself, forcing deep breaths through my nose and out through my mouth. I had a plan. Tonight I was going to meet Sione and Janna at the hotel, then head down to the beach. We'd split up and find boys of the right age and family, watching for anyone else who was asking the same questions. Then we'd compare notes, find the killer, and make sure he — or she (Sione was right; it was possibly a woman) — never hurt anyone ever again.

I couldn't have Jake back. But I'd have the killer, and answers to my questions, and revenge. And that was going to have to be enough.

CHAPTER EIGHT
Sione

†

GETTING DRESSED ALWAYS MADE SIONE FEEL
better—putting together those pants with these shoes, putting together a version of himself to show the world. Leaving
his messenger bag behind when he'd gone to lunch had been a
mistake; something about the weight of it over his shoulder
always made him feel more secure.

But after he was ready, there was nothing to do but wait.
Neither of the girls showed up at his hotel room. He checked
his cell phone thirteen times just in case the sound wasn't

working, but there were no texts or missed calls, and when he finally got up the nerve to call, Janna didn't pick up. He didn't even have Keri's number.

As the light outside got dimmer, he felt more and more like giving up on the whole night. Janna and Keri were good-looking girls; guys would spill their guts to them without wondering why they were being asked about their siblings and how long they were going to stay. Sione was pretty sure it wouldn't work like that for him. He would more likely get bashed.

But he and the girls had to find the killer's next target, almost as urgently as they had to find the killer.

And he was worried about what Jake's anomalous death might mean. No one else had died during summer, so close to the end of another year. What if the killer was escalating? What if he or she was going to kill two boys next year, too? Or increase exponentially? The thought of a dozen families, bereaved as his had been, got him to his feet.

Walking to the esplanade, Sione caught sight of his reflection—hunched under the weight of his bag, mouth tight—in the art gallery window. He squared his shoulders and forced a smile. No one would want to talk to someone with a face as miserable as a cat's bum.

At 9 PM there was still plenty of light on the beach, but some of the groups gathered there had lit fires anyway, drift-wood burning that magical blue-green, flickering in the warm breeze coming down from the hills.

The good news was that he spotted Janna nearly right away. The even better news was that she was wearing a corset—pink and black stripes set off by a sparkly Hello Kitty brooch. On nine out of ten girls, it would have been way too much. On Janna, it was amazing.

The bad news was that Takeshi and Aroha had apparently also just arrived, and Takeshi had seen the corset, too.

"It's Kitty-chan!" he said as Sione approached.

"Oh, right, it's a Japanese thing," Janna replied, beaming at Takeshi. Didn't she remember she was supposed to be talking to other guys? There were plenty around a bonfire farther down the beach. Some of them were looking her way, even.

"My sister, Keiko, she likes Kitty-chan," Takeshi explained. "And Miffy also. Do you know Miffy? She is a rabbit." He sounded too enthusiastic, and for a moment, Sione felt some sympathy for him. It was hard to be out of place. Even small things could be significant when they were reminders of home.

"I do!" Janna said triumphantly. "Did *you* know that Miffy was actually Dutch?"

"Dutch?" Takeshi asked, pulling out the electronic dictionary.

"From the Netherlands."

"Hi, Sione," Aroha said. Pretty sharply, actually. From the way her eyebrows lifted, he could tell she was already sick of being shut out of the conversation. He risked a small grin at her, and she grinned back.

"Oh, hi," Janna said. "I wondered when you were coming."

"Can I have a quick word?" he managed to say, and Janna went aside with him, smiling at Takeshi as she went.

"Have you talked to anyone else yet?" Sione asked, trying not to sound accusatory.

The smile dropped. "A few. Where's Keri?"

"No idea."

"That's weird. She's usually crazy punctual."

"I thought we were meeting at my room? Coming together?"

"Oh, were we?" she said. "I thought we were meeting at the beach at seven. I was wondering where you were." She laughed. "I was just getting good and angry at you—what a waste of energy! Okay, anyway, I talked to a couple of guys, but none of them fit the bill."

"No older brothers?"

"A few, but none staying until New Year's." Her eyes strayed back to Takeshi. "Look, can I ask you to talk to people for a bit? I don't want to give Takeshi the wrong idea."

Sione felt his already-withering hopes dry to dust. "I..." He choked. "Janna..."

"Hey," she said, and squeezed his hand. "Friends, right?"

"Sure," he said, and stumbled away from her before he could see her turn back to Takeshi with the come-hither look she'd turned on for him once and never again.

"Hey," a soft voice said behind him.

Sione turned. Aroha was looking at him—not exactly with sympathy but with kindness. "Do you want to get a beer?"

"I don't really drink," he said. But as soon as he said it, he wanted the light dizziness of being drunk, the feeling of not having to worry about anything that was happening to him.

"Me, neither. But you look like you need one. And they probably have Coke?"

"Sure," he said. "That's ... nice of you."

She shrugged and set off toward one of the tables on the

other side of the beach. "I got dumped four weeks ago. Sucks, doesn't it?"

"I wasn't exactly going out with her," he admitted. "She doesn't owe me anything."

"Doesn't matter. Still sucks."

"How did you deal with it?"

"Oh, all the ways the movies say girls should. Ice cream. Bitch sessions with friends about how he was never good enough for me in the first place. Didn't key his car—probably should have. He loved that thing way more than me."

Sione managed a rusty laugh. "So what's next?"

Aroha glanced up at him, an odd little smile on her lips. "Rebound relationship, I guess."

Sione might have come up with a response to that, but just then he noticed that the two guys grabbing beer cans from a cooler at the table looked familiar. The bonfire flared as someone threw on another log, and the light revealed their faces.

"Hey!" he said, in surprise as much as greeting, and the two older boys turned to face him. Luke and Mark were summer friends—of Matthew's, of course, not his—Tongans from Upper Hutt. And Luke was a perfect candidate for the killer: the right age, an older brother, and living somewhere the killer hadn't struck recently.

Okay. He could do this. "Hey, guys. How's it going?"

The brothers looked at each other, faces strange in the flickering firelight.

"Oh, yeah," Mark said after a long pause. "Little Felise. Want a beer? What's up?"

Sione winced. They hadn't recognized him right away. He

took a can of beer and cracked it open, just to give himself something to do. "Uh, not much, eh," he said, trying to remember if they knew about Matthew. Mum had sent the news to so many people, but she might have missed the regular Summerton crowd. "So, you guys going to be here for the—"

Luke broke in. "Who's your friend?"

"I'm Aroha," she said, and held out her hand. Luke looked down at it, then at Mark, and his full mouth twisted into a sneer.

That expression didn't look right on Luke's face. The air felt weird, tingling around them.

"That's a Māori name," Luke said. "You Māori, A-ro-ha?"

"No," she said. "Blame my mum. She liked it." She tucked her rejected hand into her pocket, shrinking herself a little, but her voice came out clear. "So how do you know each other?"

"We knew his brother. Used to be a little band of four. Matthew, Mark, Luke—and him." Luke jerked his chin at Sione. "Except it's funny, eh? We got white names, and Sione got the Pasifika one." He dragged out Sione's name the way he had Aroha's: *see-oh-nay*, mocking emphasis on every syllable.

"Why's that funny?" Aroha asked cautiously, and Sione wanted to stop her, because he could recognize the setup for a put-down even if he didn't know exactly what it would be.

"Because *Sione's* the potato," Luke said, and stood there smirking at them while Sione's stomach went into free fall.

He couldn't believe it. Not from Luke. These guys never wanted to bother with him, but they'd either ignored him or let him tag along when they went swimming or played beach cricket with Matthew and the others.

They'd never done this.

Aroha stiffened again, this time with anger. "Hey—" she began.

"Hay's for horses, beer's for men," Luke said, which didn't even make sense, and he grabbed at Sione's beer. Out of instinct more than anything, Sione kept his grip on the can.

"Hey, man," Mark said. "Take it easy, eh? Sione's okay."

Luke snorted. "Yeah? I should take it easy on you, Little Felise?" He pushed Sione's shoulders, sending him stumbling back in the soft sand. "Take it easy, you little faggot?"

"Oh, fuck *you!*" Aroha snapped. "Sione, let's go."

He wanted to leave, but he couldn't turn and meekly follow her. He had to say something, let Luke know this wasn't okay, ask him what he'd done.

But he thought he knew.

Too smart, too rich, too small. Not a real man.

He could feel his mouth opening and shutting like a fish's.

"Sione," Aroha said again, flickering glances at Luke as he sauntered over, an ugly, unfamiliar smile firmly fixed on his face. He loomed over Sione, blocking out the moon.

"Bro, nah, come on, let's get another drink," Mark said, and was reaching out for his brother's arm when Luke pushed Sione again, knocking him onto his ass.

"*Hey!*" someone shouted behind Sione, and then Janna barreled past him and shoved Luke in the chest.

Luke took a step backward, probably more out of surprise than at the impact, and pushed Janna out of the way.

She shrieked, and fell into the sand—not hard, but Sione could finally move, in her defense if not his. He threw the can of beer straight at Luke's face. It flew uselessly past his cheek, but Luke shouted and grabbed for him.

But Takeshi was already there, standing between Janna and Luke, the muscles in his bare arms standing out as he clenched his fists and stared Luke down. Mark was saying something to Luke, trying to get him to calm down, but if Takeshi threw the first punch, Sione knew Mark would probably help his brother. It was important to back up family. Takeshi looked pretty strong, but Luke and Mark would destroy him. Sione staggered to his feet, trying to make himself ready to fight.

"*Police!*" a huge voice roared. "Come on, break it up!"

And Sergeant Rafferty appeared, bigger than Mark, bigger than Luke, huge white hands grabbing Luke at the scruff of the neck like a cat would a kitten. "Who taught you to hit girls, sunshine?" he asked, and his voice was soft and heavy.

Sione saw it cross his face, the exact moment when Luke realized that he'd pushed a local white girl in front of a local white cop. He didn't protest Sergeant Rafferty's hand on his neck. His eyes flickered over Sione's face, oddly pleading, as if he couldn't work out what was going on, as if he couldn't work out how he'd gotten to this moment, what he'd done to make this happen.

It was exactly how Sione felt, and *he* hadn't pushed anyone. Aroha was explaining what had happened, voice high and angry over Mark's faltering explanation that Luke had been only joking, and Sione turned away, feeling sick. He hadn't done a damn thing.

"And you're okay?" he heard Sergeant Rafferty ask, and looked over his shoulder. Janna was flicking sand out of her

cleavage, looking more irritated than anything else, but the
sergeant wasn't talking to her.

"I'm fine," Takeshi replied. "May I go?"

"Sure. You're sure you're okay, though? We've got the ambos
on standby."

Takeshi hesitated—probably because he couldn't work out
ambulances from *ambos*—and then looked at Janna.

"We're okay," she said, and stepped toward Sione as the sergeant, still shooting worried glances at Takeshi, walked away
to make sure the Gospel boys left the beach. "What happened?" she asked.

"He called me a potato," Sione said. His voice sounded
weird—well, of course it did; it was the first thing he'd said
since the whole thing began. His messenger bag was *heavy*—
why the hell had he brought it to the beach? Did he think it
would make him look like less of a dick?

"What—" Takeshi began, and Sione broke.

"Brown on the outside, white on the inside, okay?" he
snapped. "*Fia palagi*. Not really Samoan. *Rich* boy in his fancy
clothes, too smart, no mates, pathetic loser who only wants to
be *white*—"

"Sione—"

He whirled away from Janna's hand on his shoulder. "I've—
I'm done, okay? You'll have to do it." He gestured at the spec-
tators, all the curious young men. "*You'll* have to."

"Of course. Sure, no problem."

"You need to—Luke's not really like that," he said. "I could
have handled it, okay? They weren't going to do anything!"
That was a lie, he knew—Luke was massive, and he'd been so

weirdly aggressive, for no reason Sione could pin down. It couldn't have been that he was with Aroha, who was watching him with an unreadable expression. Those guys hit on palagi girls all the time. He'd seen them.

Sione was afraid it was just him, Matthew-less him, with no reason for anyone to be tolerant or halfway nice. Had Luke really hated him all these years?

"I could have handled it," he repeated to Takeshi's confused face, and took off up the hill, bag thumping against his side.

CHAPTER NINE
Janna

★

JANNA WATCHED SIONE RUN THROUGH THE dunes toward the road. *God, the poor guy.* Of course, this meant that now she was stuck doing all the work herself.

"I guess it's just us," she said. "Aren't you lucky, Takeshi? Two pretty girls at the beach."

"All the people will envy me," Takeshi said calmly. The way he pronounced *vee* made Janna's knees wobble in her boots, and she was seized by the totally inappropriate urge to stick her tongue in his mouth and taste the cuteness.

Someone stumbled past them and threw up into a patch of sand grass, which sort of killed the impulse.

"Lightweight," Janna said, and cast a practiced eye over the beach. Most of the people were strangers, but there were a few people from school. Hemi and Kyle were talking to each other by a cooler, Kyle's hands making the motions that said he was thinking through a new beat. They saw her and waved.

At the very end of the beach was a *big* group, a lot of tourist kids mixing and dancing, none of them the boys she'd managed to screen before Takeshi and Aroha turned up. *Excellent*, she thought, and led the way.

Sand, Janna had discovered years ago, was a great excuse for stumbling into handy, boy-shaped support and requiring him to hold her up. Takeshi seemed to understand this important obligation and did not disappoint, his arm steady under hers.

She stopped dead when she realized that two of the figures at a table were familiar. And *not* young.

"Ew, it's the Maukis brothers," she said, and used her free hand to point at the two men. Octavian was taller and Tiberius wider, but otherwise they looked creepily alike, dressed in near-identical black shirts and black jeans, with the same neat beards and slicked-back hair. "They think they're twenty-three or something. It's so gross."

As if on cue, Octavian grabbed a dark-haired girl's plastic cup of something, taking a sip and laughing at her outraged look as if this was normal flirting, or something. Which it might have been, if he wasn't at least twenty years older than she was. The girl moved away, her body language screaming,

Ick! Ick! Ick! Octavian followed until she joined a group of girls, who closed protectively around her, and only then did he back off, looking for someone new.

"That's foul," Aroha said. "Those guys are the artists, right? We bought a painting from them last year, but it's really crap. Mum ended up putting it in the guest room. They were so smooth to her, it made me sick."

"They're disgusting. Right, Takeshi? We met Tiberius at the art gallery this afternoon," she explained to Aroha.

Takeshi looked baffled. "There was a...hat," he said vaguely. "No, uh, crown." His hand went to touch his hair. *"Omoi."*

Janna remembered the colored light cut into little pieces and the feeling of being covered in golden warmth, like the glory that sometimes swept through her with Cherry Bomb in her hands and a song to storm through. But the memory was weirdly hazy. *God, Janna, get a grip. Romance is so bad for your brain.*

Aroha seemed to be allergic to silence, especially charged silence between two people smiling at each other. "So!" she said, a little too brightly. "What are you planning for uni, Janna?"

She was obviously just making conversation, and Janna tried not to grimace at the topic. "What about you?" she countered.

"Engineering," Aroha said promptly. "And you? Music, maybe? Commerce?"

Janna shrugged. "I don't want to go."

Aroha probably didn't mean to sound so shocked. "You don't want to go to *uni*?" she asked, and Janna realized that she was one of *those* people, the ones for whom university was guaranteed, probably for a couple of generations. The ones who went to private schools and got music lessons and tutoring and had no idea how lucky they were. Aroha hadn't had to babysit every brat in Summerton for years to buy an old car and a secondhand bass; her parents probably just *gave* her anything she wanted.

"Not everyone goes," Janna said. "*Most* people don't."

"But you're—" Aroha said, and bit her lip. "I mean, you seem really smart."

Janna felt her hands twisting at her belt. "Well, I'm not. I suck hard at everything in school except Music and Drama, and I screw up the writing assignments there. I *probably* have a learning disability, actually." This wasn't nice. Aroha hadn't meant to hit one of Janna's sore points. But Janna could feel the anger crackle off her skin, and now Takeshi knew she was *stupid*.

"Janna is going to play the bass," Takeshi said, and squeezed her shoulder. "She is very good."

Janna felt her anger leeching away into the warm patch where his hand rested. She untangled her hands from her belt and tried to smile. "I mean, I'll probably end up being a waitress who plays on the weekends, but I'm going to give it a shot."

But she didn't believe that, not really. Someone had to make it, and it was going to be her.

"I'm really looking forward to hearing you at the Beach Bash," Aroha said quickly. "Oh, and I forgot, Dad got us this for tonight." She opened her bag to show them a bottle of wine and then closed it again. "It's an apology for the car crash." She shuddered. "That was so weird. I was looking straight ahead, and I didn't even see you until after we hit."

"Probably the shock. Say thanks to your dad for me," Janna said, deciding to forgive her. "How about you, Takeshi? Are you going to uni?"

Takeshi ducked his head. "I will do a bachelor of science degree."

Aroha laughed. "And then a master's degree, and a PhD at the International Space University, and then —"

"I want to be an astronaut," Takeshi said softly. "I want to be a mission specialist."

He was looking right at Janna when he said it, and she felt that drumbeat hammer at her heart again. Cute, sweet, smart, and *ambitious*. Someone like her, with an impossible dream, as driven as she was.

Then he deliberately banked the fire in his eyes and looked humble and apologetic. "It's very difficult. JAXA chooses only a few people to be international astronauts. But I will try."

"You'll succeed," she said firmly, and saw pleasure and surprise flicker across his face. Didn't people tell him that?

"I need to speak perfect English," he said. "That's why this exchange, it is good."

"How long have you wanted this?"

"From the time when I was six." He shrugged. "People laugh at me. They think it's too much. Too big dream."

"No, not too big," Janna said, and took his hand. His fingers were muscular and dry and fitted neatly into hers. They both had strong hands, too. "My brother wanted to go into space," she said, mostly to herself. Her mum had gotten pregnant at the same age Janna was now and married seven months before Schuyler was born. Schuyler had been pretty good about having to entertain his much younger sisters, usually with hours of playing school. Long before Janna could read, she'd known the names of the planets and the details of rocket propulsion.

"I'll just...I'll just go get this opened," Aroha said. "Borrow some cups from the table. Might talk to a few people. That's Ainsley—I met her last year; she's great."

Aroha was trying to give them alone time. That was so sweet, and incredibly inconvenient.

Janna wavered. She could wander off with Takeshi right now, explore him and his dreams and the night full of stars.

Or she could work toward avenging her brother, who would never go into space.

She squeezed Takeshi's hand one more time and moved forward, toward Aroha and the table and the guys clustered around one edge. "Here," she said to Aroha, but tipping one of the guys a smile that would encourage him to talk. "Let me help."

✒

The night was a total bust.

Guys talked to her, no probs, but bringing the conversation around to family and how long they were staying got really obvious, really fast. And to make matters even worse, Patrick found her and started on band business without even saying hi, right in the middle of a conversation.

"I signed the contract," he said, picking up a bottle of beer and scowling at it. "Gave it to Tiberius just now. That guy's a skeeze."

"Mmm," Janna said, turning away from him. "Sam, you were saying that you're going to be here until the twenty-ninth? Not for New Year's?"

"I'm going back to Nelson for New Year's," Sam explained, and was probably very disappointed when Janna nodded, turned back to Patrick, and drifted down the beach with him.

"I thought you already had a summer hookup," he said. "Why all the chitchat?"

"I'm trying to make sure people stay for our set at the Beach Bash," she improvised.

"Oh, yeah, good thinking. I've been planning some publicity. Our names aren't on the posters; they got printed before the lineup change."

"The Beach Bash *is* publicity for Vikings."

"We could put flyers up," he said. "Talk to local businesses. My cousin Xiao-Xiao has a show at Radio Greymouth, and she said she'll do an interview, and Mum said I can have the car to drive us down...."

Janna could just imagine what Sione and Keri would think of her taking a day off the killer hunt for a publicity road trip. "I'm busy. Can't we do it by phone?"

"Studio is better. This is important," Patrick said. He sounded surprised at having to remind her; he and Janna had always been the ones who really cared, who made the others turn up and practice long after they were bored.

"You've scheduled four practices over the next week, Patrick. Kyle or Hemi can do it."

"They work all day; they don't have time for the drive. And you're better at this stuff anyway."

"I'm doing things, too, you know."

Takeshi and Aroha were staring out at the sea, caught in the Summerton Effect. Patrick shot them a look. "Right," he said skeptically. "Get serious, Janna. You know that's not going to last past New Year's. Vikings needs you to —"

And he was *right*. She knew he was right, but it hurt weirdly to hear it. She turned on him. "Shut up." He opened his mouth, and she stuck her finger in his face, glad that she was that extra inch taller than him. "No, shut *up*! I turn up to practice, I work my ass off for this group! Don't you question my commitment!"

"I thought you wanted to get out of Summerton," Patrick snapped.

"I do!"

"Yeah? Look at Cara Wells. She was *so* close, Janna. She had that pop-opera thing totally working for her, she did a couple of TV appearances, she was all lined up for a big career, and then what did she do? She gave up and came straight back to this stupid town for no reason at all." He made a scornful face. "'Oh, I was so homesick!' Yeah, right. She couldn't hack it. And now she sells popcorn at the movies. It takes more than talent; it takes drive! You *need* commitment all the time, not just when it suits you."

Janna felt something turn over in her stomach. She'd always thought Cara's failure had been her own fault, too. But Keri had that theory, and Sione said the numbers backed her up.

No one moves into Summerton. No one leaves.

She twisted to look at Aroha and Takeshi, still staring at the bonfire light reflecting on the water. In the shifting light of the flames, their faces were placid and calm.

104

Like cows lined up for slaughter, waiting for the stun gun.

It wasn't natural, the Summerton Effect. It wasn't right.

"Magic," she muttered.

"You've *got* magic," Patrick said impatiently. "We all know that. You light up a stage. What I'm talking about is —"

"Yeah, shut up," she said absently. Patrick sighed in loud disgust and took off, probably to harass Hemi and Kyle.

Summerton was a *perfect* town. Always sunny, always safe, always the same. No one moved into Summerton. No one left. And Sione could say what he liked about irrelevant patterns, but it *was* a pattern.

She nearly laughed at herself. A spell to keep a whole town perfect — that would be some *serious* magic, with a lot of skill and power behind it. But the blankness in the tourists' faces — the dumbstruck awe that she'd always made fun of — didn't seem so hilarious anymore.

She wouldn't mention it to Sione and Keri. Not just yet. They'd only laugh at dumb Janna with her wacky beliefs and stupid ideas.

She started to make her way back to the table, planning to dump her bottle and touch base with Takeshi before she went after the next guy. But as she walked, she nearly stumbled over a woman sitting in the lee of a piece of driftwood.

"Crap, sorry," Janna said, and then, recognizing her, "Oh, hi, Sandra-Claire."

"Hi, Janna," the blond woman said without much enthusiasm. "How's it going? I hear you're hanging out with Keri again."

The Summerton grapevine at work. "Yeah, she's good times."

"She's a bitch," Sandra-Claire said, again without any particular emotion. "A little bitchy control freak who thinks she's got everything all worked out and won't let anyone tell her different without throwing a fit." Her lips twisted. "Jake dying didn't fit her *plans*, did it?"

"Are you feeling okay?"

"What do you fucking think? And the dwarf doesn't make anything easier."

Janna recognized the way Sandra-Claire tilted her head and squinted for focus; she'd done it often enough herself. "You're drunk."

"Not drunk enough." Sandra-Claire pushed herself up unsteadily. "Drop by the shop sometime after Christmas; there's new stuff in that you might like. But don't bring your little friend."

The magic shop, where Sandra-Claire assisted Daisy Hepwood. Where there might be explanations for *unnatural* things.

"Yeah, okay," Janna said. "I think I will."

CHAPTER TEN

Keri

⚡

BEING ACID-BURNING ANGRY TIRES YOU OUT.

When my alarm went off, I jerked awake, immediately realizing I hadn't met Sione and Janna for the beach party.

I'd completely screwed up the plan. Heartbeat jolted into full speed, I rolled out of bed, reaching for the bag hanging off the door handle and the cell phone inside it. I'd call them, explain, hear what they had to report. We'd set a new time to reconvene. It was okay. We still had time.

The new plan fell apart when I took my first step toward the door.

In the night, Jake's T-shirt had fallen out of the bed, to lie in wait for my shuffling morning feet. It tangled around my ankles. I should have been able to catch myself easily, but the world tipped around me, my balance completely off, and I fell, feet together, arms wide. I turned, trying to tuck in my arms and take the impact on my shoulder. Too slow, too late. My fingers caught on the carpet, twisting me even more off balance. All my weight crashed onto the outside point of my left wrist.

I heard the wet crack before I felt it. Nauseating waves of heat and cold spread up my arm and down my whole crumpled body. Only after that was the pain.

I moaned, the first sound I'd voiced, and instinctively curled around the hurt. That small motion set off new earthquakes of agony, aftershocks shuddering through me until I could force myself still. It took a moment to adjust to this new reality. How could this have happened? How could my own body have betrayed me like this?

"Okay," I said, panting. I was cold all over now, except for the burn in my arm, yet I could feel sweat prickling at my spine. "Okay, you know what to do."

I called out for Mum first, knowing that it was useless—the house was quiet, and she hadn't investigated the thudding impact of my body on the floor. I had to get myself up, then, thinking every motion through slowly and carefully as I rolled onto my knees, pushing myself up with the good hand—the right, thank God. My cheek was stinging now, too, and there was a red rash from the carpet on my knee. "Good girl," I told myself when I was upright, left wrist cradled across my body. I could hardly stand to look at it, the wrongness of the angle, the puffy redness around the bony knob at the side. The first-aid kit under my bed was well stocked, but I couldn't do anything about this by myself. This wasn't the greenstick fracture I'd had when I was seven.

For a moment, panic rose up my throat as I thought about what could happen if I'd done real damage, what a serious injury could do while I was still growing, what it could mean for rugby. I pushed it down to a hard lump in my stomach. Panic wasn't part of the plan. Go with the plan.

"Good girl," I repeated. "Phone now, then wait."

Summerton had one ambulance year-round and an extra for the holidays, to handle the bonus incidents of drunk people falling down and cutting themselves or walking into the bush and scratching themselves up. One came and whisked me away: sirens and lights, the full deal.

I would have been embarrassed by all the fuss, except by that stage I was feeling even more sick and sore, despite the splint that cushioned my arm against the bumps. I insisted on walking into the hospital, though, and the ambulance woman let me do it. Another positive was that I was still wearing yesterday's clothes; turning up at the hospital in pajamas would have been the worst.

"There's going to be a wee wait for Dr. Ryan. Is there anyone we can call for you?" the admitting nurse asked — not Janna's mum, but a young man I didn't know.

It was getting hard to remember the positives. My tongue

felt thick and swollen, and I had to concentrate hard on not cutting myself with my own teeth. "My mum," I told him. "Call Lillian Pedersen-Doherty at the Chancellor Hotel. You have to tell her I'm alive first."

Then I started falling forward, head heavy on my neck. The nurse caught me by the shoulders before I could face-plant into the desk, and the ambulance woman grabbed me around the waist. The nurse was shouting something, but his hands shoving into my shoulders had set off another massive cataclysm of pain, and his voice buzzed dark explosions into my mind.

For the first time in my life, I fainted.

So it wasn't the best morning ever.

When Sione opened the door to his room, he looked worse than I felt. But his eyes went immediately to the cast.

"Yeah, don't ask," I said.

"What *happened*?" he said anyway.

I rolled my eyes. "I fell down," I said. "It was really unlucky and stupid, and I'm pissed at myself. But the good part is I'm not dead, although it'd be great if you could tell that to my mother, because now I'm under house arrest so she can be sure I don't fall into the ocean and drown."

"But you're here," Sione pointed out. "Uh, are you sure you should be?"

"I'm fine," I said, in the face of all the evidence. "Anyway, I convinced Mum to bring me here instead of home, but when she finishes her shift, I have to go home with her, which is dumb, because I hurt myself *at* home. It was so weird. I couldn't get my balance. I felt like the house had tricked me. Like it had turned my body against me." I sighed. "I'm sorry about last night. I had a fight with my brother's evil ex and just went to sleep, I guess. Where's Janna?"

"Coming. It's okay about last night."

"No, I completely screwed up. How'd it go?"

Sione stared at his shoes. "Not…great."

I sat on the bed, pulled momentarily off balance by the cast. Six weeks of this. Maybe eight. I was going to go out of my mind. "How do you mean?"

In the end, I had to drag what had happened out of him word by word, and I was pretty sure he was still holding back. I decided to get the rest off Janna later, but I had enough information to work out that Sione's friends were dicks and that if I ever caught up with them, they'd be sorry.

Sione looked uncomfortable, too. "I had a thought," he said, "about what happened, after the fight. I don't know if it's important but—"

"Out with it," I said.

"Luke knocked me and Janna down. And Aroha was there with me. But when Sergeant Rafferty turned up, he was only really interested in if Takeshi was okay, and Takeshi hadn't been touched. I mean," he said, sounding as if he were trying to be fair, "Takeshi was *ready* to fight. He just didn't have to, because Rafferty turned up then, and he asked if Takeshi wanted an ambulance. He seemed…concerned."

"So it was Takeshi he was really worried about?"

"That's what I think."

"You worked this out last night?" I said, really impressed. I could never think in the middle of a fight or remember it properly later—it was all adrenaline and speed to me, the same as flying down the field with the ball tucked under my arm. When my body worked that smoothly, my brain didn't need to record what was happening.

"I think a lot," he said bitterly.

My skin was prickling, like it had when my wrist snapped. "I think it's him," I said. My voice was weak. I made it louder. "It's him, and he's probably going to try to kill Takeshi next year."

"We don't have any proof," Sione said, but I could tell he believed it, too. There was something that looked a lot like hate at the bottom of his eyes. "And the problem is, we were going to go to the police when we'd worked out who. We didn't think it *was* the police."

I hadn't ever planned to go to the police. "I know where Dad keeps the keys to the gun safe and ammo locker," I said. I knew how to use the rifle, too, even if I wasn't a hunter like Dad or Jake.

Jake, who'd been shot in the head by Sergeant Rafferty. My mouth tasted strange and metallic, like the memory of blood.

Sione didn't look horrified; I'd expected him to freak out. Instead, he frowned, like I'd handed him an interesting logical puzzle. "You'd get caught," he said.

"I don't care."

"I think you would, later. And even if you didn't, your parents would. I mean, they'd be able to visit you and everything, but you'd be in jail. In some ways, they'd have lost both their kids. Not to mention that a story like 'Māori girl kills white cop' would be all over the news. The media and radio talk shows and all that would be hassling your parents for months, maybe years. And we still don't have definite proof. Wouldn't you always wonder if you'd killed the wrong guy?"

He sounded so reasonable, so smart and perfect and right, and I really hated him.

I got up and walked over to the table, then back again, energy leaping under my skin with nowhere to go. "Fuck you," I said, kicking the bed and making it jump under him. "Fuck you, Sione Felise. Just because you're a wimp."

"Yeah," he said, sounding defeated. "Yeah, I know."

It wasn't worth trying to fight someone who wouldn't fight back. I slumped back onto the bed and stared at the tourists in the picture on Sione's wall dancing under the thunderclouds.

It was okay for *them*. They weren't real, and they didn't have to worry about real consequences.

We needed proof. I needed a new plan.

"Okay," I said at last. "Here's what we do."

CHAPTER ELEVEN
Janna

★

JANNA REALLY HAD MEANT TO GO STRAIGHT up to Sione's room to make her case, but Aroha and her family were coming out of the restaurant as she entered the lobby. Takeshi smiled straight across the long, light-filled room, and her heart expanded in her chest like an inflatable air bed.

Which was bad. The whole point of summer romances, for the three years she'd been having them, was that they should be hot and heavy and *fast*. She liked them the same way she liked playing gigs, at parties or Smokefreerockquest: slick skin and heart-pounding rhythm and the certain knowledge of what move came next and where her hands should be—and then the song was done and she moved on to the next one, which could be just as good, or even *better*. There was no time to think and no need to; she just threw herself in and made everything happen.

But she and Takeshi were playing something slower. They hadn't even *kissed* yet.

"Hi," Takeshi said. "You look very pretty."

"We're off to the beach," Aroha said. "Want to come?"

"No, I'm visiting Sione," Janna said, leaning into Takeshi's side. He slipped an arm around her waist—not grabby, just solid. "Are you looking forward to Christmas?" she asked him. "Is it different from in Japan?"

Takeshi blinked. "Japan is not a Christian country."

Janna was tempted to say "Neither is New Zealand," but tomorrow was a public holiday for a Christian celebration, so she wasn't sure how well that argument would go.

"So you don't have Christmas," she said instead.

He shrugged. "Well, a little Christmas. Christmas is for boyfriends and girlfriends. It's a love holiday. New Year's Day is our holiday for family. It's a religious day, too." He thought for a second, and Janna, recognizing the pause that meant he was putting a sentence together, waited instead of speaking. "It's strange here," he said finally. "No winter for Christmas and New Year's Day. No snow."

"Do you think you'll miss it?"

"Yes, my family, and the food. At my...uh, my community, a little after New Year's, we write on paper. Our dreams for the year, we write them. And we burn them in a fire outside. A fire in the snow. I will miss it."

"I've been telling him we could do that here," Aroha said.

Takeshi looked politely blank.

"We have fires around New Year's, too," she persisted. "You saw them on the beach. They aren't religious, though."

"They used to be," Janna said. She didn't know why she wanted to argue with Aroha all the time; she liked her fine, and Aroha wasn't even interested in Takeshi. Maybe it was because Aroha was a year younger and still thought she knew best about everything. And this once, Janna knew better. "It was a pagan tradition, lighting bonfires for a good year. But that was a winter thing, in the Northern Hemisphere."

"Oh, yeah," Aroha said. "And the druids burned people, right?"

Takeshi's eyes widened.

"No, that was probably made up," Janna said. "By the Romans."

"But I saw this documentary where they'd nominate a guy to be the king, and he'd have a great time, and then they sacrificed him in winter. To make the next year good."

"Nah, that was based on some stuff that was probably made up—" Janna said, and then horror rushed over her like a dump wave. The pagan Summer King myth was just that, some old guy taking old stories and spinning them into a book where ancient societies all over the world had sacrificed kings to make the land fruitful and the kingdom strong. But it was a really attractive idea. People liked to believe in it. And when it came right down to it, all neo-pagan rituals were made up—that's why they were *neo*. Ritual worked, if you did it right; putting will into the world, calling on deities or just the energy of the universe got results. And if you wanted a lot of energy, for a spell big enough for a whole town...

Summer Kings, sacrificed for prosperity and luck.

And Tiberius Maukis had picked up The Pride of Summerton and crowned Takeshi with it, right in front of her.

"No!" she said, her voice harsh.

"Janna! What is the matter? Are you sick?"

She looked up at Takeshi, gripping his muscular forearm. He was supporting her with his other arm. She hadn't felt her knees give way. "No," she said, and let him help her up. "No, I just...I have to talk to Sione. Right now."

"You went completely white!" Aroha said.

"Food poisoning," Janna said. It was totally unsexy, but it was the first thing she could think of. "I've really...I'm going." She stumbled into the elevator and pushed the button for the sixth floor three times until the door closed and she was free to slump against the wall, fighting back the desire to scream.

Bursting into the room and snarling "It's *magic*!" didn't quite have the effect she'd expected.

Sione just pulled the door shut behind her, and Keri didn't even pause as she scribbled something on a piece of paper. It looked like a map.

"We're pretty sure it's Sergeant Rafferty," Sione said. "But we need proof."

"We're going to break into his house," Keri said. "Serial killers take trophies. We find those, we've got him."

"Didn't you hear me?" Janna spotted the bright white cast on Keri's arm. "Oh, wow, what happened?"

"Don't ask," Keri said. "I think Sandra-Claire hexed me, the evil cow."

"Sandra-Claire wouldn't hex you," Janna said tentatively.

"Sure she would," Keri told her, yanking at the sling knot. "She hates me."

"She wouldn't curse you," Janna insisted. "She knows evil magic comes back to you."

"An ye harm none, do what ye will," Sione said in a posh voice. Janna blinked, and he forced a laugh. "What, you don't think we have any Goth kids at my school?"

Well, that was reassuring, sort of, Janna thought. Maybe Sione would be on her side. But she would have to correct his misconceptions first.

"I was actually referring to the Rule of Three, which states that any energy put out will return threefold to the practitioner, not the Wiccan Rede," she said. "Some witches believe the Rule of Three, and some don't, but I know Sandra-Claire *does* believe, because she lectured me on it for, like, half an hour the first time I bought a book from Inner Light. She wouldn't curse you, because something even worse would happen to her."

"I was joking," Keri said with heavy patience. "Magic doesn't work. Man, this thing itches already."

Janna tugged at her shirt and wished she could summon some of Stardust's confidence right now, when she really

118

needed it. "Magic does work, though," she said. "That's what I meant. The boys were killed *with* magic. And it's not Rafferty. It's Tiberius Maukis—probably Octavian, too."

That got Sione's and Keri's attention. Sione's mouth went round with shock, and Keri lifted her head from her plans and glared, a narrow-eyed look that said she planned to be angry with *someone*, and Janna was getting close to the top of the list.

"*Listen*," Janna said, and began to explain her theory. It didn't come out all that well; words describing fictional ancient rituals and what she'd seen in the gallery didn't sound right in the sunny hotel room with its ocean view. They let her finish, but by the time she was done, Sione was fidgeting with his shirt cuffs and Keri had her good hand on her hip. The other hand kept dipping down, trying to mirror it, but the cast got in the way.

"You think the Maukis brothers are Wiccan," Keri said flatly.

"Ugh! I hope not. Definitely not right-hand path. But that crown is magic. I *saw* it. Tiberius isn't doing it just to kill the boys, like a serial killer would; he's using their deaths for what he *really* wants. Think about it! Why are all the victims about the same age, with younger siblings?"

"Because serial killers often have narrow victim preferences to support their pathology," Keri said. It sounded like a quote. She frowned. "Though not usually across ethnicities or using different methods. But it's possible."

"Well, think about the *other* stuff," Janna insisted. "Why is Summerton so successful, while the other towns on the coast aren't? Why is everyone employed? Why doesn't anyone do meth or die in car accidents? Why did people keep coming even after the Steps to Heaven disappeared? That was the major tourist draw, and it vanished, but it didn't make any difference. Summerton got *more* popular."

"Well, it's really beautiful," Sione began.

Janna whirled around to face him. "Is it? It looks nice to me, but only nice, like any other town along the coast. Is it *really* beautiful, or is that just what outsiders see? Why does it never rain from Christmas to New Year's, prime tourist season? On the West Coast! That's *impossible*."

"I never thought of that," Keri said slowly.

"And why did you never think of it? Why does no one move in, Keri? Why can't anyone *leave*? And why don't we think about that, either?" She felt tears prickling at her eyes and blinked them away. "It used to rain in the summer holidays. Don't you remember? Before Schuyler died, it rained."

"Coincidence," Keri said. "Microclimate."

"This Summer King," Sione said. "Tell me again. He's sacrificed, and the sacrifice ensures a good year." His dark lips twisted, like he was trying to be scornful but couldn't quite manage it. "With his life energy or something?"

Janna nodded, willing him to believe. "Something like that. The Maukises specifically choose older brothers. There's a lot of ritual significance there."

For a moment she was afraid the ceremony had already happened in that one crowning, that Takeshi was already doomed. Better to believe he wasn't, she decided, because then she might be able to do something about it. So she went on, talking herself into belief. "The Maukises probably finish the spell on New

Year's Eve, because that overlaps with the time the boys stay here, and it makes ritual sense, too; the end of the year is something people celebrate—there's energy around that. And the town gets another year to be"—she looked out the window at the shining bay—"*perfect*. Perfect Summerton."

"But they're both crossed off the list!" Keri said.

Ugh, all their work with the electoral roll had been completely useless. "You're not *getting* it. I bet they don't even have to be near the boys when they die. Octavian and Tiberius do a ceremony, the boys go home, and, in winter, they die. They might even think it's their own choice. And this year, it's Takeshi."

"Jake didn't die in winter," Keri pointed out, and Janna's train of thought nearly derailed.

"Well, maybe he found out about it?" she suggested. "Or it was a top-up for the spell. Maybe the Maukises are doing winter *and* summer deaths now?"

"This is crazy, Janna," Keri said. "Hypnotism, I might believe. Maybe the Maukises—or Rafferty—plant a suggestion and the boys go home and kill themselves. But all the rest, the stuff about the good year and the rain...Magic doesn't make any sense, Janna! It's not how the world works!" Her small fists were clenched, the left one as well as it could around the cast, and her voice trembled. Janna suddenly got just how much Keri needed the world to make sense.

"I'm sorry," Janna said, as gently as she could. "But that's what I think happens. It fits all the facts."

"Except the fact that there's no such thing as magic." Keri looked at Sione. "You don't believe this, do you?"

Sione fidgeted again, glancing at both girls in turn, then staring at his shoes.

"Oh, for God's sake," Keri said.

"Why are you sure it's Rafferty?" Janna asked.

Sione told her, still unable to meet her eyes, and Janna frowned. "That sounds more like gut instinct," she said.

"Yeah, 'cause instinct makes less sense than magic," said Sione.

"Oooh, look at you, all brave." Janna meant it as a joke, but Sione didn't smile.

"It's not a game, Janna. It's not a fairy tale—"

"Nothing to do with fairies—" she protested.

"Or a fun summer fling, okay? This is our family."

"Mine, too!" Janna said, stung. "You think I'm playing around? I am totally *serious*, and neither of you will listen to me!"

Keri sighed. "So we break into Rafferty's, Sione?" She looked at Janna. "It's probably a two-person job, tops, so if you don't want to come—"

"There won't be anything there! It's the Maukises!" Janna said, then hesitated. Rafferty had looked really concerned about Takeshi at the beach... "Wait. If he's working with them, and I guess that's possible, he might have witchcraft supplies. Look for an athame—that's a ritual dagger—or a chalice."

"Are you kidding me?" Keri demanded.

"I honestly am not." Keri's face went hard again, and Janna jumped in before she could speak. "Look, I'd come if I could, but someone should keep an eye on Takeshi. And I'm going to try to get a look at The Pride of Summerton. Just...look for them, okay? I know you think I'm crazy, but just do it as a favor! Do it to shut me up, if that's what it takes."

"If it makes you feel better," Sione said. He was looking at Keri when he said it, and if his tone wasn't exactly firm, it was close enough to it to be surprising, coming from him.

Keri nodded. Grudgingly, but she did it.

This was a victory, Janna decided, and exhaled at last.

"Tomorrow's Christmas, and I don't know if Rafferty'll be working or not," said Keri. "We can't break in then."

"And I promised Mum I'd go to midnight Mass tonight," Sione said.

"The gallery will be closed tomorrow, too," Janna said, realizing. "But it's open Boxing Day. I can check out the crown then."

Keri nodded. "So everything's on hold until after tomorrow." She put her map in front of Sione. "Okay. Let's plan."

It was all right if Keri pretended to ignore Janna, as long as she looked for magical evidence anyway. Once she saw proof, Keri would have to believe.

CHAPTER TWELVE
Sione

✝

WHEN KERI'S MOTHER CAME FOR HER AT FIVE,
Sione put on his politest smile, the one he used at church or for
greeting Dad's business buddies, and opened the door. Small,
he thought, like Keri, but blond and pale and polished—a por-
celain woman. Lots of the mums at his school were like that,
though he bet their clothes cost more.

"Hello, Mrs. Pedersen-Doherty. I'm Sione. Nice to meet
you."

"Yes," she said, and shook his offered hand. Approval

flickered on her face momentarily, for his manners, for his clothes, before it was replaced with blank friendliness. "Nice to meet you at last."

Sione figured the last two words were aimed at her daughter and got out of the way as Keri rose from her spot at the desk and went to the door. He had finally worked out what was strange about her movement: Most people with a cast moved as if they suddenly had an extra limb and had to be careful with it. Keri looked weird because she *didn't* look weird; she carried the cast like a weapon and went around daring the world to get out of her way.

Mrs. Pedersen-Doherty seemed less impressed than he was. "You left your pills in the staff room," she said.

"I don't need them," Keri said.

"Dr. Ryan said two on the hour, every four hours, with some food."

"She said, 'If you need them.' Which I don't. It doesn't hurt."

The older woman's forehead developed new wrinkles, and Janna jumped to her feet. "How are you, Mrs. Pedersen-Doherty?"

"I'm fine, Janna," she said automatically. "How're your mum and dad?"

"Good, thanks."

They all stood awkwardly for a moment. Then Keri walked forward, forcing her mother back. "Let's go. So you can yell at me in the car." She was moving too fast to see her mother's expression and went down the hall without looking back. Sione looked into Mrs. Pedersen-Doherty's face in time to catch the weariness and the pain, and the terrible fear that lay under both.

"She's okay," he said impulsively. "She pretends it doesn't hurt because she's embarrassed, and she doesn't want to worry you."

Keri's mother jerked, and Sione realized what he'd said. He felt his face fill with blood from forehead to throat and knew she was close enough to see the color under his skin. Megablush. Supremo-blush. Sione Felise, World Champion Blusher. "I mean...I'm sorry."

"Yes," Mrs. Pedersen-Doherty said quietly. "Thank you." She nodded at Janna, who was shifting from foot to foot, and followed Keri to the elevator.

"Whoa," Janna said. "You're a braver man than I am. And more observant."

"Well, you know...when your mum's a therapist, it sort of gets to you, too." He closed the door and moved into the room, and only then did he realize that they were alone in his room together. Janna was looking away from him, fidgeting with her buttons.

He remembered stroking the back of her neck, amazed that she was letting him do this, amazed that she was sighing in his ear. *Don't think about it*, he told himself, but the memory after that was the one with her lips on his and the terror and excitement that had swept through him as he opened his mouth to hers.

"So," he said, and cleared his throat. "What are your plans for tomorrow?"

"Takeshi and Aroha have to spend Christmas with her

parents," Janna said. "And I have morning Mass and presents and Christmas lunch, but I think I can come visit you in the afternoon. Mum knows you're here by yourself."

"I guess she feels sorry for me, eh?"

Janna nodded, oblivious to his tone. "Yep. She wanted to invite you to join us, but I explained you'd probably feel weird about that."

Sione stared at her, trying to find the words. "Did you?" he said at last.

Something in his voice must have gotten through, because she looked uncomfortable at last. "Was that wrong?" she asked. "I just thought…maybe you'd like to be alone. The first Christmas and all that. I don't really—it was pretty bad for us, that's all I can remember. You can come if you'd like. It's no trouble."

"No trouble," Sione repeated. He wanted to trouble her, that was the thing—give her sleepless nights like he'd had, make her wait for him to show up online, have her be happy to speak with him even about horrors, afraid that she would say the wrong thing and drive him away.

Instead it was all about *Takeshi*.

You don't own her, he reminded himself. *She doesn't owe you anything, definitely not herself. You've got no right to be jealous.* But it was so, so hard. "My parents are calling tomorrow," he said. "I couldn't come anyway."

Janna curled her fingers around the edge of her shirt and pulled it straight. "Okay, then. Good night," she said, and brushed past him as she went for the door.

Sione felt a hole open inside him, just under his rib cage,

and went to shower so that he could pretend to himself that he wasn't crying.

◢

Mum rang at nine. Sione listened over the crackly line to her voice, the familiar lilt of the island accent she'd kept even though she'd now lived longer in New Zealand than she'd lived on Upolu.

"I heard something, Sione Felise," she said. "I heard you got in a fight. Is that how I raised you?"

"I didn't," Sione said quickly.

"I heard the police got involved, and there was some girl—"

"No, Mum, no. It didn't happen that way."

"You tell me what way it happened right now! If you think I won't come back there and take you home, you've got another think coming."

"It was just some guys, Luke and Mark, you know them. Luke was a bit drunk, playing around." He could feel the sweat prickling in the recess of his spine in this air-conditioned room. Mum didn't make empty threats. She'd fly home and haul him back to Auckland by his ear, or send one of his Auckland cousins to do it. "It got a bit noisy, but no one was hurt. It was all a misunderstanding." He added, truth sour on his tongue, "You know me. I don't fight."

"Hmmm. Were you drinking?"

Sione remembered the can he'd flung at Luke's head, arcing through the air like a big silver bullet. "No, Mum."

"And the girl?"

"Just my friend Janna. And we weren't fighting over her.

You met her last year, remember?" That, he realized immediately, had been a mistake.

Sure enough, Mum's voice sharpened again. "Oh, that girl? Who wears the clothes?"

"That's just the fashion, Mum. She's nice." That was a lie, he thought. Janna was exciting and beautiful and dramatic, but not exactly nice.

"She's someone seeking self-esteem in how boys react to her *fashion*, is what she is."

"I think Janna has plenty of self-esteem, Mum."

"Hmmm. Well, your father and I both trust you, Sione. We trust you won't let us down."

Sione thought that only Mum could give the I'm-not-angry-I'm-disappointed speech before she even knew there was something to be disappointed about.

"Are you sure you're all right?" she asked after a long breath that echoed in his ear.

"Yes," Sione said. "I'm okay. I miss Matthew." And Janna was all mixed up with his last memories of Matthew; that was part of the problem. Maybe he *should* go back to therapy.

"We can come home, if you need us," she said instead. "I've been thinking all day that I was wrong to let you go by yourself. How'd you talk me into this?"

"I'm a very responsible and independent young man," he said, trying to joke. "It's okay, honest. I'm fine. You don't have to go anywhere."

"You're a very responsible and independent seventeen-year-old, but still my baby boy," she countered. "You could get a bus ticket back to Auckland. Your auntie Betty is at home with the new bub."

He had to get her off this track right away. "How'd you hear about that thing on the beach?" he asked.

"Kirk Davidson told me. Sione, I think maybe—"

"I'm doing fine," he said. "I am. It hurts, being here, but it's kind of good hurt. It's clean. I'm getting it all out." He was thinking about Mr. Davidson's cold eyes, the way he watched Sione going in and out of the hotel. And he and Sergeant Rafferty had talked to each other about the accident, about the fight. Maybe they were working together.

Mum sighed, and he heard all his weary grief in her voice. "My mum's been giving me a hard time, eh?" She switched to fast, casual Samoan, with its soft *t* sounds. It was a perfect imitation of Nanny Isolina, but she spoke quietly. Sione could picture Mum checking over her shoulder, hunching over the phone to make sure she wasn't heard. "'Where is my grandson? Where is my baby boy? What is this "closure"? Ah, your Auckland way is so cold! Where is the family? You forget how to be Samoan!'" She went back to English. "I told her my Auckland way paid for her house, and she told me that all the money in the world couldn't replace family and proper respect. And of course, she's right."

Sione winced. "Sorry, Mum."

She laughed into the phone. His mum had a great laugh. "Is Summerton still beautiful?"

Sione remembered Janna's theory and scrunched his toes into the carpet. "Always."

"It's a real miracle, that place. Okay, your dad was going to say hi, but it's time for evening prayer. We'll call tomorrow."

"Give my love to the uncles and aunties and cousins," Sione said. "And Dad and Nanny Isolina and everyone."

"They give theirs to you. *Tofa*, Sione."

"*Tofa soifua.*"

He held the phone to his ear until it clicked and went silent, and felt the gap under his ribs open up again.

◢

When he filed into the small wooden church and found a seat at the edge of one pew, Sione felt conspicuous. He'd automatically put on his white church shirt and *ie faitaga*, what he'd wear in Upolu, or to Samoan Christmas Mass in Auckland. But almost everyone in the church was palagi, and most of the men were wearing dark pants and colored button-ups. The family beside him nodded and smiled and made room for him, though, and by the time the service approached Communion, the familiar ritual of Mass had worked to make his world better. He felt calm and safe for the first time since he'd gotten on the bus for Summerton.

He knelt with the rest of the congregation to proclaim the mystery of faith. "Christ has died, Christ is risen, Christ will come again," they chorused, and he thought, as he did every time now, *Matthew will come again, too.*

Some people thought that people who committed suicide wouldn't be resurrected. Sione had never believed that God would be that cruel to people who'd had a rough time already, but he'd been a little bit relieved when he'd realized that being murdered lifted Matthew out of that category.

With a start, Sione saw that most of the people around him had sat back down, waiting for their time to go forward for Communion. He must have looked especially pious—or like he was trying to seem as if he were.

But before he got up, he squeezed his eyes shut. He could definitely use some extra help.

Dear God, thank you for your love and inspiration. If it's your will, please help me stop this.

Guide me and protect me and my friends.

Amen.

That feeling of warmth and safety increased. He stood up and shuffled forward with faith that his prayers would be answered.

CHAPTER THIRTEEN
Keri

DAD GOT HOME AT NINE THAT NIGHT, BRING-
ing fish-and-chips and a jam doughnut for me.

He'd arranged the food on one of the good cream
plates and put everything on a tray. There was even a napkin
and a flower, which he'd stuck into one of the small shooter
glasses.

It was a rose from the garden, not anything fancy, but I felt
my throat clog as he carefully lowered the tray onto the sheets
over my lap. It was probably the painkillers that made me feel

so weird. I shoved a chip in my mouth and bit down on the salty warmth, blinking hard.

"Missed you, kid," Dad said, and smoothed my hair away from my face. My hair caught in his rough palms; all my life, my dad has had working hands, calluses forming even through the thick gloves worn by the road crews. When I was little, we used to go on driving holidays all over the South Island, Mum singing as she drove, Dad flinging lollies from the big bag in the front seat to me and Jake to keep us quiet. And every now and then, especially along the West Coast, Dad would look out the window and say, "Worked that."

My dad helped make the roads that tie the island together, moving people up and down and coast to coast like blood traveling through the body. It's maybe not a job many people think is very important, but we were proud of him, Jake and me.

He sat on the end of the bed. I wriggled my legs around, adjusting for the sag.

"It's been a shit month," he said. "Your mum's worried about you."

"I'm okay." I made a face and lifted the stupid, heavy arm. It was aching again, but I tried to move like it didn't. I didn't want to take more of the pills. "Apart from this."

"She said she slapped you the other day."

I had to think hard to remember it. So much had happened since. "Oh, yeah. It's all right."

He scratched at the gray stubble on his chin. "You really okay with missing Christmas? Your nanny wants her *moko-puna*, eh."

"I don't think I could handle it. And Mum needs the company."

"I could stay here."

"Nanny Hinekura would go mental if you did that," I said.

He gave me the respect-your-elders-young-lady look. "Don't talk that way."

"You have to go. It's only for one night, right?" And Dad needed his family. I made myself smile. "Guess you can't eat all the pies."

"I'll be back first thing Boxing Day. Got the garden to take care of." He was grinning a bit around the edges. "Thing is, I got you something."

"You did?" I said, trying to keep the surprise out of my voice. Dad wasn't in charge of gifts. He was in charge of the lawn, and the cars, and teaching Jake and me how to drink responsibly. He did a lot of things well, but presents wasn't one of them. The last thing he'd bought for me on impulse had been a Barbie, when I was (1) thirteen and (2) well over my pink stage. I braced myself as he handed me an envelope. *Look happy*, I told myself, *even if it's a gift voucher for a manicure or something.*

But I didn't have to pretend. I took one look at the red and black card that read CANTERBURY AND CRUSADERS MEMBER: KERI PEDERSEN-DOHERTY and felt joy tingle down my limbs, even the broken one.

"Canterbury membership," I breathed. "Oh, Dad. Oh, *Dad*. This is the *best*."

"We'll still have to buy tickets," he said. "And get to the games."

"But we *can* buy them." Even the finals—guaranteed seats, if we paid.

Of course I supported the West Coast, but they weren't going to win anything in the next century or so, not with the big rugby teams poaching all their best players. And Canterbury was a big team. The biggest.

The only thing that could have been better would have been season tickets to the national women's team's games, and I didn't think you could even buy those.

For a whole five seconds, I forgot Jake was dead.

Then Dad looked at his knees and hunched a bit, and it came back to me, fresh and horrible. I hitched out a breath, and then another one.

"Oh, kid," Dad said, and smoothed my hair again. "You don't have to be tough today."

Sometime later, when I lifted my head away from his chest, there were big wet spots all over his shirt. Mum was standing in the doorway, arms wrapped tightly around her stomach. Dad held out a hand, but she shook her head. "Early morning tomorrow," she said. "I just... Remember to take your pills, Keri."

"Okay," I said, too tired to fight about it.

"I love you," she added, and walked out, back stiff, before I could reply.

Dad poured me a Coke to wash down the painkillers, told me I could skip brushing my teeth, and tucked me in. "I'll put this in the fridge," he said, taking the plate. "Good night, kid. Merry Christmas."

I yawned in acknowledgment and snuggled my cheek

against the pillow. I felt emptied out, and the pills on top of that made me feel kind of drifty and soft. I knew it wouldn't last, but it was nice while it did.

⬛

Christmas morning was sunny and warm, like almost every Christmas morning I could remember. But the house was empty again, and that was completely the opposite of Christmas. Mum was already at work. I ate a festive breakfast of reheated chips, drank the last of the milk, and decided that it was time to get clean. After nearly two days without a shower and in the same clothes, I felt disgusting, and probably smelled worse.

I wasn't sure I could make the cast waterproof enough to risk a shower, and getting some soak time in sounded good. But it turned out that a bath wasn't the soft option, either.

Our tub was old-fashioned: deep and solid, with cold, slippery sides and a wide mouth. I'd planned out what to do, but I hadn't thought through how much the broken arm changed things. My body felt like it was fighting me, like it had when I'd first fallen, and I nearly tumbled in twice just trying to put the plug in. I *did* start to fall when I reached across to turn on the tap and saved myself only by shoving hard at the bottom of the bath and tipping myself back out, staggering backward across the vinyl tiles, free arm windmilling like a cartoon clown.

I slammed hard into the bathroom door, went "oof!" as the round handle dug into my back, and slid down the door onto my bum, where at least it would be hard to fall any farther.

Somebody should have applauded. Instead, I got the chirping of fantails outside the window and my own breath coming out in heavy pants.

"Okay, plan B," I said, voice echoing in the white space, and went to call the hotel.

Sione sounded pretty much how I felt, which surprised me until I remembered it was his first Christmas, too. But he said yes to my coming over and a less certain yes to what I wanted to do.

The problem, I decided, staring into my wardrobe as I tried to pack the bag I'd need, was that I didn't dress fancy enough. I could probably yank on a sports bra for underneath, but all my shirts were T-shirts or polo necks—things impossible to pull over the cast and my head by myself, one-handed.

I gnawed at an already-shredded fingernail, sighed, and went into Mum and Dad's room. Mum's clothes took up most of the wardrobe, including a bunch of button-up blouses in pastel shades. I grabbed a pink sleeveless top with shell buttons down the front, which was the least girlie-girl thing there.

I started to leave, then paused.

The Christmas present Wii that Jake would never play sat on the wardrobe floor.

I picked it up before I could think too hard about it, balancing the box on my hip, and went back to my room to write Mum a note.

When I got to the hotel, I went around to the service entrance. There was leaving the house in defiance of Mum's orders, and then there was doing it right in front of her. The last thing she needed was temptation to go nuclear in the lobby.

"Huh," I said when Sione opened his door. "You look like shit."

He grimaced, but it was true; his clothes were as crisp as ever, but the dark circles under his eyes were almost black, like an enraged makeup artist had gone at him with eyeliner. "Thanks. You, too."

"At least you don't smell. Let's be the Looks-Like-Shit Club." I dumped my bag on the end of the unmade bed. The hotel room looked a lot less tidy than usual—clothes had exploded over everything, and his messenger bag had been tossed on the table in the corner, spilling half the contents over the polished surface. A black skirt thing with pockets— *lavalava*, I thought—and a white shirt were the only neat pieces of clothing, carefully folded over the desk chair.

"Merry Christmas," Sione said when I turned around. He was holding out a small box wrapped in silver paper.

"Thanks," I said, trying not to sound too surprised, and carefully unwrapped the box. It was a pair of earrings, little silver ankhs. Stylish, and witchy, and completely wrong for me. I didn't even have pierced ears.

I looked at the earrings for a second, while Sione shifted from foot to foot, and then decided not to point out that they were very obviously a gift for someone else. "These are great," I said instead, and put Janna's earrings in my bag. "I didn't get you anything, but there's a surprise in the bag. If you want, you can set it up while I have my bath."

With that reminder, he went into the bathroom. I heard

the rush of water, and then he came out to help me tape the plastic bag over the cast. He did it well, which surprised me, but when I mentioned it he ducked his head.

"Matthew broke his arm playing rugby last winter," he said. "I helped him."

He was staring straight at the floor when he said that, radiating so much misery that I moved without any plan at all. I wrapped my good arm around him and, when he didn't move, managed to get the cast around his waist, too. I couldn't squeeze properly, but it was enough; I felt his sigh shaky against the side of my neck, and he relaxed into the hug. I stayed there a second more, wondering if he was going to cry, and wondering if I'd have the patience to stand there if he did, but he pulled away and wrinkled his nose.

"You do stink."

"I told you so," I said, and went to the bathroom with my clothes. "I should have given it another couple of days. Got a really cheesy ripeness going."

"That's disgusting," he informed me through the closed door. "Oh, hey, a Wii!"

The clumsiness that had attacked me at home wasn't bothering me here; I managed to get into the bath with no problems, with my arm resting on towels folded onto the curved rim. I soaked until my toes wrinkled, soaped myself down one-handed, and soaked again. From the main room, I could hear rhythmic beeping and the occasional groan or cheer as Sione wrestled with the Wii.

When it came time to get dressed, the sports bra was easy enough. But it turned out the buttons on Mum's fussy sleeveless top didn't go all the way down the front—I'd have to pull it over my head after all. I strained at the shiny, unstretchable fabric, sweating and cursing, and undoing all that relaxation, until Sione knocked on the door and asked if there was something he could do.

I opened the door, and his eyes went wide.

"Could you help me put this on?" I asked. "Sorry."

This close to him, I could see the blood darken under Sione's golden-brown skin when he blushed, practically feel the heat on my skin as he wordlessly took the shirt and helped tug it over my arms and then my head. I tried to interfere at one point, but it just slowed things down, and there was only so much I could ask him to take. So I suffered allowing him to dress me without doing anything myself.

"Thanks," I said when he was done and backing away. He nodded, deep in one of his silences. I was beginning to recognize it now, the way he retreated, the same way I recognized how Janna turned away from things she didn't want to acknowledge by dancing down new conversational paths.

I hadn't planned on this. I'd wanted to find revenge for Jake, not find a new friend, or an old one.

But I was probably stuck with them now.

I thought that we really should go over the plan again, make sure we knew where and when to be, and what to look for when we got into Rafferty's house.

"Do you want to play Wii?" Sione asked.

"Yeah," I said. "That sounds nice."

CHAPTER FOURTEEN
Janna

★

JANNA DID PRETTY WELL OUT OF CHRISTMAS, mostly gift vouchers, but that was okay, since no one in her family was any good at picking out things she wanted.

"It's a shame your friend couldn't come," Mum said while Petra and Mariel folded up wrapping paper and stowed it in the craft cupboard.

"He needed to wait for the call from his parents," Janna said. Sione had said so himself, so it wasn't technically a lie, even though she was positive *he'd* been lying.

"He could have taken it here," Dad said. "We wouldn't have minded."

Mum stiffened at this interference, and Janna tried not to roll her eyes. This was exactly why she'd lied about the invitation to Sione. A family Christmas wasn't any good when your family was *broken*, and it was definitely nothing to invite your friend to, especially when your friend already took everything nice you did as the next thing to a marriage proposal.

So far today her parents had fought over Mum's ham recipe ("You know I hate pineapple; why pineapple glaze?"), how much Dad had spent on the girls ("Didn't we agree there'd be no more bribery attempts?"), and whether Janna's dyeing her hair bright pink just before Christmas morning Mass deserved a grounding. On the last one, they'd swapped sides halfway through and hadn't even noticed.

Maybe she *should* have brought Sione. Introduced him to what happened to love, van der Zaag style. That would have stopped his mooning after her; who'd want to love a girl with those genes?

She'd always wondered why Dad hadn't left Summerton permanently after the divorce, instead of moving back after six months and making both him and Mum suffer when they bumped into each other in the supermarket. They still slept together sometimes, Janna knew; it was gross enough to know your parents had sex, but way grosser when your *divorced* parents had sex and then tried to act as if they hadn't. At least they'd stopped deluding themselves that maybe they'd get back together for real, but the push-pull act was almost as bad. They might have been able to change, if Dad had left for good.

If Dad had been able to leave.

Janna pushed her chair back from the table.

"We haven't finished discussing your hair, madam," Dad said.

"I didn't do it to make you mad," she protested, holding a strand at arm's length to stare at it. It was a *nice* pink, a kind of bright cerise. "I just had the dye there, and I woke up and couldn't get back to sleep and I thought I might as well."

"Everyone looking at us in Christmas Mass, that's what you wanted," Dad said.

"They might have been looking at you, Peter, since that's the only time you go," Mum snapped.

Janna got up and left them to it, rubbing her Christmas-extended belly. She scraped and stacked the plates, including Schuyler's unused one, and ran water over them.

"Dad," she said.

Her father paused mid-sarcasm and blinked his pale blue eyes at her. She'd inherited those eyes; so had Schuyler. The kids took after Mum.

"Why did you come back to Summerton?"

He glanced at Mum, obviously preparing a shot, and then appeared to think better of it. Mariel was watching from the corner, dark-eyed and solemn.

"I missed you," he said. "I missed this town. I was home-sick, every night. I felt empty and sore. Something was missing, and I knew it was here. I had to come back."

So the spell was obviously wide-ranging—as it should be, with a boy's life energy going into it every year. And powerful, if none of the other witches around had noticed it. Keeping an

144

eye on Takeshi might not be good enough. A protection spell for him would be better. Janna could do that, maybe. But she wasn't happy about doing it from one of her books. Most of them were for Northern Hemisphere witches anyway.

Sandra-Claire would probably give her advice, but Keri would go into fits. So it would have to be Daisy, who'd ask questions. She'd better come up with some answers.

Tomorrow, she thought. *After I get a good look at that crown.*

"Janna, we're pulling crackers now," Mariel said. Her hands were on her hips, and her chin pulled down stubbornly, in an expression she'd made for as long as Janna could remember.

"You can't cheat this time," Petra told her. "Only grab the *end* of the cracker."

"Bossy, bossy," Janna said, and gathered with her family under the brightly colored tree.

She did cheat, of course. It was what big sisters were for.

CHAPTER FIFTEEN
Sione

†

SIONE HAD NO IDEA HOW TO DRESS FOR breaking into someone's house. He kept thinking about the news reports Mum hated, where the solemn-voiced reporters would say, "The perpetrator was described as a large Māori or Polynesian male in dark clothing." He'd never seen a report about a medium-sized Polynesian male in Calvin Klein jeans and a funky button-down.

"Too good to make the news," he said out loud, and giggled

quietly into the mirror until the urge to laugh abruptly faded and he went back to feeling sick to his stomach.

He almost wanted Janna's magic theory to be right. At least that way Matthew would have died *for* something—something sick and terrible, sure, but not just to give a serial killer his thrills. And he wasn't sure he wanted to find *trophies*. Matthew had been buried with all his fingers and toes, but what if there was, like, a wall of hair clippings?

He got the person at reception to call him a taxi. The taxi driver was an Asian-looking man who didn't talk much, obviously sharing most Summertonians' antitourist prejudices. He raised a bushy eyebrow when Sione gave him directions to a residential house instead of the bird-watching sanctuary or one of the bushwalk entrances, but that was all. Sione slid down into his seat as they went past the art gallery, just in case.

Keri's place was a white weatherboard house with a wooden fence. There was a rock garden in the front and a trampoline in the back, with worn blue pads, and a vegetable garden. There was a man working in the vegetable garden, too, solid like Keri, but bigger and a bit darker, with a square face and heavy hands. He straightened as soon as he saw Sione and lowered his spade.

"You're the Felise kid," he said.

"Yes, sir."

"I'm not a sir."

"Sorry, Mr. Pedersen-Doherty."

"Just Doherty. It's Lillian and the kids with the double barrel." For a moment his face went hurt and tired. "Lillian and Keri, I mean."

"I'm sorry," Sione repeated, and meant it this time. The man's face had closed up again, but he gave Sione a small nod.

"I hear your brother died earlier this year."

So, not really a family for light conversation.

"Yes."

"Pretty rough, isn't it?"

"Yes, sir." He winced at the slip, but Mr. Doherty appeared not to notice.

"They say it gets easier."

This was awful. He should have asked Keri to get her dad out of the house. "Kind of. It still hurts. It gets easier to do other things, that's all. And you do more of those and you, um...you don't forget, exactly. You can't forget. But it takes up less space in your head. You can concentrate more on your life."

"Is that right?" Mr. Doherty said, like it was some new and fascinating revelation. "Keri's inside."

Sione blinked at the abrupt change in conversational direction, but started to escape while he could. Mr. Doherty already had the spade back in his hand. "Thanks, kid," he said, and stabbed the rich earth again before Sione could work out if he was meant to respond.

Keri's inside wasn't much of a direction. "Hello?" he called down the dark hallway. There were only a few doors, but he didn't want to open them. Keri had told them what she could about the crime scene—that was what she called it, *the crime scene*, like something separate from herself—and he didn't want to walk into a room where someone had been murdered. It wasn't like he could go into the garage at home, either.

"I'm here!" Keri yelled, sounding impatient, and he followed her voice to the right door. "Just...fuck!"

He pushed the door open as a series of thumps punctuated Keri's curses. She was standing, good arm over her head, books tumbled around her feet. The top shelf of the bookshelf she was standing in front of was completely clear.

"I just tugged one down and they all fell!" she complained. "I don't know what's wrong with me. My sense of balance is way off."

"Here, let me," he said, and knelt down to gather up the books. They were serious-looking nonfiction books with titles such as *The NZ Army Guide to Wilderness Survival* and *Without a Doctor: A Home Health-Care Handbook*. They were all hardcovers, and heavy. No wonder Keri had yelled. He looked up at her. "You're bleeding!"

She touched the corner of her mouth and looked at her fingers. "One caught me in the face."

"Sit down," he suggested, and grabbed a tissue from his messenger bag. He bent over her and moved her chin so that her face was in the sun, dabbing at the cut. She made a protest sound and closed her eyes against the light.

Keri has a pretty mouth, he thought. Not full, like Janna's, but neat and tucked in at the corners in a way he liked. He hadn't seen her smile that much, but she looked good when she did.

He was suddenly very aware that he was alone with her in her bedroom. Unwillingly, he remembered the swell of her breasts beneath her bra as he'd tugged that terrible polyester shirt over her head, the firm muscles outlined under the skin of her stomach. That skin would be soft if he touched it, and the muscles strong underneath it.

Keri opened her eyes and took the tissue from his hand. "Thanks."

"I think you're going to have a bruise," he said, proud of how steady his voice was.

"I'm collecting them," she said. "I fell on my ass again last night and whacked into the door handle twice this morning. If this keeps up, people are going to start thinking my parents hit me."

"Hard to know what to say when you really did walk into a door," Sione agreed, and was rewarded with one of those rare smiles.

It vanished immediately. "Give me the myths and legends one?"

It was the thickest, with a worn blue cover—if that had been the one to smack her in the face she'd have more than a little cut on her lip. He was surprised she had anything on that topic and wondered if she'd thought about Janna's black-magic theory, too, but she took it from him, frowning, and flipped it open.

Sione blinked. Someone had cut out the center part of the pages and glued the outsides together to make a box. Nestled in the space was a slim black cylinder of ridged rubber. It looked like the handle of a tool without the tool part.

"Extendable baton," Keri explained, and flicked her wrist. The sections hissed out, like a low-tech lightsaber.

"What are you doing with that?" he blurted.

She gave him a careful look. "Self-defense. I don't want to go prowling around Rafferty's house unarmed."

"So why is it in the box?"

The look got more careful. "Mum doesn't always like the way I see things." She tilted her chin. "It was a birthday present from Jake. He knew I liked to be prepared."

"That's useful," Sione said. It was a dumb thing to say, but Keri nodded, looking slightly relieved. She collapsed the baton again and put it on her desk, where it joined a selection of plastic bags in three sizes, a pair of tweezers, a pen torch, hand disinfectant, four pairs of latex gloves, and a little blue toolbox labeled LATENT PRINT KIT NO. 1. Keri pointed at everything in turn, obviously checking off an internal list, and then opened a desk drawer, muttering to herself.

Keri had clearly put way more thought into the logistics than just making an entrance plan and deciding what to wear. Sione could feel his eyebrows trying to crawl up his forehead. He turned away before she could see his expression, and went to put the fallen books away. There was half a shelf of fiction, all things like *The Whale Rider* and *To Kill a Mockingbird*—school books. The rest was nonfiction. Survival manuals, true-crime stories, disaster histories. Biographies of rugby players, triathletes, and swimmers, which he supposed were for fun.

"Aha!"

He turned around. Keri was triumphantly brandishing a Leatherman multi-tool. She beckoned him over, and he obediently opened the messenger bag for her to throw everything in. At least now he knew why she'd asked him to bring it. Keri generally had reasons, he was realizing, but she didn't always get to the part where she made them clear to you. The baton she kept, sliding it into the long calf pocket of her worn cargo pants. It was swallowed by the fabric, so you could barely tell anything was there.

Someone knocked on the door, and they both jumped. "You kids want a drink?" Keri's dad called.

He's checking on us, Sione realized, and thought again that they were alone together and of what that could mean. It was less urgent than the sick panicky desire that sometimes grabbed him around Janna. More...nice.

"No, thanks!" Keri yelled back, looking entirely unbothered by any thoughts along those lines. "We're heading out."

Her dad opened the door. He looked even bigger in the door frame. "Aren't you grounded for leaving on Christmas without telling anyone?"

"No."

"Really."

"I have to get permission from you or Mum before I go anywhere," she said reluctantly.

Her father tilted his chin the exact same way she did and waited.

"So can we go?" Keri asked at last. "I left a note for her; I didn't just *leave*."

Her dad grinned. "Be back by five. Your nanny's calling then. I told her you'd be here."

Keri made a face. "We'll be back ages before that," she promised, and hustled Sione out of the house. She tripped on a fold of carpet on the way out and stumbled into him. He caught a whiff of something in her hair as she used his shoulder to steady herself, mumbling apologies. A scent like chemical apples, not the burnt flower smell that hung around Janna. She smelled fresh and clean, and he hoisted the messenger bag, smiling to himself, and followed her down the street.

Sergeant Rafferty lived next to one of the primary schools, only a few blocks from Keri's place, exactly as Keri's map had shown. It was a sturdy house made of gray slate, with a green painted roof.

It didn't really look like the house of a serial killer—or a wicked witch—but what would? A garden with skeletons for scarecrows? A house made out of gingerbread?

Keri didn't want to enter the yard from the street, in case someone was watching, so they went into the school playground, which was full of kids trying out their Christmas presents and parents squinting in the bright light. Nobody seemed to be paying them any attention. Sione had been told to watch them anyway, in case someone did start to stare. It was easy to pick locals from tourists, he found; local kids played nonstop, yelling and running around with kites and water pistols and scooters, but tourist kids and their families, however energetic, would all occasionally pause, and, at different times, take a moment to gaze at the deep-green tangle of bush or the translucent blue sky, or the shimmering bay, and breathe in the beauty of Summerton.

It was creepy, he thought, and then did it himself, completely unaware until Keri tugged impatiently on the strap of his bag.

"Round here," she said, and Sione obediently followed her around the corner of a classroom block and into a little alley created between the classroom walls and the sergeant's wooden fence.

"Give me a boost," she ordered, and he tossed his bag over first, then cradled his fingers for her foot. She was lighter than he'd braced for and cleared the fence easily. Sione considered the problem for a second, and then got himself over at the cost of wood-dust smudges on the knees of his jeans, powdery brown visible against the dark denim.

The backyard had a vegetable garden, which was losing a fight for ground against some red currant bushes, a green swath of grass, and a washing line, with a row of big blue shirts ruffling in the light sea breeze. Sione wished they wouldn't move like that—it made him think more about being caught by their owner.

Keri was crouched between the leafy potato plants, working her hands into a pair of latex gloves and watching the house. He thought of nature documentaries, and leopards sitting in trees—it was the same kind of restless anticipation. If she'd had a tail, it would have been twitching.

Keri considered the back door for a moment. Sione had been startled when she'd put lockpicking on the backup plan list. He wasn't keen to try it, no matter how sure she was that she knew what she was doing. Luckily, there was a small window high on the wall, cracked open a couple of inches. Plan A it was.

"Bathroom window," Keri whispered, kicking off her shoes, and Sione made a foothold for her again without being asked. He was worried about Keri's arm—and after all, she'd said her sense of balance was off—but he didn't think it would be a good idea to point that out. She was looking really unstoppable.

Keri got the window open by bracing her good hand under it and shoving up from the shoulder, which really meant she was shoving down into him. Sione stood firm, surprised at the way he didn't wobble. He hadn't been certain he was strong enough for this. He'd always been the weak one. The little brother.

Keri slithered in cast-first, without any sign of the clumsiness that had attacked her at home. He waited for thumps and bangs, but there was nothing but silence until the back door suddenly swung open, nearly giving him a heart attack right there. He picked up her shoes and walked into the house, taking the pair of latex gloves she handed him without comment.

And that was it. They were in.

The house was quiet and warm and neat. *A bachelor pad*, Sione thought, looking at the leather La-Z-Boy in front of the TV, with a hollow worn into the seat. There were lots of CDs and DVDs in the living room and not many books, and in the kitchen there was a clay plaque with unsteady letters declaring the sergeant the world's best uncle above the fridge, which held cheese, half a container of takeout lemon chicken, and an unopened six-pack of beer. In the single bedroom were lots of uniforms, and polished shoes, and socks and underwear, and a couple of jerseys stuffed into a training bag with rugby spikes and a ball. On the wall was a framed diploma proclaiming Francis Rafferty the holder of a bachelor's degree in Russian issued by the University of Otago on the third of July in the year of our lord 1978, and a Royal New Zealand Police College certificate from 1979.

There wasn't a wall of hair clippings. Or a careful collection of the dead boys' possessions. Or pictures of them in a file anywhere. Keri got grimly excited over a little locked box in the office desk, but Sione found the key in a saucer on the fridge, and the box turned out to hold a picture of an old lady and a gold ring. Probably Rafferty's mum and her wedding ring.

Sione was starting to feel weird about the whole thing. He was still fairly sure Rafferty was the killer, but *fairly* wasn't *absolutely*, which was why he'd wanted proof in the first place. Going through his stuff without finding any made Sione feel like he was doing something wrong.

It must have been even worse for Keri, who had known the sergeant all her life. Not that it showed on her face. "The stuff Janna told us to look for isn't here, either," she said. "No daggers or chalices or anything. Or even a copy of *How to Hypnotize People and Make Enemies*." She put a cushion back on the couch and glared at the room, like she was trying to force it to give up its secrets.

"*Mmmr?*" something said behind them, and even Keri yelped a bit as she spun around.

It was a gray, tiger-striped cat, gangly and half-grown, blinking yellow eyes at them. Sione tried to get his heart back under control. It must have been in the front garden and come inside — there was a cat flap in the back door, now that he thought about it. It hadn't just *appeared*.

And anyway, witches have black cats, Sione thought. *"Mrowr,"* the cat said, and twined through his legs, begging shamelessly for food.

"Funny," he said, bending to scratch it behind the ears. The fur felt weird against his latex-covered fingers, but the cat shivered and pressed into his hand for more. "I don't think of murderers having pets."

"Yeah, well. Hitler liked dogs," Keri said, and then froze, her eyes going huge.

"What —" Sione began and then he heard it, too, the *chutter-chug* of a parking car.

Keri was already moving before he could make his brain work again, tugging him into the bedroom and dropping to her belly. "Under," she said, and wriggled. Sione went down on the other side, holding his breath against the dust and dragging his bag behind him. There was just enough room for both of them, beside the crumpled *NZ Listener* copies and a couple of dog-eared paperbacks.

The front door opened, and he realized that up until then, he'd still been hoping it was the neighbor's car.

The cat went into a frenzy of meows, indicating that it hadn't been fed in a year and was going to die on the spot.

"Hey, Sam," the deep voice said, wearily affectionate. "Yeah, yeah, you're starving. You little scavenger."

Floorboards creaked.

Sione looked at Keri. "Kitchen," she mouthed. She was sliding her baton out of her pocket, a move he thought was pretty smart right up until she put it into his hand. "Need my good hand free to get out," she whispered in explanation, her breath hot against his ear. "But don't move unless we have to. Then hit him and run."

Sione nodded and adjusted his fingers, sweaty in the gloves. The rubber grip squeaked against the latex—a tiny noise, but he froze, hand stuck in a rigid claw.

There was the clatter of small things falling into a bowl, and the meowing was replaced with ecstatic purrs. It was so ordinary that Sione couldn't stand it, not with his heart pounding so hard that he thought blood was going to explode out of his nose. This was the part of the horror movie where the stupid teenagers got caught. They'd be in danger, then think they were safe and exhale, and then the music would swell as they turned around and screamed....

Keri touched his leg. "Don't worry," she mouthed, and he nodded, pushing the fear back down. Had Matthew been scared? Or had he been hypnotized—*or enchanted*, a voice inside his head insisted, in Janna's tone—and thought it was all his idea to sit in the car and wait for the fumes to put him to sleep?

That might even have been better.

Sione stopped thinking about Matthew when Rafferty walked into the bedroom, instead becoming completely *here, now*, with Keri's hand resting on his thigh and his breath quiet and hot against the carpet. The wardrobe opened, and he caught a flash of blue as Rafferty threw something into the laundry basket in there—*his uniform shirt*, the thinking part of Sione supplied after a moment. Had Keri put everything back right in the

158

wardrobe? Would he notice something out of place? They'd been fast, they'd had to be, but they'd tried to be careful, too, working according to the grid pattern Keri had devised.

Did Rafferty already know they were there? Was he playing with them?

There was the *hiss-hiss* of an aerosol and a sharp, spicy scent. Deodorant.

He's just changing his shirt, Sione thought, and relief rolled up from his toes. Of course he was—a hot summer's day, a long shift—why not go home and change on your break? Keri hadn't relaxed, though, and he tried to remember the lesson of the horror movie kids. Don't think you're safe, not yet.

Someone's cell phone rang.

For a heart-clutching moment, Sione was sure it was his.

But no, he'd left it in the hotel room, and the noise was coming from above.

Rafferty muttered something, and then spoke more clearly, presumably into the phone. "Yeah?"

A pause, then, "No, I can't ask Frank where he takes his passengers!...Because he'll bloody wonder why I'm asking. The kid's probably just visiting the Pedersen girl."

That's me, Sione thought. *I'm the kid. They're talking about my going to see Keri in that taxi.* The shivers had turned into a tight tingling all over his body.

There was a tense silence. The person on the other end was apparently long-winded, and Rafferty broke in again.

"No! Look, no, you listen to *me*. It's got to stop, you understand? They're just kids. What can they d—...I fucking *know* they've all been kids. But we've never tried to *hurt* them.

159

Just . . . we don't need to . . ." There was a heavy note in his voice. "That's not the idea, that's all. Okay. Okay. *Fine.*"

That was good-bye.

"Damn it," the sergeant said into the silence, soft and heartfelt. "The fucking *witch.*"

He stamped out of the bedroom and down the hall with a speed that made the floorboards triple their creaking, *ratchet-ratchet-ratchet.* The door slammed, and the car started.

"So much for magic," Keri whispered.

But in the echoes Sione felt his brain fall apart and put itself together around a new and very different world.

Witch.

"It doesn't mean anything," Keri whispered, as if she were reading his remade mind. "He could have meant it like, you know, you bitch. We definitely know he's involved."

Sione didn't really feel up to having an argument under a bed. "And he has an accomplice," he said, whispering, too, because he was still tight all over. "They know I left the hotel in a taxi. So they know we know something. And we know they know that."

"And he doesn't think we can do anything," Keri said in a voice like a clenched fist. Sione gave her back the baton and wriggled out. He caught sight of himself in the mirror and winced. His curls were fuzzing and tinged with gray, dust motes sparkling a halo around his round face.

"Can I head back to your place to clean up?" he asked, brushing as much of the dust out of his hair as he could and frowning at his stained jeans. "If someone's watching the hotel, I don't want to go back looking like I broke into some-one's house."

"Good thinking," Keri acknowledged, and patted at her own head. Then she carefully picked up every one of their loose hairs, the curly black and the straight, and stowed them in one of the plastic bags. "DNA," she said in response to his look. "Let's go."

They left through the back door and retraced their steps through the school playground, which was full of different noisy kids. Sione felt different, too.

They started back toward Keri's place, walking in silence.

"Hey," he heard behind them. "Hey, potato."

He should have expected it, he thought, as he spun around and wondered how badly this was going to hurt. It always hit the horror movie teenagers when they thought they were safe.

Chapter Sixteen
Keri

⚡

EVEN IF THE BIG GUY HADN'T SAID WHAT HE had, I figured I could have picked Sione's ex-friend Luke out in a crowd. It was the way he looked at Sione — raw hatred, the kind where you wanted to know what someone had done to deserve it, because that kind of hate shouldn't just come out of nowhere.

But I knew Sione hadn't done anything. If anything, he was too nice, too easy.

I did a quick risk assessment, working out our available

resources and going through a few strategies. There weren't many pluses for our side. There were two of us, and we had home-ground advantage — or at least, I did — and my baton.

And Luke was much bigger than us, I had my stupid broken arm, and I was betting that Sione wasn't much of a fighter.

"Hi, Luke," Sione said. His voice was tight, and I wanted to shake him. Didn't he know not to show fear?

"Let's go," I said.

"Got another girl to bodyguard you, Sione?" Luke asked. "You a real player, man. Or are you just putting in a little girl time?"

"Where's Mark?"

"Not here to save you this time, runt."

"I don't want to fight," Sione said.

It was a dumb thing to say. Luke strolled closer — loose steps, hands swinging, he knew exactly how to be threatening — and stared down at him. "Yeah? I don't reckon that's your choice."

It was clear that the situation was going to get physical; all of this was just to gear up to the battle. Luke would have to be incredibly stupid to pick a fight with a local, in the middle of the street, in the middle of the afternoon, but I reckoned he was going to do it.

Plans whirled through my head. If we gave him time to make the first move, we could get hurt too badly to back him off. But if we started it, and Rafferty turned up, he might take Luke's side. It might be convenient for him to get us watched, kick Sione out of town. . . . I slid the baton out of my pocket and gripped it unextended, hesitating.

"Yeah, I want a word with you, faggot," Luke said, and I moved.

The baton hissed out and clicked into place, and I struck—not with much style, but I was very, very angry, and I put all my rage into the hit, reaching around Sione's recoiling body to thrust straight into the other guy's stomach.

Luke folded, gagging, and I whipped my arm back. He straightened and started forward, fury in his eyes, but he was lunging for Sione, not me, even though I was clearly the bigger threat. What a dumbshit. I crouched and swung the baton at his legs. It didn't quite trip him, but I managed to tap at his ankle, and what would have been a punch at Sione's face turned into a grab at Sione's shoulder for balance, ripping the strap of his messenger bag.

The bag thumped to the pavement, contents scattering everywhere. Plastic bags started fluttering away, and my fingerprint kit split open, dust spilling onto the street. But there was something that I hadn't seen before—a little clay figurine that bounced, end over end, to land at my feet.

Without thinking, I stamped on it, hard.

As it shattered, I *felt* the hostility evaporate, like a summer storm on hot asphalt. Luke straightened, tension draining out of his big body. He looked at me and then at Sione, face blank with confusion.

"What the *hell*?" Luke said. He moved toward me, hand outstretched. I raised the baton in warning, and he stopped, letting his hand fall to his side. "Are you all right? I"—he looked at Sione, who was looking nearly as shaky—"I'm sorry, man. Hell!"

"Go away!" I snapped.

"What was that?" he said. "What was I *doing*? Jesus! I'm really sorry, Sione."

"Sure," Sione said.

"I wouldn't…Those things I said. I mean, I don't know, man, there was something…You're all right, man." He was shifting from foot to foot, wanting to apologize better, but uncertain of his reception.

"It's okay," Sione said automatically, but he was looking at me. "I think you'd better leave."

"Yeah," Luke said, and took a step away, then another. "Yeah. Sorry!"

I thought it was probably safe to put the baton away, so I did that and grabbed one of the plastic bags to scoop up the shattered clay pieces as best I could with my free hand.

Sione bent and grabbed his messenger bag, shoveling everything back into it. I didn't really care about the bag of loose hairs at this stage, and the fingerprint kit was already ruined. It meant he could be doing something while Luke shuffled away, though, so I didn't argue.

But the pause was enough space to poke at the bigger figurine pieces. It had definitely been a person, and pretty well-made, even from unfired clay. I could see a leg there, and a shoe, and something that looked a bit like a messenger bag. And that bit there was half a head, the curls drawn in little lines, and the slant of the eyebrow above the remaining eye somehow conveying the expression that meant Sione was doing numbers in his head. Sione's face, on that little clay man.

Every hair on my arm stood up.

"You didn't put this in your bag," I said in a voice that I could hardly recognize as my own.

Sione didn't look up. "No." His breath caught, and he straightened. "What is it?"

"It's you," I said in the same flat voice. I shoved the plastic bag into his hands and started marching. By the end of the block, I was at a dead run, ignoring the ache as my cast jerked up and down. Sione was keeping pace with me, begging for an explanation.

"Janna's right," I said, and tried to ignore the way my breath hiccuped. She couldn't be. Not about *magic*. Still, I went on: "I think I can prove it."

Now that I was paying attention, I could *feel* it, the way my body weight shifted as I went through my front door, tipping off center, as if the world were swaying around me. I slowed down. Now was not the time to have another inexplicable— *ha!*—fit of clumsiness.

"Hey, kid," Dad said as I did a careful robot walk past him in the hall, Sione in my wake.

"Forgot something," I said.

I got even less sure-footed as I got into my bedroom, fingers slipping on the doorknob, feet trying to tangle as I walked slowly across the threshold. More confirmation for my theory. My blank shock was being slowly erased by the intense anger simmering in my gut. They'd broken my arm. They could have *killed* me.

Like they'd killed Jake.

I went cold all over.

Things went blank for a while. The next thing I knew, I was sitting on the bed. I couldn't remember how I'd gotten there, but Sione was crouching at my feet, holding my hand, and whispering, "Keri? Keri, what's wrong? Should I get your dad?"

I had the feeling he was repeating himself. It felt like the same sort of blackout I'd had about finding Jake, and that scared me enough that I managed to make words.

"I'm too clumsy," I said. "But only in here." That was about the best I could manage, but Sione got it right away, and even through my shock I realized again how smart he was. He let go of my hand and started tearing the room apart.

It was much faster than at Rafferty's house, where he'd been so careful and methodical I'd wanted to scream. Now he just went through everything—under the bed, in the bookshelf, rifling through my underwear drawer with a focused expression that had nothing to do with my plain cotton undies. I sat on the bed and concentrated on breathing. The air felt thicker around me; it could have been my imagination, but I thought the ground was just waiting for me to fall again. Lying down on the bed might have been safer, but I wasn't going to give in that much.

He found it in one of the desk drawers, stuffed into a pile of old essays, a little clay figure just like his. Shorter, though, and a thinner face, and straight hair, and the tiny clay features were mine.

"Break it," I said, and he dropped it on the floor and lifted his foot.

"No!" I said, too loud, and he paused. I wanted proof. "Just...snap it. If that doesn't work, we'll try smashing."

He nodded. Brown hands clenching, he broke the figurine cleanly in half.

The air cleared like a strong wind blowing off a fog. I gasped and stood up, as well-balanced as ever. My body relaxed back into itself, and I realized just how bad that curse had been, to take away what I'd always had, the sureness of myself and my limits.

And it made sense that they'd attacked Sione through his sense of himself, too, getting Luke to strike at Sione's uncertainties about himself, his place in the world. That was nasty; a really vicious brain had come up with that.

I took the pieces from his hand. Close up, I could see the little clay ropes looped around the arms and legs, the bits that had tipped me over, wrecked my body. The Maukis brothers must have made the statues—that made sense, if they were already involved by making this Summer King crown. And Rafferty was tied up in it somehow, the phone call proved that. But whom had he been talking to on the phone? The Maukises had deep, oily voices—I was pretty sure the person on the other end of that conversation had been female. Four of them.

"Someone had to have put it in my bag," Sione said, obviously thinking along the same lines as I was. "The only time I left it was when we all went out for lunch, that second day. When Kirk Davidson kicked us out of the room. He could have told them when I left the hotel."

Five, then. The four men and an unknown woman.

Doing *magic*.

"I cannot believe this shit," I said, even though I clearly could. There wasn't much point in denying direct evidence;

that was the principle I was banking on as I slid the two halves of little me into a plastic bag.

"We should warn Janna," Sione said. "And tell her she's right."

"Sure," I said, and handed him my phone, leaving the actual admitting-we-were-wrong part to him.

Now that the shock was wearing off, I felt unsteady in a different way. The world shouldn't work like this; that was why I made plans, to be ready for every eventuality. Adding the impossible to the things I had to be prepared for was really unfair.

Janna apparently had her phone switched off. Sione left a message and looked at me.

"Magic," he said. "Uh, can't say I did any research in that direction. Do you know much about it?"

"Hardly." I snorted and sat up straight. "Wait, though. I know someone who knows a *lot*. I'm sure she can help."

CHAPTER SEVENTEEN
Janna

JANNA WAS WONDERING HOW SHE'D EVER thought Patrick Tan was hot enough to go out with for nearly a whole year. God! He was so *stubborn*.

"All you have to do," she explained again, through a smile that was trying not to be gritted teeth, "is distract whichever Maukis is there for about five minutes. Come on, Patrick, it's not hard."

"I know it's not hard," Patrick said. "I just can't figure out any reason why I should do it. In fact, I can't figure out why you even want it done."

"I'm flighty," Janna suggested. "I'm full of wacky rebellious teen girl ideas."

He pushed back his straight black bangs, a gesture that had once made her want to kiss him until their lips buzzed but now made her want to get a really good grip and *yank*. "I'll trade you a favor for a favor."

She relaxed her fists. "What do you want?"

"You do that radio interview."

"No," she said flatly.

"Okay." He shrugged and made as if to get up.

She grabbed his wrist across the shiny red table, holding him before he could just walk out of Mimi's Muffins. "*Wait. Okay, I'll do it.*"

"Huh. You do want this bad." He hesitated. "You're not planning to rob them or anything, are you? Because these guys are the ones who hired us."

"I'm not that dumb," she snarled.

"I never thought you were dumb," Patrick said quietly, and for a second she remembered why she'd liked him. Under all the sarcasm and control-freakery, he could be loyal. And even nice, on occasion. "Are you in some kind of trouble?"

"Of course not," she lied, and then surprised herself by hugging him hard. "Thank you so much."

"No problem," he muttered, and then froze. "Uh..."

Janna stepped away and twisted, and met Takeshi's eyes through the café window.

The worst thing was that she hadn't done anything wrong. But she couldn't help feeling guilty, and she felt it show on her face.

Takeshi saw the guilt, flinched, and walked on.

Janna went for the door. A gaggle of tourists came in at that second, and by the time she'd fought her way through and scanned the street, there were no tall Japanese boys in sight. "Oh, *crap!*"

"You forgot this," Patrick said behind her. He was holding her bag.

"Thanks," Janna said, and yanked it away.

"Do you want to go after him?" Patrick asked. His face was carefully neutral.

"Yes," Janna said, and sighed. "But no. I'll make up with him later. Let's get this done."

What Janna had privately nicknamed Operation Enemy Territory started out well. Janna lurked in the library by the alleyway door, pretending to browse the magazine racks, until Patrick's text buzzed the phone in her hand. She switched it off and slipped through the alley door, across the tiny gap, and into the art gallery. It was silent and seemed unoccupied, but as she crept up the stairs she heard people talking in the big room at the top.

When she bent low to the steps and peeked around the corner, though, there were only tourists gazing at the colorful abstracts. The office door was partially closed, Patrick's black-jacketed back to the gap. He was blocking the view the Maukises would have of her — good.

Janna stood up, took two steps into the room, and froze.

The stone plinth was empty. The Pride of Summerton was gone.

"Looking for something?" Octavian Maukis said in her ear,

and Janna nearly tumbled back down the stairs. He caught her, grunting at the impact.

Janna strained to get her balance back and whipped around, her mind working frantically. How much did he know about what she knew?

"Where's the crown?" she asked.

"Taken away for cleaning," he said, his eyes mocking her. "I didn't know you were such a fan."

"Takeshi really liked it," she said, and straightened up. Stardust wouldn't let this middle-aged man frighten her. Oh, but Janna was scared. *Play stupid*, she thought. "So I thought — it's pretty dumb." From somewhere, she managed to pull a giggle, high-pitched and scatty.

Octavian blinked. "Thought what?"

"I thought maybe I could make him something like it. Not in glass, *obviously*, I could never do that, but maybe if I, like, *bought* a crown and glued some stones on — they have some really pretty crystals at Inner Light, or maybe even sea glass if I can afford it — I could, like, *pretend*. I was going to take some pictures. So I could copy it." She pulled her phone out and waved it in his face, and stuck it back in her jacket pocket, hoping he hadn't noticed it was turned off.

"You should have asked," he said after a moment.

She gave him her best Stardust smile. "But then you might have said no."

He laughed and, for the first time, did his standard cleavage inspection. "Well, tell you what. When The Pride comes back, you can take as many photos as you like. I'll even tell you about the creation process."

173

"That would be the *best*!" Janna said. "When's that?"

His eyes flashed back to her face. She kept her smile shining, bright and stupid. "After New Year's."

She made panic into pouting disappointment. "Oh, *no*! Takeshi leaves on New Year's Day."

"That's a shame. But you could send it to him." Was that the shadow of a smirk? "Afterward."

"I guess so!" she said, trying not to wrap her hands around his throat and squeeze.

"You're welcome, Janna. I look forward to seeing you at the Bash."

"Thanks!" she said, and clattered past him down the stairs. A big hand brushed her back as she went, not quite low enough to be something she could snap about. Oh, the Maukises were so good at walking those lines. She'd been much happier when she thought they were *only* sleazebuckets.

Okay. Okay, so at least she'd nearly confirmed that it had to *be* the crown. If she could only find it before the ceremony, she might have a better idea of what to do. Hands twitching at her clothes, she waited in the street outside until Patrick loped down. After this, she had to go get that protection spell, but she could at least thank him first.

"Did you get what you came for?" he asked.

"Not exactly. Did you see The Pride of Summerton in the office?"

"No, just some paintings and a couple of half-finished statue things. What do you want with the crown, Janna?"

She told him the same story she'd told Octavian, but Patrick was much less likely to be distracted by teeth-baring

174

smiles and perky bouncing. "Yeah, right," he said. "Like you've ever done crafty stuff. You don't even take Home Ec."

"Takeshi is making a new woman of me," she said sweetly.

"I hope not," he said, and then scratched the side of his face. "Okay, whatever. I'll pick you up for the interview. Practice after."

She spotted Aroha first, her hair shining in the sunlight, and then Takeshi walking behind her. Takeshi's head was down, Aroha tossing some statement at him over her shoulder. "Yeah, fine," Janna said.

Patrick followed her eyes. "Good luck," he said quietly, and took off.

Janna took her courage, screwed it up to nine, and went for an interception course.

"Hi!" she said.

"Oh, good, there you are," Aroha said. "Recovered from the food poisoning? Good! I'm off to do a thing with some stuff in the place. You two have fun!" And she flicked her curls, turned on one sandaled heel, and marched into the nearest shop, bell jangling cheerily in her wake.

Janna felt as if she should have been taking notes on how to pull off an exit, but she was too busy trying to catch Takeshi's eye.

"Hi," she said again, more shyly. Her stomach was doing yucky swooping things. She had to stay close to him to protect him, of course. She hadn't planned on caring this much.

"Aroha says I am stupid," Takeshi said. "Patrick is not your boyfriend?"

"No. He's a friend, and he was doing me a favor, that's all. I hugged him to say thank you."

"Oh." He didn't look reassured. "You have many friends."

All of that damn boy-scouting on the beach. "Yes. But *just* friends."

"I think that"—his face creased in frustration—"I *thought* that you maybe don't like me. It's okay. But I will like to know, please."

"I like you," she assured him.

He looked her properly in the eye and smiled, and Janna felt as if she'd been hit by the Summerton Effect herself, unable to look away. "I like you, too," he said.

"But you're going away," she said, and bit her lip. She hadn't meant that to escape, especially not sounding so *plaintive*.

But he looked as sad as she felt. "Yes. I go to Auckland in six days. Hiroshima in six months." He hesitated. "I'm here now."

"Yes," Janna said. *Harden up, girl!* she ordered herself, and put her arms around his neck. He took a step closer, his eyes glinting. *Embrace the summer*, she thought. *Embrace the guy.* That was the Stardust motto.

So she kissed him, in the middle of the street, and didn't care that this news would reach her mother's ears at the speed of sound. His lips were soft and warm, and his hands were steady and strong on her back, and whatever happened next, this moment was music; the perfect chord, one Janna could hear again and again in the echoing sound chamber of her heart.

Chapter Eighteen
Keri

⚡

IN THE CITIES, THERE WERE HUGE BOXING
Day sales that took over TV advertising for three days, right
before the New Year's sales hit. In Summerton, the few chain
stores in town—and now that was feeling like something else
I should have noticed—put up the signs, but the homegrown
shops would advertise a few specials and leave it there. No
storewide blitzes or lines outside the doors. And the locals
tended to stay away; it was just dozy visitors and their yappy
kids.

Inner Light had a good location on the main street, the windows full of posters for the Beach Bash, with that ugly Pride of Summerton crown in the corners. I scowled at it. There were a few tourists poking around the store, all of them with the same post-Christmas stunned look. I felt the baton swing against my calf and took a deep breath, stepping into the scented store with the little plastic bag clenched in my fist. Fortunately, Sandra-Claire was nowhere in sight, so I lurked by the book section, waiting for Daisy Hepwood to finish selling a dream catcher and four scented candles, then went up to the counter, Sione bobbing in my wake like a duckling.

"Is Sandra-Claire here?" I asked, hoping that the answer was, *No, she's caught the plague and had to go home to vomit out her lungs.* I had my suspicions about that female voice on the phone with Rafferty, though it was hard to believe that even Sandra-Claire could kill Jake, whom she'd really seemed to love.

"She's on break, dear," Daisy said, and then she saw the plastic bags in my hand and her eyes narrowed behind her pink-rimmed glasses. "Why don't you two come into the back?"

I followed, relieved. If she'd recognized the broken figurines as some kind of black magic, it would cut out a lot of the explanation I'd rehearsed on the way here.

But as we entered the storeroom, she smiled sweetly. "So what did you want to ask me?"

I held up the bags. "We think this is some kind of voodoo," I said. "This one made a guy attack Sione."

"I don't know very much about voudoun," Daisy said. "That's quite a different area from mine."

"But it's black magic?" I pressed.

178

"Oh, Keri. Black magic and white magic are systems imposed upon magic by the superstitious. It's a matter of perspective."

That hadn't been what Janna had said, with that stuff about the left-hand path and the Rule of Three. But she'd said not everyone believed it, either.

"I felt it," I insisted. "I felt something stop when I smashed it."

Daisy *hmm*ed thoughtfully. "Putting it in your friend's bag was certainly a nasty trick. But most things of this type only have the power we give them. That's probably what you felt when you smashed it—the resolution of your fear."

I frowned. I hadn't imagined Luke being so aggressive and then stopping. And what about my broken arm? I held up the other figurine. "Well, in my room—"

"In my bag," Sione said, and I was pissed at him for the interruption. But his pupils were blown, his brown eyes nearly completely black, and he was staring at Daisy in horror. "We never said we found it in my bag."

I might not have understood, even then.

But Daisy flinched.

"Oh no," I whispered, as it all came together in my head. "I'm so stupid. It's you."

I was hoping for denial, for puzzlement, even for outrage at the mere suggestion. But Daisy whirled in her crochet cardigan and pinned me with her eyes, and I felt the world implode. "Drop it, Keri," she said. "Or things will get much, much worse for you."

"You..." I said, and couldn't make my mouth go further.

"This has nothing to do with you," she said, her eyes boring into me. "Leave it alone."

"You?" Sione said. *"Why?"*

She made a flapping gesture at him with her hands, and focused on me again. "Summerton's a great place, Keri. Successful, beautiful. No crime, no drugs, no untimely deaths. Do you really want to destroy all that?"

"No untime—You kill people," I said, my tongue thick and heavy.

She didn't look evil. She looked sad. A hard, distant kind of sadness, removed from the flinching agony that hit me every time I remembered Jake was dead. "Young people die every day," she said. "For foolish, wasteful reasons. Or to defend their country and people, to make them safe. Just leave it alone. I don't *want* to hurt you. But this is important."

"This is *wrong*," I said. There were arguments I could make, good ones, about choice and freedom, and murder instead of war, but I couldn't seem to manufacture any of them.

"You sick old bitch," Sione said, the last word sitting awkwardly in his mouth. It was the first time I'd heard him swear. He meant it, though, and I was, in spite of everything, a little bit shocked to hear that word applied to Daisy—good Daisy, caring Daisy.

She'd come to help Sandra-Claire collect Jake's T-shirts, and she'd been nice to me. She must have put the clay figure in my desk that very afternoon, but all I could remember was the way she had been sympathetic while Sandra-Claire was her usual bitchy self.

But the swearing made Daisy look at Sione properly for the first time, before her face took on the same dismissive expression. He was just a tourist to her, I saw. Not a real person;

maybe that's how she explained it to herself. All those deaths, all those families and friends; maybe that's why it had been so long between when Schuyler was killed and Jake; maybe that's why Mr. Davidson had been sorry for my loss. They cared about the Summerton boys, but not the rest.

"Watch your tongue, young man," she said, not even using his name. "You think a broken arm or a car crash is the worst thing that could happen?"

My skin crawled all along my spine, broken arm tingling. The car crash had been her, too? Janna and Sione could have been killed. And I didn't want to die, not like Jake had, in an explosion of blood and noise. She saw the fear in my face and stepped forward. "How would your parents cope with that?" she said softly.

"I thought you would help us catch the killer," I said, and something quivered in her face before she shut it down again. "I never thought it could be you."

"I'm *trying* to help," she said. "The best way I can, Keri. You know what it's like out there."

Outside perfect Summerton, she meant. In the big, bad world.

"You leave her alone," Sione said. His voice was shaky but loud, and I could feel the tension in him. He didn't know Daisy. He'd attack her, maybe, but only if I gave him the cue. And even though she'd admitted it herself, I couldn't. I just couldn't make it across the distance between us, from my fist to her face.

The bell sounded in the shop's main room. "You can leave by the back door," she said, and returned to the shop, cheerily greeting her customers.

That was all she was going to give us.

"Did she put a spell on you?" Sione asked, his voice thick and low.

"I don't know." Without her staring at me, it was easier to think, but I had the shameful sensation that I hadn't been unbalanced by anything more supernatural than my own fear and confusion. "I don't know what to do."

"We will," Sione said, sounding a lot more confident than I did. "We'll work something out. Let's get out of here."

I moved toward the door, but he hesitated, glancing at all the pretty glass bottles and the jars of herbs and containers of crystals. "Give me your baton," he said.

I fished it out and handed it to him. He extended it—he had to flick his wrist twice before he got it right—and stood there for a long moment that made me itch all over with anticipation.

Then he screamed.

It was a war cry, a ragged, howling noise I'd never have thought could come from Sione. He took two fast steps toward the shelves and swung, smashing the contents to the floor, glass shattering as bits of dried herbs flew and danced in the air. He cleared the first three shelves in quick back and forth motions, still making that terrible, hurting sound, then grabbed the side of the shelf unit itself and yanked.

But it was too firmly anchored to the wall, and he couldn't shift it by himself. I stepped up, wrapping my good hand around the same strut.

"Now," he panted, and we yanked, dodging back as the whole thing crashed down, hurling books and incense burners and things I couldn't guess at to the floor.

I was laughing, tears streaming down my cheeks, and Sione grabbed my hand, grinning as he raced me to the door.

The whole thing had happened so fast that Daisy couldn't even get back into the storeroom before we escaped. I heard her shout once behind us as we ran down the alley and cut toward the esplanade.

Somewhere along the way, I stopped laughing and crying at the same time and just cried. Not for Jake, or Schuyler, or Sione's brother, not really, but for Daisy, who had been nice and had somehow become someone who could kill teenage boys because she was so afraid of losing the place she loved best. We had to call Janna again and let her know what had happened; we had to think of a way to protect Takeshi and get revenge; we had to do a lot of things, but all I could manage right then was sitting on one of the benches looking over the sea and sniffing furiously, trying to make as little noise as possible as I mourned my brother's murderer.

Sione didn't fuss, which was good. He just put his arm over my shoulder, letting me know he was there without trying to pull me toward him. Then he stared at the sea, falling under the sway of the Summerton Effect every now and then, until my breathing got somewhat back to normal.

He turned and looked down at me, at the same time I looked up, meaning to thank him.

It was just a coincidence, that mutual turning toward each other, but his eyes darkened with an expression I thought I recognized, and his mouth dipped toward mine, his arm suddenly tight around me.

I could have let him do it, just for a little human affection, but after everything he'd done, Sione deserved more from me than lies.

And besides, my body decided for me, stiffening in unmistakable rejection. Sione jerked back as if I'd bitten him, and his arm fell away. "Sorry," he said. "Sorry. I got it wrong."

"It's not you," I said.

"Right," he said, and he sounded so defeated I sort of wanted to kick him.

"No, you dick," I said, and punched him in the shoulder instead. I couldn't quite believe I was going to do this, say out loud what I didn't even usually put into words in the privacy of my own head. Something that no one living knew. My voice lowered, so soft only he could possibly hear. "I'm gay. I like girls."

There. Said.

As coming-out reactions, it probably wasn't that bad. Sione just opened his mouth and closed it and looked puzzled. "Oh," he said at last. "Really?"

"Really. Is it a problem?"

"No! No, no, I just..." He lapsed into silence again. "I mean... it's okay with me. Not that you need anyone's permission or anything. I mean—"

"I get it," I said. "Thanks." And I was grateful, though God knows it's sort of pathetic when you're grateful for people treating you the way decent human beings should treat each other. Sione seemed pretty decent to me. But you never knew. He was Catholic, after all, and he hadn't liked being called a faggot, which could have been because he thought it was a word that guy shouldn't have been using, or because he thought being gay was a bad thing.

And something seemed to be bothering him. "Do you," he said. "I mean, you and Janna. Do you like her?"

"Oh, God no," I said, and tried not to think of how she'd looked the other day, lying facedown on her bed, naked, edged in light. You could like girls without *liking* them. "Yeah, I don't know if you've noticed this, but Janna's straight. And high maintenance. And hates sports."

He laughed. "I just wondered, you know. After you got married behind the bike sheds, aged seven."

"Heh," I said. "I don't think it counts if you eat the rings. But you can't tell her, Sione. You can't tell anyone. No one knows."

"No one?"

"Just you, now." I felt tears gather. "Jake knew; he'd known for months. The only one. I planned to tell Mum and Dad after the holidays. I didn't know how well they'd take it, and I didn't want to spoil Christmas." Another thing Daisy had robbed me of, without even knowing; the support to take that next step. Jake had been so good; he hadn't cared at all.

You're my girl, K. Anyone hassles you, let me know.

"I'm so sorry. But Janna's your friend. She won't—"

"You don't know," I said. "You don't know how it is."

"Yeah, 'cause no Samoan kids get hell for coming out."

"I didn't mean—okay, for one, you're not gay, and for two, you live in Auckland. I know it's got to be tough there, too, but *this* is a small town, and everyone knows everything. I can hope that a lot of people won't care, but a lot of them will, and I can't get away from them. Dr. Ryan's a lesbian. Someone found out ten years ago and spread it, and everyone thought she'd leave, but she didn't. And now I know why; it's Daisy's awful magic keeping us all here. Some people are horrible; they won't get checked out by her, they wait for the other doctors, and they say things. And she's an adult, and, like, a girlie woman, you know? Makeup and skirts and that stuff."

His face stayed confused.

"Look at me!" I tugged a lock of my hair. "I keep my hair short because I swim a lot and it dries faster, but people will say, of course, it's because lesbians aren't real women, whatever that means. I play rugby because I love rugby. I *love* it, but people are going to say it's because I want to be in the girls' changing rooms, that I want to be in the scrum, pressed up against them. I don't even *join* the scrum." I made myself take a deep breath, but my voice came out too high and wavering anyway. "Horrible things, they'll say shitty, shitty things about me, Sione! I know what happens. I could be bullied, or get the silent treatment, or find all my books tossed into the toilet." I'd read about this happening to other kids, imagined everything that could happen to me, late at night, preparing for the worst. "It could be my friends doing it, it could be my teachers, it could be the team. And I won't be able to get away!

"The plan was to leave town, get to the city, come out then. It wouldn't matter so much if I was only home for holidays. But Daisy—" My voice cracked. "They'll make me come back for good, and everyone will know. I hate her and Rafferty and those slimy Maukis guys! I hate them so much! They killed my brother to keep me here, keep me safe, and never thought about what that meant."

Sione rubbed my shoulder, hesitant at first, and then with more assurance when I didn't shrug him off. "Well…if I were

186

a chick, I'd be honored to go out with you," he said. "And I'm really honored you trust me enough to tell me." It was such a weird mix of old-fashioned and sweet that I nearly started crying again. But really, how many emotional outbreaks was I entitled to in one short day?

And besides, he spoiled it by adding, "I should have figured. Everyone has a good excuse for not liking me."

"Oh, *please*," I said. "Stop it. That's not true."

"What?"

I rolled my eyes. "Aroha really likes you, you dick. Anyone can see that. And you don't have to like her back, but it is just *stupid* to go around claiming no one likes you in the face of the evidence. What you mean is that *Janna* doesn't like you that way. It's not about excuses."

He looked thunderstruck. "Aroha likes me?"

"Obviously." I stared at him. "You really didn't know?"

"She said something. I thought she was just...you know, making fun of me."

"No way. I mean, you're this super-smart, shop-wrecking badass. She'd be lucky."

He still looked shocked, but he managed a small smile at that. "That was pretty sweet, wasn't it?"

"Sweet as," I said. "Sione Felise, crime-fighting vigilante." I grabbed my cell phone while he was still smiling and scrolled through the list for Stardust. "Let's try this again."

Chapter Nineteen
Janna

KISSING TAKESHI WAS THE *BEST EVER*. HE DIDN'T grope her or try to slide his hands up her shirt or down her pants, and in fact, when she got to the stage where she wanted him to touch her, she had to actually put his hands on her before he got the idea. But then he stroked her back with strong, sure fingers, and she melted against him and offered him her mouth again, sinking into all that good heat and soft moisture until he drew back, breathing fast and shallow, and kissed the corners of her eyes.

It was so sweet a gesture that Janna felt her heart do the weird air bed–expansion thing again, and she grabbed his arm to try to slow down.

"I'll miss you," she said. What was *wrong* with her?

"I'll miss you, also," Takeshi said, and kissed the corner of her mouth. "Don't forget me, okay?"

"No," she said, and tipped her face up to his again.

"Janna!" Mariel yelled, and pushed the woodshed door open. "Are you here? Keri's on the phone for—oops."

Takeshi blinked at her in the sudden wash of light.

Janna jumped off the workbench and tugged her shirt back into order, glaring at Mariel through the cloud of sparkling dust motes. "Don't you know how to knock?"

"I didn't know your new *boyfriend* was here," Mariel protested, which would have been fair enough if Janna had been in any mood to be fair. "I didn't even know you *had* a new boyfriend, and you're not supposed to be in the woodshed with boys *anyway*."

"You're not supposed to just barge in on me!"

Mariel gave her a scornful look and marched away without closing the door. "Don't have sex in the *woodshed*!" she shouted over her shoulder.

Janna flushed all the way up to her hairline and hoped that Takeshi's English hadn't been good enough to catch that. But no luck. He was blushing, too, though on his darker skin it wasn't quite as obvious as her own red face.

"Well, I wouldn't anyway," she said. "It's not very comfortable. There's no bed."

Takeshi's laugh was sudden. "A bed is good," he agreed shyly, and that probably answered a question that had been bugging her. She felt envious of whatever girl had first shared a bed with Takeshi's quick smiles and careful hands, and then pushed the feeling away. It wasn't like she would let him get weird over *her* history.

"I'll just talk to Keri," she said, hoping it wasn't very important so they could get back to kissing. "Come in with me."

Ten minutes later she stood in the hallway sick and shaking while Takeshi held her hand and waited for her to tell him what was wrong. But she couldn't do that, because then he would think she was crazy, and he'd start avoiding her and she wouldn't be able to protect him from the Maukises and Kirk Davidson. And from Sergeant Rafferty and Daisy Hepwood, whom she'd really, really *liked*. Whom everyone liked. It had been so much easier to hate the Maukises.

"My friend Keri is in trouble," she said, which was true. They were all in trouble, oh *God*. She'd almost gone to Daisy for help with that protection spell. Thank goodness she'd decided to make up—and then make out—with Takeshi first.

"You have to go?" he asked, looking troubled but not grumpy. Another point for him. Patrick would have grumped. She probably wasn't supposed to compare new boys with old boys, but she couldn't help it, even at a time like this, when it should have been the last thing on her mind.

"I do," Janna said. "Sorry."

"I hope Keri is okay." He pressed his lips together. "Can I help you?"

Grumpiness she could have dealt with. Concern made her weak in the knees. *Oh, girl*, she thought. *This is really* not *a good time to go all gooey.*

190

So she plastered on her flirtiest smile and kissed Takeshi and tried to be brazen badass Stardust, who wasn't scared of anything and didn't worry about broken hearts *or* curses.

"I'll see you later tonight?" she suggested, and straightened to whisper in his ear. "Maybe we can find a bed?"

He jerked, and she was scared she'd gone too far, but then she saw the pleasure in his eyes. He squeezed her hands. "Maybe," he whispered back.

She let him out the front door, trying to look less worried than she felt as he walked away. She was pretty sure that New Year's Eve was the danger zone, but right now she didn't want him more than a meter from her at all times.

"I'm telling Mum about the woodshed," Mariel announced from the living room door. "Unless you give me your mascara. The good one, not the clumper."

Janna threw a cushion into her youngest sister's face and stalked outside to steal her bike.

◢

She hadn't remembered until she was almost at the garage that it was Boxing Day, and most service places were closed. But Mr. Mangakahia was there, wiry body swimming in his grease-stained overalls, and he let her in to take a look at her car.

The Corolla was retrievable.

"She'll be right," said Mr. Mangakahia, and slapped the dented hood. "Bit of panel-beating will see her through."

It was the best news Janna had heard in months, and she

could feel joy trying to bubble out of her, but there was so much fear crushing it down. "Can I grab my stuff?"

"Was gonna ask," Mr. Mangakahia said. "Lots of junk in there."

Normally, Janna would have swept everything into the plastic bags he gave her, but she went really slow, putting each item in one at a time. Even so, she almost missed it. She'd been looking for a detailed clay figurine like the ones Sione and Keri had described, but there was nothing like that in there. Instead, she found a little ghost figure clumsily made out of paper, like someone had taken a square of paper and drawn down the four corners, twisting the middle a couple of times and tying it with a bit of string to make the head. Only the straight lines for hair, drawn with black Sharpie, and the big, blue ink eyes, gave any indication that it was anything but a piece of rubbish.

No wonder Aroha's dad hadn't seen the Corolla.

Janna couldn't feel any of the tingling the others had described, no bad luck clinging to the car. Maybe the paper doll's power had died after the car crash, or maybe it needed to be recharged with closeness to her, and she'd been too long away. Or maybe dyeing her hair had changed her appearance enough that the doll couldn't find her. She didn't know enough of what Daisy had done to be sure. *Voodoo doll*, Keri had said, but Keri didn't know anything about magic, and Janna knew at least a little bit. Nearly every tradition used human figures of some kind. Daisy wasn't a *bokor*; she was a witch.

A witch who'd well and truly taken the left-hand path. A *wicked* witch.

She ripped the doll in half just to be sure it was safe, the soft paper shredding at the tear. It was a napkin, she realized, and she turned it inside out, blinking at the restaurant logo.

The Kahawai. *But the last time I went there was when Sione came to meet us*, she thought, and then froze, because it wasn't until now that she'd put it together.

They knew from then, she thought. All her wide-eyed smiling at Octavian had been a waste; probably from the second they'd all met for that first dinner, the siblings of three dead boys, their enemies had guessed that they were on the right track and had tried to put them off it. That car crash could have killed both her and Sione — maybe the Fisher family and Takeshi, too.

Mr. Davidson. He must have been curious when Sione came back to town alone and followed him to the restaurant.

"Janna."

"Mmmm?" Janna said, and came back to herself. The napkin was nothing but shreds now, white confetti that drifted from her hands as she started. She shoved the bits in her pocket and tried to smile. "Sorry, I...you said something?"

"I'm heading home, love," Mr. Mangakahia said, wiping grease from his hands onto a rag.

"Oh," Janna said weakly. "Okay, coming."

She was beginning to realize the full scope of the spell. Just protecting Takeshi wasn't going to be enough. Even if they succeeded, there would be a next year, and a next year, and one after that, and she and Keri would still be stuck in this town, trying to watch the tourist boys and hoping that "bad luck" wouldn't kill them.

They had to stop the whole spell. Somehow persuade Daisy and her allies to never do it again. Or break it themselves, with stronger magic, and how could she possibly do that? It had to be a pretty powerful spell. Maybe the deaths of the boys just renewed it, like some spells needed to be repeated every full moon to stay strong. Maybe interrupting this one sacrifice would ruin the whole thing.

The truth was, she just didn't know enough. Daisy hadn't let her join her coven, and now she knew why. Stupid, stupid Janna.

She wheeled Mariel's clunker out to the street and hesitated. The Chancellor was uphill, the main street down.

The others were waiting for her, and Keri would be mad, but she *had* to find out more about this if they were going to win. And even if Daisy was evil, and most other adults potentially untrustworthy, there was one person who knew about magic that she thought she could safely ask. Someone young enough to not be involved, someone who'd known and loved a victim too much to harm him, someone who'd sat alone in the dark in the middle of the beach party, drinking to ease her pain.

Keri *really* wasn't going to like this.

Janna turned downhill, coasting all the way to Inner Light.

The shop looked mostly empty, and Daisy was nowhere in sight, but Janna lurked on Copper Road, making a big deal out of eating an ice cream until she was sure Daisy had gone for the day. Sam from the beach came by and tried to flirt with her, which gave her a little more padding time, and when she got rid of him and went in, it was ten minutes until closing. Sandra-Claire was leaning her elbows on the counter, looking more sour than usual.

"Hi," Janna said.

Sandra-Claire's spine snapped upright. "Do you know what your midget mate did?" she demanded.

"Um," Janna said, deciding that she should play innocent on this one. "No."

"She freaking *destroyed* the storeroom! It took us hours to clean up! Daisy had to go home with a migraine, and there's still a heap of things to put back on the shelves."

"Wow," Janna said. "What happened?"

"I don't know. Daisy said she was making all kinds of crazy accusations. Says Keri's *grieving*, won't let me call Lily and George. I said vandalism isn't grieving, but she shut me down. That girl is trouble, definitely. She always hated me, couldn't stand that me and Jake were in love." Sandra-Claire shook her sheets of blond hair over her shoulder. "Daisy's too nice," she concluded. "So did you come to look at the new stuff? Some great books in."

Sandra-Claire had never quite figured out that Janna didn't want to read.

"Are you in Daisy's coven?"

"Nah, my coven's in Nelson. I really only see them on the Sabbats—Samhain and Beltane and that."

"I know what Sabbats are," Janna protested, but felt reassured all the same. "Who is in her coven, do you know?"

Sandra-Claire gave her a long look. "That's none of your

business," she said. "Or mine, either. I think Daisy's coven are mostly old-school, you know—don't want people knowing about their faith. People can be so freaking prejudiced. Why do you want to know, anyway?"

"Just curious," Janna said. "Actually, I was hoping you could help me with a protection spell."

"To keep someone from harm?"

"Yeah."

"It has to be selfless," Sandra-Claire warned. "You can't protect someone against a rival lover, for example—that'll come back to you, and you'll lose him for good."

"You still believe in the Rule of Three, then?"

"Of course."

"Does Daisy?"

Sandra-Claire's gaze sharpened. "Why do you keep asking about Daisy?"

"She wouldn't let me join her coven, that's all. I wondered what I did wrong." Janna tried to look embarrassed, which didn't come easily.

It must have been convincing, though, because Sandra-Claire relaxed again. "Don't take it personally. You're under-age. And she wouldn't invite me, either. I think it's a pretty tight group." She came out from behind the counter and started scanning the shelves. "So, protection spells. I've got a couple of options for you. Let's see what suits you best."

The biggest, best protection you've got, Janna thought, and prepared to learn better than she had in her entire life.

CHAPTER TWENTY
Sione

✝

SIONE WAS RELIEVED WHEN KERI FINALLY got hold of Janna. He'd been thinking about "accidents."

"Stardust turned her cell phone off to sneak into the gallery," Keri reported at the end of the conversation. She tossed her own phone onto the hotel room table and sank into a chair beside it, moodily shoving at the carpet with her toes. The hotel didn't feel like the haven it had before, but they'd checked all the places Keri said might hold bugs, and she'd decided that Mr.

Davidson's spying couldn't be very high-tech, or he'd have known they were breaking into Rafferty's today.

"Did she see the crown?"

"It's been taken away. For 'cleaning.'" She made sarcastic quote marks, one-handed and then looked at him. "She wants to check her car for one of those figurines."

Sione thought of anomalous Jake, who didn't fit the murder patterns, and wondered if an "accident" had happened to him.

"I don't think they want to actually kill us," Keri said in answer to what he hadn't voiced. "Daisy thinks she's doing good by killing those boys. Getting rid of us would be harder to justify."

"Unless we start making real pests of ourselves. Like maybe if we started telling people," he suggested, wondering again. He was pretty sure that wasn't it, though; if Jake had known or suspected something, he'd have told his sister first. Anyone could see they'd had the kind of closeness Matthew and he had never managed. If he'd been gay, he could *never* have trusted Matthew enough to tell him first.

"We've still got the same problem as before," Keri said, unaware of how envious he suddenly was. "No proof. And this is even worse because we've got no method or opportunity that anyone would listen to. People don't *believe* in magic."

"People" had, until today, clearly included Keri, but Sione thought it wouldn't be wise to point that out. He looked out the window in an effort to avoid her eyes. The afternoon light glittered on the sea.

"Hey," Keri said. She was tugging at his sleeve. A moment ago she'd been ten feet away.

"I did it again," he realized, feeling sick. Even *knowing*, he couldn't stop being caught in the illusion of Summerton's beauty.

Keri's face was full of sympathy. It was an odd expression on her. "Janna's going to come here after," she said. "Wanna play Wii bowling?"

It turned out that Sione was pretty good at bowling. He got strike after strike, while Keri scowled at her losses.

"I think your arm is pulling you off balance," he offered at one point.

Keri gave him a long look. "Nope," she said finally. "My balance is fine now. You're just better than me." She put the controller down on the coffee table and shook out her hand. "Where is she? I had to be home at five. My mum's going to have fits."

It was five forty now.

"I wonder if other things are magic that we just don't notice," Sione said, and sent a ball into the gutter, sort of on purpose.

"I think they must make us not notice," Keri said, and knocked down three pins. "That has to be a big part of it. Otherwise people would really start to wonder, you know? They don't. They just go, 'Oh yes, Summerton is so pretty and so safe for the children. Why would we leave?' We noticed only because we *had* to think about it. Because all your spreadsheets made the pattern so clear. Where the hell *is* she?"

Someone knocked on the door, which could have been a

199

spooky coincidence if Keri hadn't been repeating that question every three minutes. Sione should have felt relieved when he let Janna in, but instead he felt a heated annoyance prickle at his skin.

Keri was glaring at Janna, too, and Sione sneered inwardly. Keri was always scowling. If she wasn't careful, her face would be stuck in that sour expression forever.

"I went to Inner Light—" Janna began, and Keri, naturally, lost what little self-control she had.

"You *what*?"

Janna rolled her eyes theatrically, like the drama queen she was, dying to stay the center of attention. "I waited until Daisy was gone. I wanted to research *protection* spells. Jeez, you can stop looking at me like I'm a moron. Sandra-Claire told me—"

"You *are* a moron," Keri said. "How could you talk to *Sandra-Claire*? She hates me!"

"She's always liked me." Janna hesitated, her face twisting, and then said, "Maybe she's nice to people who aren't total bitches."

Keri looked as if someone had slapped her.

"I don't want you doing magic on me, Janna," Sione said. "Keri's right. You're not the brightest bulb in the socket." He couldn't believe he'd said it, but Janna went dark red, humiliation and rage warring on her face, and he was glad, so glad that he'd finally managed to hurt her.

"God, get over it, Sione!" she spat out. Her eyes were huge, her pupils little black points in the middle of all that glistening blue. Her stupid, pretty face, the only reason anyone liked her.

"I kissed you *one time*, to make your brother jealous. You were *second prize*, okay?"

Sione felt it like a kick in the gut, and Keri followed up, laughing right in his face.

"You really should have expected it, Sione," she said. "Everyone knows about Janna."

"What?" Janna demanded. "What do they *know*, Keri?"

Keri smiled, an evil thing. "They know you'll kiss anything, if it has a pulse and a dick. What gets me is that you always try for the guys who are brighter than you—not that that's hard. Do you think smart is a communicable disease? Maybe you can fuck yourself into a couple of extra IQ points."

"You fucking bitch! Just because no guys want you, you *midget*."

"Or girls," Sione said, and Keri's face went gray. For a moment he felt alarm, but there was a sly voice in the back of his head, wet and rotten, whispering all the worst things to say.

And he was glad the voice was there. He *wanted* to say those things. "Maybe you're pissed because Janna won't ever kiss *you*, dyke."

Janna hooted. "Oh, *now* it makes sense." She pointed at Keri's hair. "You're not just a freak, you're a *lesbo* freak."

Keri put her good hand on Sione's shoulder and shoved, hard. "You're an asshole," she said. "An untrustworthy little shit. Trying to buy friends, Sione? No wonder no one likes you, *potato*."

White-hot with rage, he shoved her back.

She stumbled, trying to catch herself against the table.

But she'd forgotten about the cast. Joyful, he watched the pain explode across her face, followed by a look of startled realization.

"Calm down," she said.

But Janna was screeching at Sione, calling him a whining dick, a coward, a loser, and he was shouting that she was a cock-teasing bitch and a dumb drama queen. It was as if she were seeing all the sick, secret, decaying things buried deep in his brain, the ones that rose up and tortured him, and he had to combat with the same, only worse, all the worst things he could possibly say. Things that weren't actually bad in themselves, but that he knew would hurt her, give him power over her at last.

Keri said something else, something about *magic*, or tried to say, but the minute she spoke, Sione turned on her, too, the poison spilling from his lips. She was a nasty bitch, a coward for not coming out, not a real girl, a horrible daughter lying to her parents.

"I don't need you!" Keri screamed over both of them. "Fuck you both. I wish *you'd* killed yourselves."

In the ringing silence that followed, Sione thought, *She's right.* He'd known it all along. It should have been him who died.

The pain of that thought was so great it doubled him over, so great that it momentarily quieted the thick, rotten voice in his head. This wasn't right. This wasn't *normal*.

Keri deliberately knocked her cast against the table again and gasped. "It's a spell," she said. "It's not real; they're *making* us like this. Pain helps."

Janna's lip curled, but there was something uncertain in her eyes. "I—"

"Okay," Sione said, and tugged hard at his hair. It did help, dampening the little voice again, and letting him see what it was. "You're right." Another one of those clay dolls? "Get out of here, okay? I'll try to find it."

Janna was pinching and twisting the pale skin of her inner wrist. "The figurines attracted trouble *to* us, around it. This is trouble inside us, imposed from outside. The spell might be somewhere else."

"Are you sure?" Keri demanded.

"Of *course* I'm..." She stopped and took a deep breath. "Sorry. No, not completely sure. He should check. But it could be anywhere."

"Inner Light? The art gallery?"

"Maybe."

"It started when you came in," Sione said. "Keri and I were fine. It started with the three of us together."

"After Daisy went home for the day," Janna said. "That total bitch."

Keri was breathing fast. She'd stopped banging her cast about, thank Jesus, because Sione was pretty sure that the gray tinge of her skin wasn't a good sign. Instead, she was yanking at her hair, like him. Short dyke hair—*no*. "They're trying to break us up, keep us away from each other," she said. "So that we can't interfere in their plans."

"Let them think it's working," Janna said.

"It *is* working," Sione said, and then winced at his tone. "I didn't mean that how it sounded."

"I know, it twists everything," Janna said. "Look, they've been ahead of us all the way! Let's get ahead of *them* for once. Let's stay away from each other. I'll stick with Takeshi and do the protection spell—"

"You're an amateur—" Keri protested, and then bit the rest of it back.

Janna talked over her. "And we'll all protect him at the Bash, so they can't come for him. They won't be expecting it."

"You *still* want to do the Bash?" Sione asked.

She flushed. "I have to!"

"She's right," Keri said reluctantly. "Let them think it's worked. Daisy thinks she scared us."

"She *did* scare you," Sione snarled. "You could hardly talk."

"You should know what that's like," Keri shot back, and then took a deep breath and knocked her cast again. She gasped. "Oh, fuck, I can't keep doing this. Okay, we keep in touch by phone, all right? In private. And as far as anyone knows, we had a fight and hate each other." She glared at both of them. "Don't tell anyone otherwise."

It was almost true anyway, Sione thought. The things they'd said to him curdled in his stomach, but worse were the things he'd said to them. He couldn't believe he'd outed Keri, couldn't believe he'd called Janna a whore. Exactly as if he were like those people who thought being gay or having sex was *bad*, when he knew much better.

The rotten little voice was getting louder again. Knowing they weren't really his own thoughts only helped a little; he suddenly had a lot of sympathy for some of Mum's clients.

They *knew* the bad feelings were all coming from inside their heads, but relying on logic didn't make it stop.

"I'm sorry," he said. "You guys, I am so, so sorry."

"Me, too," Keri said.

"Me, three," Janna said. She was looking at Keri, though, her face wrinkled. "Are you really gay?"

Keri flinched. "Yes."

"That's okay! I mean, it's okay to be gay. I—look, I won't tell anyone."

Keri looked at the clock. "I have to go. I don't hate you," she added, all in a rush. "Not really. I know it's not real. But I have to go."

"Me, too," Janna said. The girls nearly brushed together in their haste to get out the door and then recoiled from the other's closeness.

For the first time, Sione was happy they were leaving him alone.

CHAPTER TWENTY-ONE
Keri

⚡

I TOOK THE STAIRS, SINCE JANNA WAS MOVING toward the elevator. Halfway down, and breathing hard, I noticed water dripping off my nose onto my shirt. That was how I knew I was crying.

Of course Mum was in the staff room, along with a couple of the housekeepers. And Kirk Davidson. It was that kind of day.

"Keri!" she exclaimed, jumping to her feet. "Oh my lord, what happened?"

"They're *awful*," I said. "Sione and Janna—what they said to me, Mum."

"What did they say?"

I flinched. "It doesn't matter, it doesn't—" I was sobbing almost too hard to speak now, and it wasn't entirely to sell the story we'd agreed on. It wasn't all Sione's fault he'd outed me, but he had, and that meant the secret was already out of my control.

Mum gathered me into her arms and rocked, as if I were seven, not seventeen. I thought of what they'd said and shuddered. Would she love me this much if she knew I liked girls? Or would she look at me and wonder, *Where did I go wrong?*

Mr. Davidson got me a glass of water, and I pretended I didn't mind his big fingers uncurling my hand to put the glass in there. I gulped down the water. The housekeepers weren't even pretending to mind their own business, and one of them was Hemi Koroheke's big sister. Great. This was going to be all over town.

Well, at least Daisy and Company would believe their plan had worked. I hoped they choked on their own smugness.

"Come on," Mr. Davidson said, and hustled everyone out of the break room, closing the door quietly behind him.

As I calmed down, breath by breath, I was able to stop crying and clean my face, but the hate wasn't gone. A real emotion that strong should have been leeched out with the tears, but this one thrummed inside me like an engine choking out greasy smoke, making my fingers itch with the urge to be away from them. *They are disgusting*, the voice whispered.

You're not real, I thought fiercely, and the voice went softer.

But it didn't disappear. I looked at the yellowing walls and tattered bits of paper on the bulletin board, so different from the glossy lobby and luxurious rooms. It was all an illusion, the beautiful hotel. All the work that went into it was planned in these grubby rooms.

Dirt under beauty. Just like Summerton.

"Oh, Mum," I said. "Can we go home? I want to go home."

She was looking at me, her sympathy swallowed up in careful appraisal. "Your father called, Keri. He said you were supposed to be home at five. It's well past six. You missed the phone call from your grandmother."

"It's their fault!" I said. It was, wasn't it? That was fair. "Janna and Sione, they made me late."

"Stop it," Mum said, her voice slicing through my protests. "Stop it, Keri, right now. I have had it with your excuses. I know you're having a hard time—we are *all* having a hard time—and one of the ways I am coping with it is that I need to know where you are and that you will keep your promises. You said you understood."

I couldn't remember saying anything of the sort.

"You are grounded," she said. "You are to stay home until New Year's Day unless you are accompanied by me, or your father if he's home."

"But the Beach Bash!" I said.

"No buts, no Beach Bash," she hissed. "So help me God, Keri, do you want me to have a nervous breakdown? I am trying to hold this family together!"

"You canceled Christmas!"

She stood up, every line in her body vibrating with tension, like a tree in a gale. "Yes," she said quietly. "I shouldn't have done that without talking to you. But you are grounded, Keri, because you promised one thing and did another. Am I understood?"

She was scaring me, with her intensity, with her tension. If I said no, would she just fall apart? And I was tired, so tired I could barely think, all my energy gone into the fight, and my grief, and the effort to keep the hatred at bay. My arm ached. "Yes," I whispered.

"Good. Because I swear to God, if you put one foot out of line, I will drive you down to your grandmother myself. She won't put up with your nonsense, and you won't have friends there to make you late, and me out of my mind with worry."

And I wouldn't be here to save Takeshi. "I understand," I said. "I'll be good."

She breathed out, a long sigh. "All right, then. Let's go home."

Dad didn't yell at me; instead he listened to Mum explaining why I was grounded until New Year's Day and nodded, looking at me with disappointed eyes.

That was much, much worse.

I didn't complain. I ate my dinner and helped load the dishwasher and went to bed.

And lay awake for most of the night, planning.

I could stay home for the next six days, being as good as gold, but on New Year's Eve, Takeshi was going to be sacrificed. I had to get to the Beach Bash, whatever happened to me, and whatever punishment came after that.

But there was time to be good before I disappointed them again.

CHAPTER TWENTY-TWO
Janna

★

JANNA HELD IT TOGETHER IN THE ELEVATOR, all the way up to the suite Takeshi and Aroha shared, but when Takeshi opened the door and said her name, she stepped into his arms, trusting him to hold her until the shaking stopped.

"What happened?" he said, careful hands gentle on her back and hair. "Janna, is something gone wrong?"

"Yes," she managed, and clutched him tighter. "Sione and Keri—a fight. We had a fight. They called me—" She stopped. She couldn't tell Takeshi the things they'd said. He would hate them, when it wasn't really their fault. Or worse, he might wonder if they were right. What if he thought she was *bad*? They'd taken all the words she was most afraid of right out of her nightmares and thrown them into her face.

"Come…" Takeshi was saying. "Come in. It's only me here." He was stepping backward, drawing her in, and sitting her down on the plush couch. He took her hand in his and patted it, which was so sweet she could cry, if she hadn't been crying already.

She gave up on that as pointless and looked around as she blew her nose on a tissue, ignoring Takeshi's polite little turn-away.

She'd never been in here before. The suite was a lot nicer than Sione's room downstairs. Takeshi and Aroha had their own bedrooms and a lounge furnished in fancy red furniture on soft cream carpet, and some sort of modern-art glass vase on the coffee table. She didn't think she liked the vase much—it was shiny, gold-veined black, too smooth and perfect—but she could tell it was expensive. Aroha's parents must be so, so rich.

What would it be like, to never have to worry about money? Not that anyone in Summerton was *really* poor, like homeless poor, or even on-the-dole poor—*and now you know why that is*, she reminded herself—but this kind of rich was something else, something she wanted almost as much as she wanted to make music. The freedom to go almost anywhere, do almost anything, and never have to worry about not having enough; that's what this kind of money meant.

"Where's Aroha?" she asked, and then, because she didn't really care, "Thank you. For this. Sorry that I'm a big mess."

Takeshi stroked her cheekbone and showed her the black smudge on his fingers. "The same when we met, beautiful Janna," he said, and smiled. "This fight?"

"I don't want to talk about it," she said. She could feel her face twisting and even knowing she must look ugly couldn't make her smooth it out again.

Takeshi took her hand. "It was a wrong fight?"

"Bad. Bad fight, yes, I don't *want* to—" He was going to make her talk about it, he was going to be understanding and persistent and gentle, and she didn't want gentle right then. And she'd have to lie, and she didn't want to lie to him anymore. Janna wanted to stop thinking.

She reached up and drew Takeshi's mouth down to hers, fierce and raw and *wanting*. It took only a few seconds before she wasn't faking it anymore; she was burning up with him, the fight forgotten. She took his shirt off, laughing as it mussed the careful spikes in his hair, and kissed her way down his chest to pry, teasing, at his belt buckle. She grinned at the noises she was drawing out of his throat and the little shudders that rippled down his smooth body, hummed as she pressed her mouth against his skin.

Sometime after that, she took his hand and led him to his bedroom, and the soft, white bed, and the joyful, tender space they made together there.

Janna went home that evening, warm and thoughtful, with Takeshi's soft black jacket draped over her shoulders. She'd asked to borrow it, and he'd given it to her with no hesitation. A thing worn often, freely given. That should help what she meant to do.

Nobody seemed to be home, which was just as well. She'd showered afterward, but Mum had a sixth sense about these things, like just before she'd decided to do it for the first time with Patrick. She'd sat Janna down for a "little chat," and Janna had expected a long lecture on the importance of saving herself for marriage (which would have been *totally* hypocritical), but instead she'd gotten Mum-the-nurse, not Mum-the-Catholic, and an in-depth review of contraception and sexual health. In some ways, that had been worse. There was nothing quite like your own mother carefully explaining the symptoms of herpes to make you want to die.

Okay, then. A house to herself and time to make the spell work right.

Sandra-Claire had been firm that, while she *could* sell Janna all the herbs she needed for any of the spells, it would be better to work fresh, with what she had on hand. So they'd gone with the simplest spell they could find.

There was flax in the overgrown back garden. Mum would probably make her and her sisters weed again pretty soon. Janna made a mental note to learn something her sisters didn't want Mum to know so that she could make them do her share. Of course, they'd try to do the same to her; it was only fair.

She sliced off some of the flax with the silver athame she'd bought last year to show Daisy she was serious. If she'd known nothing could get her into that coven, she would have saved the money, but it was probably just as well she had it now.

What was she doing, playing around with homemade spells in the backyard? She'd never been initiated; she knew what she knew from books she struggled through and what she'd picked up from conversations at Inner Light, and here she was trying to fight Daisy Hepwood, who'd been a practicing witch long before Janna was born.

Janna gave herself a full minute to freak out, counting out the seconds while the panic made her fingers shake. Then she took the flax inside and got to work.

Stage fright was never a reason to back out of a gig. Patrick would have laughed right in her face.

In the end, the hardest part was unpicking the lining at the inside back of the jacket. Janna stabbed her finger a couple of times and hoped that her blood wouldn't spoil the spell. Twisting a little person shape out of the flax was easy enough, even if it made her think of the napkin poppet in her car, and the clay figures Sione and Keri had talked about. Thinking about those two made the gross voice in her head start whispering again, and she had to stop and breathe calmly before she could go on. It was a good thing she hadn't started the actual spell yet. She'd have tainted it, with all that twisted fury.

She found a piece of blue cloth in her mother's sewing drawer and spread it on her bedroom floor, kneeling in front of it. On top of the cloth, she set two long blue candles, and a squat red one, which she wound a silver ribbon around before lighting. Janna let the candles burn for a while, thinking of Takeshi. His quick eyes, sometimes frustrated with the things he couldn't quite put words to. His drive, his enthusiasm for the unknown—new cultures, new worlds. His shoulders, muscles gleaming under a light layer of sweat, and his mouth, curving upward as he happily took everything she had given him in the big, white bed.

Janna unwound the silver ribbon while the red candle still burned and wrapped it around the little flax figure, from crooked head to spindly legs. The sap was sticky and smelled fresh and strong. She could have made up a chant to go with it, but she always felt silly doing that, and it seemed important that she be secure and certain in this. Instead she settled for saying Takeshi's name, three times, and finishing with "Keep him safe" as she tucked in the ends of the ribbons. She wasn't asking anyone in particular to look out for him, because she wasn't sure whom to ask. But it was her will, with all the emotion she could gather behind it, and that had to count for something to any spirits or gods that might be listening in, didn't it? She slipped the figure into the jacket lining and sewed it up again, then blew out the candles and stood, her feet prickling with the new blood flow.

There. Give the jacket back to him and make sure he wore it on New Year's Eve, and he was as safe as she could magically make him. And as for physically—Janna struck what she imagined a kung fu pose might look like in her mirror. "Bring it," she said, and tossed her hair. It was only play, but she really felt like Stardust for a second, powerful and strong, impossible to scare. For the first time, Janna wondered if everyone had a secret self, named or unnamed, waiting for their time to emerge. Who might Schuyler have been, alone in this room that had become hers?

All this daydreaming was making her sad, and the clatter

from the hall announced the kids were returning, no doubt stinking of chlorine and complaining of sore eyes.

Sure enough, Petra and Mariel were in the kitchen, wet hair dripping everywhere, fighting over who should have the first go with the blender. Lurking in the hall, Janna felt a huge surge of love for them, so overwhelming that she thought it should trickle out her fingers in ribbons of light, ribbons to wrap around her sisters to keep them always warm and treasured and loved.

Of course, such weakness could not be revealed.

I'll make sure they have a future. Anywhere they choose, she thought, and stepped through the door. "Oi, you brats," she said. "Give it a rest. *Some* people are trying to concentrate."

CHAPTER TWENTY-THREE
Sione

✝

ON THE THIRD DAY AFTER THE FIGHT, WHEN the housekeeper once again came in after noon and found him still in bed, Sione decided that he'd better do something so he could stop telling so many lies to his mother. Every day, he'd been talking about walks on the beach and bird-watching and long, quiet sessions of communing with nature, and promising her that he was getting out of his room and away from his computer. Somehow it was easier to lie about what had happened than to think about it long enough to tell her. The one time she'd mentioned "those girl friends of yours," he'd swiftly changed the subject, feeling sick to his stomach, and she'd let it go.

He'd just about managed to stay in touch with Janna and Keri, but the spell was getting stronger, creeping into his dreams so that he woke up exhausted and hating. They were down to exchanging text messages now, unable to cope with each other's voices on the phone. At least that had meant Keri's itemized lists of plans had stopped coming; they'd grown increasingly paranoid, and more and more dictatorial on what he and Janna should do and where they should be, with backup plans for the backup plans.

But being able to contact any of them was increasingly something that concerned him.

He screwed up his courage and sent them both a text: WILL WE BE ABLE TO COME TOGETHER AT BASH?

IF WE TOUGHEN UP, Keri texted back. Trapped at home, she always answered messages right away. Sione stared at the screen, wondering how much of that was a sneer at him.

Janna's message came later, beeping at him when he got out of the shower. TLD U. USED SPELL. ALL GUD.

He rolled his eyes at it. One out-of-practice witch trainee couldn't do that much, could she? And she refused to tell them what kind of spell it was.

CM SEPRATE THO, she added a few seconds later, and Sione had to see the sense in that, even though he had no idea how he was going to get backstage, where Takeshi was apparently going to be. Keri had given him four ways to do it, ranging from sneaking through the security fence to faking an injury to get him to the medical tent in the backstage area.

Her micromanaging made him angry. But over the last three days, what didn't? Everything about this hotel reminded him of either Matthew or the girls. The picture over the bed, of the bright people at the Beach Bash under the gathering clouds, was impossible to look at without feeling sick. At any rate, he didn't want Maukis art anywhere near him. He'd asked the housekeeper to take it away.

That was more words than he'd spoken to anyone but his mum and dad since the fight.

Something had to give. He put the camera and phone in his bag and slouched down to the lobby.

Keri's mother was at the reception desk, and he nearly turned to go back, almost missing the red-haired girl in the lobby, curled into a chair with a book. But she moved her head, and the light streaming through the enormous windows caught strands of golden light in the pile of fuzzy curls. He walked toward her, trying to pretend that Keri's mum wasn't staring a hole into his back.

Of course, when Aroha looked up from her reading, he had no idea what to say.

"Sione!" she said, and bounced to her feet. "Hi! Haven't seen you in ages! How's it going?"

She likes you, Keri had said. And if she wasn't trying to make a fool out of him . . . No, she'd said that before the spell, when they'd still been friends. So it had to be true.

How did you talk to girls? Matthew would know.

"Oh…okay," he mumbled, and nodded at the book. "What're you reading?" That seemed safe.

She shrugged. "Some sci-fi thing of Takeshi's."

"He reads science fiction?" He craned to look at the book and was surprised that he could read the title. "In English?"

"Yeah. Although I think he read this one in Japanese first. He reads English a lot better than he speaks it. It's the other way around for me, with Japanese."

"But you borrowed it?"

"Stole it, really. But he wasn't using it," she said, and rolled her eyes. "He's busy."

With Janna, Sione thought, automatically bracing for the way the thought of her curdled his stomach.

"You don't have a thing for him, too?" he said. He was going for joking, but it came out twisted.

But Aroha only looked resigned. "Ew, he's my host brother. But this was supposed to be—God. My parents treat these Summerton trips like a second honeymoon, even though they always make me come, too. But they go off together to be lovey-dovey with each other, like they're our age. It's pretty gross. And I thought, since he was coming, that I'd at least have someone to hang out with. But he's spending all his time with Janna, and it's okay, I get it, summer romance, but today I got kicked out of our suite." She winced. "Well, not kicked out, exactly. They were just…I said I might go for a walk, and they looked so grateful, I thought I'd better do it before they went to his bedroom anyway. But I stole his book. So, you know, we're even." She tried to smile, but it was weak around the edges.

220

Abandoned and lonely, with nothing to do and no one to be with. Sione felt a pang of sympathy so sharp that it went right through the fog that had been hanging around his brain since the fight with *them*.

"I was going for a walk," he said. "Wanna come?"

Which was stupid, of course — the last thing he should do on a walk to clear his head and put together alternate plans to protect her host brother was invite Aroha along. But her face lit up like the fireworks on Guy Fawkes Day, and he couldn't feel sorry about it.

During that walk, he discovered something interesting: Because he knew Aroha already liked him, he didn't get as nervous about talking to her, and she talked enough to fill in his gaps anyway, without expecting him to take an even share. Which made it easier for him to talk. They discussed their schools, and books they'd both read, and movies they'd both seen. She laughed, more than once, as they wandered up through the hills.

So did he.

He'd liked Janna because she was exciting and dramatic — and because she was Matthew's kind of girl, but she'd kissed *him*. And he'd wanted to kiss Keri because...well, because he'd seen her with her shirt off and been full of adrenaline after the confrontation with Daisy.

He was wondering if he might like Aroha because she was Aroha. Maybe he *should* have a rebound relationship. Talking to girls was pretty easy when it was the right girl.

"So you play drums?" he asked. "I bet you're good."

"I'm okay. Dad hates the noise, but Mum loves it. She was a punk-rock chick in the early eighties."

Sione tried to match that to the red-haired lady he'd seen after the crash. "Really?"

"Really. Riot grrrrrrrl! Angry feminist music, you know." She gave him a look that was partly challenging. "Mind you, they had a lot to be angry about."

"No lie," Sione agreed. "My mum, she was a social worker before she moved into psychotherapy. She's got some stories."

"I bet. I'd like to meet her." She blushed, and Sione stopped, amazed. On her it was a hectic flush, a bright wash over her pale skin. "I mean . . . I don't mean that—"

"She'd like to meet you, too," Sione told her, and started walking again. Mum would probably be interested in any girl he introduced to her, but he thought she'd like Aroha as Aroha, too.

They were on one of the easier trails, a footpath, really, with matai trees towering greenly on each side instead of buildings, and the cheeps of fantails instead of traffic noises. The manuka were in flower, little white blossoms everywhere. Aroha stopped to grab an empty chip packet that someone had dropped.

"I hate litterers," she said, stuffing it into her pocket. "Who would want to spoil this place? It's so beautiful."

Sione held his tongue and nodded.

The path broke out, finally, into an empty wooden platform just over a tarn. The water was so clear that Sione could see the rocks at the bottom when he leaned over the rail, even make out an eel slipping through the waterweeds to his left.

Aroha took pictures, but he was content to stand and watch, without the mindless devotion that still caught him in town. Was this far enough away from Summerton? Was it only the area around the bay that held people in that worshipful trance?

"What are you thinking about?" he asked to break the silence.

Aroha lowered the camera and turned to him slowly. "Takeshi said Janna said your brother died," she said, and winced when he flinched at the name. "Sorry, I shouldn't have —"

"It's not that," Sione said, and kept on talking before she asked what it was. "I mean...yeah, he died. Suicide. Carbon monoxide poisoning."

"I was thinking about it. I'm an only child. I can't even imagine what it would be like to lose a sibling."

"Matthew was an only child before I came along," Sione said. "He said he liked it better that way."

"I'm sure he was just joking."

"Nah, he meant it."

Aroha gave him a dubious look, and he felt himself starting to get annoyed. "Look, he was my family, okay? We loved each other, and we would have been there for each other in emergencies, but he didn't like me very much, and he wasn't real shy about showing it. I embarrassed him."

Aroha looked stunned now, and he felt mean for pricking the bubble of all her brotherly dreams. "I'm making it sound worse than it was," he said. He remembered being told to go away, stop hanging around — a thousand little stings about his height, his clothes, his brains—but concentrated instead on a happy memory, one of the shining, true things Matthew had done. "There was this one time—it was in Summerton, actually. I was about eight, and I hadn't learned to swim. Shameful, right? What kind of eight-year-old Samoan can't swim? I'd dog-paddle, but I wouldn't put my head underwater, even in the lagoons. I was afraid of what could be there. It was stupid."

Aroha's eyes were intent upon his face, and he realized how pretty they were, a clear, true blue. "No," she said quietly.

"It was. Dad was really angry about it. He tried to bribe me into learning, and then he tried to punish me when I wouldn't—"

"Jesus."

"No, he was right. It was important. It's not safe, not knowing how." He thought of his father's first home, of the gray-green water that had terrified Sione, and the cousins who had leaped, long-limbed and fearless, into the lagoons and run splashing into the ocean.

"And Matthew taught you?"

"Well, now you've spoiled the ending," Sione told her. She surprised him by laughing, and he felt himself grinning back. "Yeah. Not in a magical Disney way. He just splashed around in the shallow end of the saltwater pool down by the beach and told me to come in. I always wanted to be where he was and do what he was doing, so when he asked me...I actually tried. Matthew loved to swim, and he loved trying to be older than he was. Being in the kids' end must have really annoyed him. But he stayed there until I could do it on my own." Sione sighed. "And then he left me there, I guess."

224

"And now you can swim," Aroha said, and leaned her shoulder against his.

"Now I can," he said, and leaned back.

They were silent for a little while. Sione could feel Aroha's breathing as it moved her arm against his, the soft slide of her jeans as she shifted her weight minutely. She might have been breathing a little faster than normal. But so was he.

A kererū flew over the lake, white flashing from the underside of the iridescent blue-and-purple wings. Aroha exclaimed, breaking the silence.

Sione found that his plan had come together after all. It just wasn't the plan he thought he had been making. He took his courage in both hands and leaped into the deep end. "This Beach Bash thing," he said. "Would you like to go with me?"

"Yes," she said, and beamed at him. "That would be great."

CHAPTER TWENTY-FOUR
Janna

★

JANNA WAS SORT OF GRATEFUL FOR THE
stupid radio interview that Patrick had suckered her into. For
one thing, it got her out of Summerton, and the chance of seeing anything that reminded her of either of *them*. Bad enough
that she still had to think of them when she tried to think of
protecting Takeshi or read one of Keri's plans.

For another thing, the interview itself was really fun.
Patrick's cousin Xiao-Xiao was like a smaller, feistier, girl version of Patrick, and Janna got a straight-girl crush on her right

away. Which made her think of Keri, which made the little voice start up again, but Janna drowned it under Stardust's charisma and lilted her way through the interview, funny, flirtatious, and just a bit wild.

"The Beach Bash is known for launching rising stars," Xiao-Xiao said. "So what's next for Vikings to the Left?"

Patrick opened his mouth, but Janna leaned forward and spoke confidently into the big, fuzzy microphone. "Who knows?" she said. "But the world better be ready for it."

Xiao-Xiao gave her a thumbs-up, lips curving in appreciation. "We'll be waiting. And that's it for 'Scene It' this week. I'm your host, Xiao-Xiao, and join me next week for a report on the Beach Bash and all the Double X action you can handle. Local community news is next, and I'm playing you out with "What They Say When They See You," by the ultra-talented Vikings to the Left." She flipped a switch and took her headphones off, grinning at them.

"People don't like show-offs," Patrick grumbled.

"People love show-offs," Janna told him, hopping off her stool. "They just don't like that they do. Smile, Patrick! We're on the radio!"

Xiao-Xiao poked him in the shoulder. "Seriously, cuz. Crack those pearly whites."

Patrick pulled his lips back from his teeth and leered into Janna's face. "It can be taught!" Janna announced. "Sort of."

"You guys want to eat?" Xiao-Xiao offered. "There's great Thai down the block."

"Nah. We have to get back." Patrick gave his cousin a quick hug and muttered thanks, and slung his messenger bag over his shoulder before picking up his guitar. That was probably the real reason he'd wanted to drive down — the chance to play live on air.

Janna dawdled enough to take another look at the radio studio, all the CDs piled against the wall in their plain wooden shelves, the LPs in plastic sleeves looking dusty in the corner. This was going to be her world, she promised herself. This was where she belonged.

Driving back, they played songs on the sound system in turn, bagging on each other's choices. Janna twice picked a fight over a song she actually liked, just for the fun of watching Patrick's face turn itself inside out with sneering at her lack of taste.

"You're so ugly when you hate everything," she informed him. "Which is, oh, all the time."

"How's being a knockout working for you?" Patrick asked. "People taking you seriously, are they?"

Janna made a face. "If music doesn't work out, you could always try stand-up. Can I drive the next bit?"

Patrick shot her a glance under his bangs. "No," he said. "Insurance won't cover it."

Janna picked at the hem of her plaid skirt. "The crash wasn't my fault, you know."

"I know. You're a good driver."

She raised her head, surprised, but he was watching the road as they passed through one of the hamlets between Greymouth and Westport. It was raining, that light drizzle that fell every-where outside Summerton. In the rain, the few houses looked gray and tired, the one car in sight rusty around the doors and wheels. Janna shivered. "Do you think people still live there?"

Patrick shrugged. "Dunno. Pretty shitty for them if they did."

"Do you ever worry about what might happen to Summerton?" she asked. "If people stop coming?"

"I don't think about Summerton much." For a moment, she thought it was all he was going to say, but he surprised her again. "I guess it would suck. That's where most of the money comes from. People would lose their jobs. The hospital might close. My dad probably couldn't be a taxi driver anymore; most of his fares are tourists."

Janna slumped. "The town would die." As she said it, she felt something clutch at her chest and understood, dimly, that Daisy must have felt that fear. That fear might have made her do what she did—not fear for herself but fear for the town, fear of an uncertain future.

It was still selfish and wrong, she reminded herself. But because Janna knew she was selfish herself, the thought made her wriggle.

"Maybe not that bad," Patrick said cautiously. "Why are you worried about it?"

"I don't know," she said.

It was totally annoying that Patrick *knew* she was lying. She *knew* that he knew. But he just leaned forward and cued up the next song and left it up to her whether she'd explain.

"I really like Takeshi," she said over Salmonella Dub's latest.

"Uh, okay?"

"I'd hate it if he got hurt."

Patrick snorted. "Anyone who tried to hurt him would have to get through you first. Hope they have nice funerals. What are you *talking* about?"

"Nothing," Janna said. She crunched into her seat and reminded herself that she was doing the right thing, and she didn't look at any more abandoned houses all the rest of the way home.

On the day before New Year's Eve, Vikings finished their last rehearsal.

"Want to run 'Elephant in the Bath' again?" Hemi asked. "That bridge is still dodgy."

"I think we're done," Patrick said. He picked through the opening chords for "Coming Down Again" and shook his head. "I don't want to overplay it. We know what we're doing."

"*I* do," Kyle said. "*You* sang 'gray as burnt rose' and not 'gray as *a* burnt rose' again."

"Gray as burnt rose scans better."

"It doesn't make sense."

"It—"

"Boys, boys," Janna interrupted, strumming a chord for emphasis. "Shut up. What are you going to wear?"

"Black," Patrick said blankly.

"Do you own anything else?" Hemi wondered. He was wearing one of his gross T-shirts, this one proclaiming him a member of "Boob Watch."

"I could wear my school uniform," Patrick told him. "And you could wear yours."

Janna gave up, put Cherry Bomb in her case, and went to kiss Takeshi while the other guys squabbled. He was wearing his jacket. He had worn it every day since she'd said it made him look cute, protection charm hidden safely in the hem. And if sometimes Aroha vanished to give them the suite and Janna ended up taking the jacket off, well, she was there to look after him then.

"You are very good," he said, and squeezed her hand. "Are you worried? On the news, they say it will rain tomorrow night. A big storm."

Kyle laughed. "Hey, check the tourist," he said. "Guys, did you hear the Beach Bash is going to get rained out?"

Hemi cackled. "Summerton really annoys the weather girls," he told Takeshi. "It never rains, from Christmas to New Year's."

"Why?" Takeshi asked, and Janna tensed all over.

But Hemi just shook his head. "Don't know," he said, bored. "Microclimate or something. The storm will come up from the South, then go out to sea and leave us warm and dry. And rocking out."

Takeshi nodded, and then tipped his head at Janna. "What will you wear?"

She kissed his forehead. "Something fun. You'll see."

"Something short, I hope," Hemi said, and yelped when Patrick punched his arm.

"Okaaaay, we're going," Janna said, tugging Takeshi up. He came willingly, laughing with his eyes. "Bye, guys."

"Get plenty of sleep," Patrick warned, and rolled his eyes when the other boys went "Ooooooooh" in unison. "Shit, grow *up*."

But when they returned to the hotel, Aroha was in the suite, reading a book and looking as if hints about going for a long walk would be totally ignored. Janna thought she'd have to settle for kisses and an early bedtime.

"Are you going tomorrow?" Janna asked her.

"Yeah," Aroha said, looking surprised. Janna reviewed the last few days and realized she hadn't talked to Aroha much, other than implying it was a great day out there and maybe Aroha would like to explore it. Oops. "I'm going with Sione, actually," she went on, looking pleased, and all of Janna's guilt vanished in the red wash of fury.

It's not real, she told herself, but every time she told herself that, she was less convinced. Even if the spell had started everything, they'd said such disgusting things to her. There was *no* excuse good enough.

"Oh," Takeshi said.

Aroha looked frustrated. "We'll get there after you guys, don't worry. What was this famous fight about, anyway?"

"Ask *him*," said Janna.

"He's not saying."

"I bet he's not." *Wimp*, said the voice in her head. *Sad little potato.* She caught the look Takeshi and Aroha exchanged and felt her anger spark hotter. "Are you two talking behind my back?"

"We just wanted to —"

"Fine. Whatever." She stalked toward the door, then whirled back and kissed Takeshi, hard and furious. Aroha hid behind her book, possibly rolling her eyes, but Janna didn't care. "Wear your jacket," she whispered in Takeshi's ear, then released him.

"Good night," he said behind her, sounding confused and a little lost.

After, she thought. *I'll explain to him after.* And then he would break up with her because he'd think she was totally crazy, but what the hell. He was leaving on New Year's Day anyway, going back to Auckland, and then to Japan, and she would never see him again. Stardust wouldn't care; she'd take the memories of a good time and a hot fling and carry on.

Janna felt like shit.

"I lay down by the long grass," she sang in the elevator, doing jazz hands with faked enthusiasm to her reflection in the brushed chrome. "I laid down my heart."

CHAPTER TWENTY-FIVE
Keri

SINCE I WAS HOME ANYWAY, MUM MADE ME do the cleaning, with a list of chores to complete each day. Everything was still tidy from her massive session after Jake's tangi, so there wasn't much point, but I did it anyway. I dusted every china thing on the mantelpiece, polished all the wedding silver, vacuumed, and ironed, all of which was even less fun with one good hand. Mum came home every lunch and dinner break to check on me and called the home phone at random times during the day. The message that she didn't trust me couldn't have been any clearer. I tried to be a good daughter and not complain about it too much.

I remembered the horrible things *they* had said, that I was an awful daughter who should have died instead.

Or had I said that? It was hard to remember. Thinking about the fight, or the other people in it, made me feel sick and small. And getting everything in the entire house to Mum's ridiculous hotel standards of cleanliness gave me far too much time to think.

I was able to give the others plans at first, going over them again and again, because I couldn't trust either of them to do it right the first time. But as New Year's Eve drew closer, I had to concentrate on things I could do without thinking of those two at all. On the thirtieth, in between wielding the duster and the toilet brush, I practiced punching one-handed and kicking with my cast held out to balance me, and swung the baton around until I had a good idea of how to be effective with it. Sergeant Rafferty and Mr. Davidson were going to be the problems. The Maukises were foul, but I didn't think they were really physical people. And Daisy was skinny and middle-aged; she wouldn't be able to put up much of a fight.

Unless it was with spells.

But everything she'd done had been quieter and less immediate—no big flashes of lightning or anything, just those dolls to put us off balance and whatever she'd done to make us hate one another. And she hadn't done anything like that again; maybe she thought she'd succeeded in warning us away, turning us against one another.

I swallowed back my nausea and tried to think again.

Tomorrow night was the Beach Bash, and I knew where Takeshi would be. Originally, I'd thought we could all stick by him, and I'd come up with various ways so that Sione and I could be around him all the time, and Janna when she wasn't onstage. Janna had been maddeningly vague, and I didn't trust her protection spell, but she was pretty sure that since the coven had started with the crown, they'd need to use it again to complete the ritual. Which meant they'd have to take Takeshi somewhere quiet. My first plan had been to find the crown, but there were just too many possibilities of where it could be, and if we got caught, it would totally destroy the illusion that the three of us had given up.

But though we couldn't locate the crown, we *did* know where Takeshi was going to be. With all three of us around, they couldn't grab him without us making a big fuss.

As a last resort, I was prepared to start screaming about magic.

I'd be labeled the crazy girl for the rest of my life, but at least the idea would be in people's heads. They'd wonder if Takeshi then died. They might start asking questions. And the one thing I knew about the conspirators was that they *hated* people looking into what they were doing. If I was loud enough, long enough, the coven would have to resist sacrificing Takeshi, just to keep their secret.

Now I was wondering how far I could rely on the other two. Janna could be distracted by anything shiny, and Sione was a coward who'd probably curl into a ball and start crying at the first hint of violence. A better plan might be to get Takeshi away and hide him somewhere, by myself, until New Year's Eve was over.

Then I'd be grounded for the rest of my *life*, stuck in Summerton until I died, unloved and alone.

But it would be worth it if Takeshi lived.

On New Year's Eve, I got up late. Mum was home, sipping coffee in her dressing gown, with her fair hair falling around her shoulders. The browny roots were getting longer, the real Mum peeking through the blond Lillian mask.

"Sit down," she said, and I turned a chair around and straddled it, crossing my arms over the back. Mum hated it when Jake and I did that, but this time she did nothing but sigh. "I've noticed that you've been very helpful," she said. "Obviously repentant. I appreciate it."

"Oh," I said. "Yeah. I'm sorry."

"I accept your apology. And I'm sorry you fought with your friends. That Sione seemed like such a nice boy."

My skin prickled. "He's not."

"He keeps moping around the hotel, no company but that red-haired girl. Poor kid. I don't know what his parents were thinking, to send him here alone." She looked at me. "Was this a lover's quarrel, Keri? Did you and Janna fight over this boy?"

My laugh was harsh, tearing at my throat. "No! No way! That's disgusting, Mum."

"Well—"

"Really, I'm done with them," I interrupted. "Do you and me have to talk about it?"

"No, not if you..." She sipped. "Anyway. I've been asked to take over the management tonight. Mr. Davidson invited you to come along and help, if you like. Earn some money. *Or* I could call in sick, and we could both stay home and have a nice New Year's Eve together." Her face tightened over the cheekbones. "Talk about...your brother, maybe. Share some good memories."

Oh, this was just fantastic. A chance to talk about Jake with Mum, one she really needed, and I had to turn it down.

"Maybe some other time?" I said instead. "I mean. It's all a bit—I don't think I can—"

She scraped a sliver of nail polish from the side of her thumb and nodded. "Well, come to the hotel, then?"

"Sione might be there," I said, almost gagging on the name. "I'm sorry, Mum, I can't. I think I'll just...have a quiet night. Watch the New Year's specials on TV."

She looked suspicious, but it wasn't as if I'd ever been much of a party girl, and I *had* been really good all week. "I'll call you at home," she said, the faint threat clear.

"That would be nice," I told her, and her face softened.

She reached out and cupped my cheek. "I love you very much."

I willed myself not to confess everything. I was going to scare her and hurt her all over again, and there was no way out of it. "I love you, too," I said, and grabbed the dirty breakfast plates.

After Mum went to work that afternoon, I drifted around the house. I'd packed a bag with all the stuff I thought I'd need and slipped my baton into my cargo pants, where it would be close at hand. But I'd decided not to leave for the Bash until later; I hoped that I could answer Mum's checkup phone call before I went and save her the worry.

There was nothing to do. TV wasn't distracting, I'd read all my books, and Sione still had my Wii, the thieving shit. As afternoon faded to evening and the sounds from the beach got louder, I started doing chores out of desperation. Mum hadn't left a list, but I wiped down the stove and cleaned the microwave and emptied out my drawers to refold all my clothes. Everything else was done.

Except, I remembered, the basket of loose socks in the laundry cupboard. We added to it every time we found a stray, but no one had sat down and matched them for at least three years. That would be soothing.

When I yanked the basket down, my favorite pair of jeans tumbled from where they'd been shoved in beside it. They lay crumpled on the floor like a shed skin as I stared at them openmouthed.

Mum hadn't thrown them out. She'd washed them and put them away, the last piece of my final moments with my brother, and told me they were gone. I wasn't the only one who'd been lying.

I was very calm. I shook the jeans out and looked them over. They'd been washed, probably several times. The marks weren't stains, really, more like shadows against the worn denim, a suggestion of what had lain in my lap and bled on me.

It was three hours until midnight and nearly dark outside. The Bash would be starting in earnest.

I unzipped my cargo pants and slithered out of them,

pulling on the jeans. They settled against me like a hug, warm and familiar. Nothing had ever fitted me as well as those jeans.

The telephone shrilled as I locked the front door, but I didn't turn back for it. I went, dressed in blue denim and my brother's blood, to destroy his murderers.

Completely.

CHAPTER TWENTY-SIX
Sione

✝

ON NEW YEAR'S EVE, SIONE SLID HIS BELT through his jeans, gave his messenger bag the routine check for clay figurines, slung the strap over his neck, and worried about Aroha. Not that there was anything wrong *with* Aroha. She was funny, she was smart, she was really pretty.

And she was honest, all the time.

No, the problem was with him, who'd been lying to her from the beginning. Who was going with her to the Bash so he would have an excuse to watch her host brother.

"Just until this is over," he mumbled to the boy in the mirror, who couldn't meet his eyes. "When it's done and Takeshi's safe, I'll tell her then."

He met her in the lobby, where Mr. Davidson was nowhere to be seen.

"Takeshi and Janna went ahead," Aroha said. "To—what?"

Sione tried to stop staring. "I like your hair."

Aroha smiled and flicked the coppery strands off her bare shoulders. They fell sleekly down her back, looking as if they were glowing with their own light. "Thanks! It's such a pain to straighten it, so I only do it for special occasions."

"I like it curly, too," he said quickly, and tried to concentrate on why he was there. "Why did they go ahead?"

"Oh. They're meeting the band there." She watched him carefully. "Was that wrong? Did you guys make up?"

"Not yet," he half lied. He risked a smile and reached for her hand as they left the hotel.

Aroha's breath caught, her fingers curling round his. She said nothing more about the fight.

Do it, he thought. *Make something true and good, before all this is finished.*

"Hey," he said at the same time she tilted her head and said, "So…"

They both stopped, laughed, and did the you-first-no-you thing, and when that was done, it was Sione's turn.

"When we go back to Auckland," he said. "Would you…I mean, I don't know, if you're interested, maybe you were thinking just for Summerton, but—" He could have gone on in

242

hypotheticals forever, but she squeezed his hand and spun around to face him.

"Are you asking me out?"

"Um. Yeah?"

"Are you asking me out because you want a rebound relationship?"

His first instinct was to tell her what he thought she wanted to hear. But Aroha deserved the whole truth for once. "I don't know," he said. "I don't think so, but wouldn't that feel the same?"

"Probably," she said, and grinned up at him. "Okay. Yes."

"Oh," Sione said stupidly. "That's really—" *Shut up*, his brain advised, and luckily Aroha seemed to be reading his mind, because that was when she kissed him.

It seemed that it might be his destiny to be kissed by girls instead of kissing them, but he thought he was going to be okay with that.

This, unlike Janna's hot-and-heavy moves, was a close-lipped kiss, quick and very sweet. Her lips were soft and warm.

"Wow," he said when he got his voice back.

"Good start," Aroha told him, and snuggled her arm tightly in his as they started walking again.

Sione felt stupidly good. He should have been worried about Takeshi, but Janna would be watching him until Sione got there to take over—well before the Vikings went onstage. Unless her greediness for fame meant that she wasn't paying attention. *That's very likely*, the slimy voice in his head argued. *You could probably distract her with something glittery on a string.*

Trying to seem casual, he increased his pace. There were a few people on the streets, all heading toward the beach, but it sounded as if most of the town was already gathered there. He could hear music—not Vikings to the Left, but a hip-hop group that he and Matthew had both loved, singing about Friday night being the scene.

He wondered if Janna had worked out that the Maukises didn't really want her stupid band. The only reason Vikings to the Left were playing after these big acts was because they wanted her out of the way when they took Takeshi.

He felt something cruel curl his lips. Maybe he'd get a chance to tell her before the night was over. Maybe before she went onstage and begged for people to love her, like she'd been doing all her life. He reckoned that would shake up her show.

They were passing the library now. The gallery was the next building, gleaming white under the waning Summerton moon. Sione thought of the glass crown.

Tiberius and Octavian Maukis stepped out of the gallery and headed straight for the beach without looking behind them.

Heading for Takeshi.

Sione stopped walking and glanced up at the gallery. The unguarded gallery, with its empty upstairs room, where Janna had last seen The Pride of Summerton.

Aroha's hand tugged in his. "What—"

"I forgot something," he said. It was the first excuse that came to mind. "I'll meet you there, okay?"

"What did you forget?" she asked, looking disappointed and suspicious.

"It's a surprise," he said. "Go find Takeshi, okay? It's for you and him. Don't let him go *anywhere*." He kissed her before he could lose his courage. It would be so easy, to just go out with his girlfriend and be happy.

Matthew.

"I'll catch up with you," he promised.

"Okay," she said, face still full of questions. "I'll see you soon." She started walking, and he waited until the gleaming red hair had turned at the next corner. After. He would tell her *after.*

He pulled out his phone and hesitated, thumb poised over the two girls' names. He should really tell them what he was doing, warn them that the Maukises were on their way.

But he couldn't make himself do it. The hate was just too strong to let him talk to them.

Okay, he thought. *I'll do it alone.*

◢

It was easy to break in, especially since the little alley between the library and the gallery protected him from view. Sione wrapped his white jacket around his fist, squared up against the door, and punched right through the ornate glass door pane.

No one came to investigate the noise. Grinning despite himself, he reached in to turn the dead bolt. The door swung open into the dark building, and Sione slipped in, crunching carefully over the broken glass in his soft-soled sneakers. There was no sound of alarm from upstairs; good, Daisy and the other two weren't around.

He couldn't turn on the lights without risking discovery, but that wasn't a problem. He'd brought the flashlight in his bag for just this kind of possibility. Not that he was OCD or neurotically overprepared, like Keri. Just ready for an attempt to save someone's life at night.

The gallery looked weird by flashlight, all those massive landscapes ghostly without their bright colors. It was definitely the perfect place for a ritual. He headed straight up the stairs, freezing every time one creaked under him.

When he reached the room at the top and swept his beam of light across the room, he nearly wet himself. But no, it wasn't someone standing there—just the stone plinth. It was only a trick of shadows that made it look so creepy, that made it seem for a moment like a man crouched and ready to attack.

The top of the plinth was bare.

Disappointment surged over him. He'd been so *sure* that they'd returned the crown in preparation for tonight and then gone to find Takeshi. If they had, he could have ended the whole sick nightmare right then, without relying on *those girls*. He could have been a hero, all by himself.

Scowling, Sione looked around the room one more time and spotted the office door at the end.

It didn't have a handy glass pane, but it also wasn't locked.

On first glance, there was nothing wrong with the contents. It could have been anyone's office—two messy desks, a computer on a separate table, a bulletin board covered in bits of paper, and a few art supplies piled in the corner.

But nested among those supplies, between a damaged canvas

and a tumbled box of paintbrushes and palette knives, were the three statues.

They were knee height and painted, made with more care than the little clay figures had been, but they were definitely of the same people—the short, sturdy girl; the young man with the wild hair; the slender girl with the pretty face. They were arranged in a triangle, back to back, and their faces were obscured by red cloth blindfolds.

Nausea roiled in Sione's stomach as the hate flooded through him. If either of the girls had stepped into the room right then, he'd have tried to kill them. Swallowing as hard as he could did nothing; acid burned in his throat.

He gagged on the taste and swallowed again, stepping forward through air that was suddenly moist and rotten against his shivering skin. The spells on *them* could remain; he didn't care. But the figure of him had to go. Heedless of the noise, he picked up the statue and swung it at the floor.

The head shattered, and it felt like he could breathe for the first time in days, as if the room had suddenly flooded with oxygen. The base, still in his hands, slipped from suddenly nerveless fingers. It was *gone*, all the hatred that had eaten at him for days.

Was it the blindfolds? Red for rage? It didn't matter. The disgusting feelings were *gone*. He laughed in pure joy and grabbed the statue of Janna, yanking off the blindfold before he broke it against the wall.

"Sione!" Aroha yelped behind him. "What are you *doing*?"

He jumped to face her, dumbstruck for only a second. She'd

followed him, obviously not fooled by his earlier hasty lies. Man, his girlfriend was *smart*.

"I'm—" he said, and gave up. "I can't explain right now." He grabbed at the Keri statue, but Aroha's arms were around his waist, tugging him away.

"Stop," she said. "Oh my God, Sione, stop!"

"I have to!" he said, but she wouldn't let go, and he couldn't just shove her away. "Look at it, Aroha! It's Keri!"

Her grip slackened as she looked, and he lunged forward out of her arms, catching the statue with the side of his fist. It toppled but didn't break. He lifted his foot to smash down on it when someone much heavier than Aroha launched into his side and knocked him face-first into the edge of the desk. Pain exploded from his cheekbone to his jaw.

A chunk of time went missing—maybe only a few seconds, because when he came to, he was still slumped against the desk.

And Kirk Davidson was advancing toward Aroha.

Aroha screamed twice, short, sharp cries as if she were cutting the air with her voice. Then she seemed to give it up and put her back to the wall, fists clenching as she prepared to fight.

Sione pushed himself to his feet. The right side of his face felt like something with sharp little teeth was gnawing at it, and he could taste blood down the back of his throat. But Mr. Davidson was looking away from him, and the toppled statue was in reach. He grabbed for it, knowing that if he missed, they were both dead.

"Run!" he shouted. "Tell Janna!" He smashed the statue onto the back of Davidson's head and fell to his knee with the force of the blow. Everything was fuzzing around the edges now, and he was dimly terrified. But the Keri statue shattered, the man stumbled, and Aroha didn't hesitate. She twisted past Davidson's grasping hands and raced out the office door. Sione heard her clatter down the gallery stairs as Davidson turned, fury distorting his bland features.

"You little shit," Davidson hissed.

Get up, Sione told himself, but he couldn't move, and the blood in his mouth was thick and raw. He watched as Davidson drew back a fine leather shoe, and he tried to at least get his arms up to cover his head.

It didn't work. The foot slammed into his broken face.

A burst of white noise sang through Sione's skull, and he fell, deep into the darkness that reached up hungry arms for him.

CHAPTER TWENTY-SEVEN
Keri

⚡

READY FOR MAGIC, I WALKED DOWN TO THE beach to find it transformed.

Nothing witchy about that, though. Every year, people did this with technology and labor. The stage alone was a miracle of engineering—yesterday that patch of beach had been nothing but sand, and now it featured a huge black platform, full lighting and sound rig, and a bunch of people on cranes with TV cameras.

Even knowing what all this celebration secretly supported

couldn't stop me from being impressed at the speed and scope of the work as I walked into the crowd.

The Beach Bash was the one time when locals and tourists of all ages mingled without any tension, so there were plenty of familiar faces around. No one said hi or even waved at me. It was as if my brother's blood made me invisible, protected me from their eyes. I felt like a ghost, drifting unseen through the crowds as I moved steadily toward the stage.

When I got close enough, I paused to survey the security precautions. They looked exactly as I'd remembered them from last year: Wire fences now enclosed the shore from sand dunes to the high-tide mark, blocking off all but two of the paths down to the sea, and lower fences were in front of the stage and the tent set aside for the performers. There were black-shirted security people standing behind the stage barriers in that standard wrist-gripping, humorless way.

I felt my mouth curve in satisfaction. Perfect for plan B.

The next act was announced, and a mob of kids swarmed the stage. Any other year, I would have been excited, too, but my focus had been narrowed down to a single point. I skirted the mosh pit and got myself to the corner closest to the ocean, where the stage fence met the wire enclosures. There was an arc light above me, but it was angled down toward the stage, leaving that corner entirely in shadow. Except for a couple of people who seemed too stoned to pay any attention to what I was doing, much less care, there was no one else there. Dad's wire clippers were sharp. Even one-handed, it was easy to snip a hole and slip through.

"Cool," said one of the stoners behind me, and that was all the notice anyone took of my illegal exit.

Once I was in the backstage area, it was easy to stay there. I was wearing a black T-shirt and beat-up jeans, like a lot of other people, and I walked as if I knew where I was going, frowning at the clipboard in my good hand. It's amazing what you can get away with if you're carrying a clipboard. The homemade ID card on the lanyard around my neck helped, too—I positioned it so the blank back showed, and no one seemed interested in taking a closer look. In fact, no one seemed interested in me at all. I looked straight ahead and kept moving toward the performers' tent.

I knew Janna would be in there, and the thought wriggled in my head like maggots. When I saw the pink hair in tight ringlets around her made-up face, I thought I was going to spew all over myself. Even the comforting blanket of gray nothingness wrapped around my heart couldn't stop my revulsion.

No. There was no way I could leave Takeshi with her. We'd have to go, now.

"Hey!" Kyle Hamilton called out. "It's Keri! I didn't know you were working this thing."

I hurried over, caught between my twin urges to protect Takeshi and to stay away from Janna, who was foul and unclean. I trained my eyes on him only, concentrating on all the details of his appearance—dark blue jeans, white T-shirt, black jacket—hoping to block her out. It was no good. Just being near her felt like being dipped in a vat of cold grease.

"Janna, you okay?" someone said behind me. Patrick Tan, probably, and the concern in his voice nearly made me ill. She fooled them all, all her boys, who had no idea how twisted and shallow she was. We were supposed to be working together, but I'd been dumb to trust her.

In fact, she was probably working with the enemy.

The little voice was huge now and finally making a lot of sense. I couldn't believe it had taken me so long to see it. She was a witch, after all, and she'd known both Matthew and Jake. It was so clear: She'd been Daisy's ally this whole time. She'd lured Matthew to his death, and now she planned to do the same thing to Takeshi, laughing at me all the way.

"Who let the dyke in?" she said, and I spun to face her.

"Who let the slut speak?" I said, and the boys around us did a quick double intake of breath that might have been funny if she hadn't been right there, sneering at me. I was in no mood to laugh.

"You don't say that," Takeshi told me, his eyes narrowing.

"You don't understand," I said. "She's *evil*. She wants to *hurt* you."

"Me?" Janna shouted. "It's you who—" She stopped. The ugly lines on her face smoothed out into absolute shock. "Oh my God," she whispered. "Keri, I'm sorry. I'm so sorry."

"You *are* sorry," I said, and put my back to her, skin itching in anticipation of the attack I was sure she was planning. Just let her try! I'd tear every stupid pink hair out. "Takeshi, please come with me. You're not safe here."

"What the hell is going on?" Patrick demanded, but Janna ignored him, crooning more apologies in my ear as I tried to persuade an annoyed Takeshi to come with me, to trust me, not *her*.

"Is she really a lesbian?" Hemi Koroheke whispered, very loudly.

"No," Janna said. "It's just a thing we say. God, Hemi, don't you know any girls?"

It was a trick, I knew. It was all a lie to make me take down my guard and then come at me again. I spun around, ready to tear off her face, get her on the ground, and kick her lying mouth, snap her shiny teeth, and—

And then it was gone.

The spell breaking was like a lightning strike, searing all the rage from my brain. "Oh, shit," I said, in the aftershock of the detonation. "It nearly worked."

Janna looked as relieved as I felt, but then she wrinkled her forehead. "But how is it gone?" she asked, and her face flashed fear at the same time it stabbed me, even under the joy of losing that slick, rotten voice. It was so *good* not to hate her anymore. "Where's Sione?"

"With Aroha," Takeshi supplied. "The fight is over?"

"*Yes*," Janna said, and hugged me hard. "The things I said, I am so sorry, Keri. I didn't—I don't think that way, you know that, right?"

"Me, neither," I said, hugging back. "I don't care who you kiss. I hate that they made me say I did."

"Are you sure you're not a lesbo?" Hemi asked. "Because I'm okay with that. That would be hot."

I flinched and, for a moment, disliked Janna of my own free

will. She hadn't done it on purpose, but it was out now. I was going to have to handle stupid comments like that for the rest of my life.

"Shut *up*," Janna snapped. "Hemi, you are a pig." He opened his mouth, and she ran right over him. "No! Girls aren't here to make your dick happy! Apologize right now!"

"Uh," Hemi said. "Uh, sorry." He shot me a glance and then looked away.

It was nice of her, but I had some mixed feelings about someone else defending me, especially when she'd been the one to put me in this position. And making Hemi say sorry sort of made it seem like she was making him apologize for calling me a lesbian, not for being a dickhead. My being gay wasn't the problem; his being a jerk was.

Still. She'd meant well. "Whatever," I said, and pulled out my cell phone.

Sione wasn't answering. Either the spell was still working for him and he wouldn't pick up or he'd forgotten to bring it, or —

Janna's own cell phone rang, and from the strain of her face as she listened, I knew it wasn't good news. "Where? Okay. Okay, we're coming. Just . . . stay put, okay? We're on our way." She whirled. "Takeshi, *stay here*, with Vikings. Don't go anywhere with any adults, do you understand?"

"I understand," Takeshi said. "But why?"

Patrick's eyebrows were crawling up his face. "What? Where are you going?"

"Sione?" I said, but Janna shook her head.

"Aroha." She swung toward Patrick. "I'm sorry, I have to go do this thing. I'll—"

"We're going onstage in an hour," Patrick said. His voice was very soft.

"I'll try to get back in time, but I—"

"Janna."

"Stardust, we have to go," I said. I had some sympathy, but I was pretty sure we didn't have time for this.

"I'm sorry, Patrick," Janna said, and grabbed his hand. "Please, please—"

"This is our *chance*, Janna! Are you kidding me? What's wrong with you? We put in all this effort and—" He scowled, recovering some of his composure. "I thought you got it. I thought you wanted this; I thought you *understood*."

"I do," Janna whispered. Her face was drawing in, tight and small. Takeshi was watching her, his hands shifting as if he wanted to comfort her. "I want it more than almost anything."

"Well?"

"I'll come back," she said.

"No. If you leave now, you *leave the band*, you understand me? You're out for good."

Janna choked back something and looked away. When she met his eyes again, her own eyes were glistening. "Okay. Sorry, guys. Takeshi, I'll explain later, I *promise*."

"What the hell?" Kyle yelled, and Hemi reached out for her arm, his face more worried than angry, but Janna ducked around them both, and we ran. How she was keeping up with me in a tight pleather skirt and spike-heeled boots, I had no idea, but she was doing it, her breathing harsh as we raced out the backstage exit, past the startled security guard, and toward the town. I wanted to console her, but I had too many other concerns to waste thought on sympathy.

"What happened?" I asked.

"Sione and Aroha snuck into the art gallery," she said, dashing her hand across her face. "He smashed statues that Aroha says looked like us, which I think must have been the spell focus. Kirk Davidson caught them and beat him up, but Sione managed to stop him from grabbing Aroha. He told her to run and find me. But he didn't follow her out."

"Oh, fuck," I said, and sped past her.

"Wait, wait, we have to go together!"

"Kirk Davidson makes five!" I said, and halted in front of Lauer's, a block from the art gallery. Janna panted to a stop beside me.

"Janna, what is happening?" Takeshi said, and I nearly jumped out of my skin. I'd been paying so much attention to what was ahead that I hadn't looked over my shoulder.

"You can't be here," Janna said, when she got her breath back. "Oh my God, Takeshi, go back to the beach, *please*."

"No," he said. He managed to pack a lot into that one syllable, standing with his feet apart and his eyes steady on us. He looked like someone with a game plan of his own.

For the first time, I realized that I'd made Daisy's mistake. I hadn't been looking at Takeshi as a real person. Even before I'd met him, he'd been nothing to me but a potential victim I could save, as Jake had not been saved. I hadn't cared about him as himself.

But Takeshi was undeniably real, ready and willing to act on behalf of a guy he had no reason to like.

Janna, who obviously did care about Takeshi as Takeshi, responded faster than me. "But—" she began.

"Sione is in trouble," he said. "You will help, and me, too."

"*Pssst*," someone hissed, and this time I managed not to jump as Aroha emerged from behind the Dumpster in the alley behind Lauer's. My head spun. It was the same place where Janna had taken me when this had all begun.

If you want to find out who murdered your brother, follow me.

"What are we going to do?" Aroha demanded. She looked different with straight hair—older, somehow. But her face was a mess: smeared makeup, red and blotchy from her crying. She wasn't crying now; she seemed to have shifted gear into rage. "Sione broke those things—he did that—but Mr. Davidson really *went* for him. I saw blood and everything. People have been going in. I saw the Maukis brothers and that big policeman; I think they might be *arresting* him. But they can't get him for breaking and entering without a counter-charge for assault. I was thinking, when my dad gets back, he—"

"No!" Janna said. "Sergeant Rafferty's in on it."

"In on *what*?"

Janna opened her mouth, and I could see she was going to lie. But I was sick of lies, and we were here, now, at the crux of it. So I spoke up first: "Black magic. Human sacrifice." I shrugged as Aroha stared at me. "Believe me or not. But if you're coming, come quietly."

Janna threw her arms in the air. "Takeshi—"

"He might be safer with us." I wasn't sure of that, but Vikings didn't have a clue what was going on; if Rafferty tried to take Takeshi, they'd probably let him go. And besides, he deserved the right to choose his own risk and not just be protected, like a prize.

"Okay," she grumbled, but I was already moving across the road, toward the alley between the library and the art gallery. Janna was whispering hurried explanations, Aroha translating sections in a voice thick with disbelief, but I was silent, careful as I balanced every step.

It wasn't until I groped for the baton in my pocket that I remembered; the pocket, and the baton, were at home, lying on the laundry room floor with my cargo pants. I was armed with nothing more than one good fist. That was another good argument for Takeshi's coming. The Maukis brothers, and Daisy, and Rafferty, and Kirk Davidson. Five of them, four of us, and us unarmed. Even with the element of surprise, it was going to be tight.

I reached the broken door and looked over my ragtag army. Aroha looked determined, Takeshi looked doubtful, and Janna—Janna looked as fierce as I felt.

I nodded at her and pushed the door open, stepping quietly around the pile of broken glass. Sione had done this? I was clearly a bad influence.

There was soft light coming from upstairs, and arguing voices, and I felt my adrenaline spike. The acoustics in the building were weird, though, and I couldn't make out what they were saying or who was speaking. But I was grateful for the noise, which covered the creaks we made going up. When we got near the top, I signaled the others to stop, and crept farther up on hands and knees, holding my cast behind my back so it wouldn't knock against the floor.

Low to the ground, I peeked around the corner and froze.

My enemy count had been off.

CHAPTER TWENTY-EIGHT
Janna

★

JANNA HAD THOUGHT AROHA MIGHT BE A problem, but the red-haired girl went inside without protest, her sunny face grim. That was scary in itself; whatever Mr. Davidson had done to Sione had been enough to make Aroha trust Janna and Keri's talk about magic. Takeshi had looked much more critical after her translated explanation, eyebrows drawn together.

But he followed, tight and warm at Janna's back, catching her elbow when one of her stockinged feet slipped on the polished wood of the steps. She'd taken the boots off downstairs, and if she'd been thinking, she would have taken the socks off, too. But thinking wasn't working properly right now, not with a fog of tears swirling in her brain.

The possible sacrifice of her boyfriend and the definite beating of her friend were sort of *priorities*, but those were big, horrible things, too huge to accept as real. What was making her want to curl up and die was the look on Patrick's face as she'd turned and run. Vikings wasn't a hobby. It was a future, it was a *family*, and she'd betrayed it.

For my other *family*, she reminded herself, and tried to focus, tried to shut out the music coming from the beach, a joyful noise that she wasn't making.

Ahead of her, Keri edged her head around the corner and went still, her back lean and tense as she balanced.

When Keri turned back to them, Janna forgot all about Vikings. Keri—determined, aggressive, hyper-prepared Keri— looked as if she'd lost hope.

Janna crawled past her to see why and felt her face sink into the same despairing lines.

There was Daisy Hepwood, all right, and Sergeant Rafferty, and both Maukis brothers, and Mr. Davidson.

And everyone's favorite English teacher, Mrs. Rackard, and her daughter Emily, who was just a bit older than they were. Nineteen. Sione's brother had been nineteen, and Keri's, too. And that provided a better explanation for the poppet in Janna's car—Emily had been the Kahawai spy.

It took Janna a second to work out why Emily's being there felt like a song in the wrong key, but when she understood, she thought she might be sick. Emily was too young—not just to be doing this at all, but to have started when it all began. She had been nine when Schuyler died. Emily must have been brought into the coven later, maybe a few years ago, maybe tonight. It didn't matter when. They were recruiting new people, spreading the poison down Summerton's generations. They would never, ever stop.

Huddled to one side of the stone plinth and talking to one another, the killers looked exactly as they did any other day. They weren't wearing fancy black robes or ceremonial face paint, and they didn't cackle loudly or wave bloody knives about. The only light came from tall candles in long, straight holders, lights and shadows dancing as the flames fluttered. This just made the human figures look even more ordinary, in their business suits and flowing skirts and sensible shoes, like opera fans at a black metal gig.

This is what evil looks like, Janna thought, clear and calm over the rush of her blood in her ears. *Ordinary people doing terrible things.*

"—didn't need to hit him that hard," Rafferty was saying to Mr. Davidson, disapproval thick in his voice.

"He was destroying the office. What was I supposed to do? At least he's not a problem anymore. But he broke those bloody statues. Why the hell didn't you lock the door, Tiberius?"

"Daisy called us to say he was coming and to bring him in by leaving," Tiberius snapped. "I didn't think you'd take so long to grab one boy, did I?"

"Why did you want him caught, Daisy?" Rafferty asked.

"You said the girl got away?" Mrs. Rackard broke in. She was tearing nervously at her fingernail.

They're rattled, Janna thought. They weren't used to mistakes, or people getting in the way—people who knew the truth.

"What's done is done," Daisy said matter-of-factly, and some of the tension went out of the room, people settling down with less-ruffled feathers. "The girls will work out that their anger was the result of enchantment, but it's not as if they could do anything about it on an hour's notice, even if they knew where to go. And Janna's due onstage then, isn't she?"

Tiberius nodded.

Ha, Janna thought.

"Well, then. One teenage girl on the loose—or even two—is hardly a problem for us."

"What about the one who got away?" Octavian demanded. "That red-haired little bitch—"

"Excuse *me*," Mrs. Rackard said, giving him the kind of look she gave Hemi for his "jokes" about girls. It was so familiar that Janna felt tears prick at her eyes. Mrs. Rackard was patient about Janna's misspellings, and let her do oral reports instead of essays, and had gone over the proper way to set out a business letter three times until Janna had it firm in her head, all without making her feel stupid. She shouldn't be here, worrying about whether Janna would disrupt her plans to kill someone.

"I doubt she's a problem, either," Daisy said patiently. "But we should get started." She glanced at her watch, her rings cutting the candlelight into colored pieces.

"Look, the Felise kid?" Rafferty said suddenly. "There's no need for him to be here. I'll take him to the hospital and say I found him on the street; even if he wakes up and starts talking, no one's going to listen to a kid with head trauma."

"Mmm," Daisy said, and then lifted her head. Her shadow on the wall looked sharp-edged and hungry. "No. We're running out of time; they'll ask you questions. You can take him after. Have you got the sand, Emily? Good. Draw the circle, just as I showed you."

Where is Sione? Janna strained, trying to make him out in the candlelight. The office door was open, and there was a shadow in there, too irregular to be a piece of furniture.

It wasn't moving.

Keri was tugging on her arm, pulling her back down, and she joined the others at the landing halfway down the stairs, where they couldn't make out what the people above were saying.

"Did you see Sione?" Aroha hissed, and Janna nodded.

"He's unconscious, I think. They argued about taking him to the hospital."

Aroha looked as if someone had punched her in the stomach.

"Didn't you say they'd have to bring Takeshi here?" Keri whispered. "Is this something they can work on him from a distance, like those statues?"

"I guess so," Janna breathed. That didn't feel right, somehow, but unless there were more conspirators out there, scouring the beach for Takeshi, it looked like Keri was correct.

"How good is the protection?" Keri asked. "Will your spell work?"

"It should," Janna said, too worried to be offended. "I felt it work when I finished, like it sort of settled into place." She tugged on Takeshi's arm. "Do up your jacket."

He cocked an eyebrow at her but obeyed. The quick slither

265

of the zip sounded too noisy in the sudden silence from upstairs, and they all froze, looking up.

But the music from the beach was still loud, and no one came down.

"Too many," Keri muttered, looking grim. "There're just too many. If Takeshi's protected anyway...let them try their stupid spell. Let them think it worked. We'll wait and watch. When Rafferty takes Sione to the hospital, we can follow, and you can say what you saw, Aroha. At least we can get Mr. Davidson into some trouble."

"He hit him *really* hard," Aroha said. "He smashed his head onto a *desk*."

Janna wanted to tear Kirk Davidson's head off with her bare hands. Sweet Sione, who wouldn't hurt anyone—that was *disgusting*. She must have made some motion because Keri grabbed her arm.

"We can't help him if we *join* him," she hissed, and wriggled up the stairs before anyone could protest.

"I thought you were the fighter," Janna muttered, and then went up after her, motioning Aroha and Takeshi to stay on the landing as backup. She was *almost* sure that the protection spell would work. She was very nearly positive.

But keeping some distance between Takeshi and the ritual was probably a good idea.

For about the zillionth time that week, Janna wished she'd studied witchcraft more. She was confident—mostly—about her own spell, and some of the things they were doing seemed familiar, but it was hard to tell. Especially lying on her belly over three stairs, with the corners jabbing her in the ribs.

Emily Rackard had produced a bag of sand, the same gray-white of the beach, and dropped it in a big circle around the seven of them. Inside the circle, they formed a square, with Emily, her mother, Mr. Davidson, and Rafferty taking a corner each, and Daisy and the Maukises making a triangle inside. The shadows from Rafferty and the Maukises, who were closest, spread over the top of the stairs. That gave Janna and Keri more concealment, but it also blocked off part of their view; Janna squinted past the three men at the far side of the circle, where Emily was raising her arms.

"We call the spirits of the East," Emily said, her voice rapturous, and Janna recognized that from her research. "We bind the spirits of the air to our service on this night."

"They're closing the circle, making it safe," she whispered to Keri, and watched as Mr. Davidson, Mrs. Rackard, and Rafferty called for and bound the spirits of each direction and element. Rafferty didn't sound very enthusiastic about it; the words were rote, like the way people mumbled "our-father-who-art-in-heaven." The binding part was freaking her out, though—newer rituals *asked* spirits for protection, not bound them to give it.

With the circle closed, they looked calmer, although Rafferty's eyes kept going to the crumpled shadow in the office. Daisy opened her big straw handbag and drew out something wrapped in black velvet.

Janna knew what it was well before the glass was exposed, to shimmer in the candlelight.

"Come, Summer King," Daisy said, holding The Pride of Summerton in her hands. "Crowned and celebrated, protected and praised, come Summer King."

"Come, Summer King," the others repeated.

And on the landing below them, Takeshi stood.

Janna never knew how she'd moved so fast and so quietly, to press her body against his and clamp her hand over his mouth. Aroha was holding on to him from behind, her arms tight around his waist.

Only Keri stayed at the top of the stairs, ready to spring into action. Delay the coven, probably, even if they hurt her getting past; Keri was probably that ruthlessly brave when it came down to it. But Janna didn't have more than half a thought to spare for Keri with Takeshi a stiff stranger against her body.

"Come, Summer King," Daisy said again, and again the others repeated it. Takeshi twitched in Janna's arms. Janna looked over his shoulder and saw her own panic in Aroha's eyes.

"No," Janna whispered in his ear.

What had she been thinking? Her stupid protection spell, a vague instruction to no one to "keep him safe," matched against strong magic that had already been moving in him days before she'd knelt on her bedroom floor with dusty old candles.

For a second, she lost hope. What was she going to do against that? Stupid, dyslexic Janna, a dumb drama queen. Stardust would laugh in their faces and defy them. But Janna wasn't really stardust, never integral to the workings of the universe; just a small-town girl with big-city dreams that would never come true.

It tangled in her head, as black and rotten as the voice that had told her to hate her friends, only this was coming from inside her. But under the self-doubt, right down at the bottom of herself, where the bass line made the song like a heartbeat made a life, Janna knew who she was.

They'd killed her brother, and now they wanted her lover. *Screw them.* She was Janna van der Zaag, and she was going to *fight.*

Janna thrust her hand under Takeshi's shirt, and stroked the bare skin at the base of his spine. "Listen to me," she whispered, hand still firm over his mouth. He stared down at her, unblinking and unaware, his body straining against hers. Okay, she could use that. She thrust herself against him deliberately and grabbed the lining of his jacket, through the shirt. She could feel the flax figure there; her hand tingled as it closed around the spell, warmer than it should have been.

"They crowned you, remember? They crowned you, and now they're calling you. Don't go. You have friends and a family and a life. You're not the Summer King; you don't have to be their sacrifice. You can be yourself. You're Takeshi Hoshino, Takeshi of the stars." There were tears prickling at her eyes. "You're going into space."

"Come, Summer King!" Daisy called a third time, her voice cracking like thunder, and the others, catching her urgency, shouted in response.

"You're *mine*," Janna said out loud, under the cover of their shouting. She clutched the spell she'd made with her own blood and, taking her other hand from his mouth, crushed her lips against his.

He was unresponsive and cold, but she pushed doubt and fear away and poured everything she was into that kiss—all her passion and ambition and appetite for life. Aroha was still gripping him from behind, and that had to help, too, sister-friend and lover both holding him back from horror and death. It *had* to help.

The tears spilled down Janna's cheeks when his mouth softened against hers, falling open. His arms went around her, and when she dared to open her eyes, he was staring into them, knowing her.

"Okay," he whispered against her lips. "It's me."

"It's me, too," Janna said, and kissed him again.

CHAPTER TWENTY-NINE
Keri

⚡

I DID NOT THINK THAT THE MIDDLE OF A black magic ceremony was an appropriate time to be making out with your boyfriend.

On the other hand, when Janna managed to tear herself away from Takeshi and give me the thumbs-up, her smile trembling with relief, I figured there must have been more happening than that.

Magic. As soon as this was done and Sione safe, I was going to — what? Set Inner Light on fire?

I was going to do *something*. This was no way for sensible people to go about their lives. I had no idea how to act here; all my years of planning out situations and possible reactions to them were useless now. That way of life had died the second they'd made Jake put the shotgun in his mouth, but I'd kept trying anyway, like a train stuck on the same tracks, even with a tree fallen across them. Magic made everything uncertain, unpredictable, impossible to plan for. I went back to watching and listening, my body straining with the effort.

"What's going on?" Tiberius demanded.

"He's *protected*," Daisy snarled, putting the glass crown on the stone pillar. Even in her rage, she was careful with it, and I noted that. "He's not coming. I can't even feel him out there. It must be the van der Zaag girl."

Ten points to Janna, I decided, and grinned into the darkness.

"What does that mean?" Mrs. Rackard asked. "We can't do it?" She almost sounded relieved, and I felt a moment's hope.

Daisy spared her a scornful look. "We have to do it, Gloria. The spell has to be maintained yearly, or it's broken for good. That's the nature of sacrifice. I told you this!"

"After the first time, you told us," Mrs. Rackard said.

"It's not my fault you didn't really believe it would work," Daisy said, shrugging impatiently. "Hasn't Summerton been successful and safe ever since? Haven't you all done well?"

"We didn't do it for that," Rafferty said.

"Of course not," Daisy said. "You did it for the town. We all knew something needed to be done, and you agreed to try. And it demands maintenance."

"But if he won't come—" Mrs. Rackard said.

Daisy smiled. "We have a substitute," she said, and pointed at the open office door.

A fist clenched around my heart.

There was a shuffle-bump behind me, and suddenly Aroha was at my shoulder.

"Now hang on," Rafferty said. "Sione Felise hasn't been crowned—"

"We can do that now, do it all together—"

"And you haven't done the divination," he said, raising his voice. "We ask around among the tourists to see which boys are right, we bring you the names, you do the divination to see which ones are going to kill themselves in the coming year, and you pick from *them* for crowning. *That's* the deal, Daisy! He wasn't on the list! For God's sake, on top of everything else, he's an only child now! We don't take boys without siblings."

What?

Could it be true? Could they have just taken the energy to protect Summerton from boys who were already planning to die?

But Daisy hesitated, her face sly in the candlelight for just a moment. I thought of Sione's careful spreadsheets, the charts he'd spent so many hours on. That many older brothers, one for every year, who were already thinking of suicide? Spread so evenly over the country, killing themselves at around the same time every year?

I had faith in Sione's math; the pattern was too deliberate to be accidental. She'd lied to them.

The only mystery was how they'd been stupid enough to believe her.

They'd been scared, I thought. Scared to lose Summerton. So when she came to them, they'd wanted so badly for it to be true. Or maybe she'd used magic to blind them.

And now, far too late, Rafferty saw through it. His face went gray and old, and I could have felt sorry for him, if I hadn't hated him so much. "You never did the damn divinations, did you?" he asked, voice flat.

"Does it matter?" Daisy asked.

"Does it *matter*?" Mrs. Rackard repeated. "Daisy! It can't be true. You said the boys were going to die already."

"Lots of boys die," Daisy said. "These ones died for something important."

Sergeant Rafferty's hands moved toward his belt. "Daisy Hepwood, I'm arresting you for murder."

My heart leaped, but Daisy's contempt was clear. "Don't be an idiot."

He was reaching for his police baton, but she tilted her head, and the Maukis brothers jumped him from both sides. Strong sculptors' hands forced his arms up behind his back. Tiberius kicked him in the gut, and the struggle was over. Rafferty wheezed and sputtered as they bound him with his own handcuffs.

Mrs. Rackard squeaked, "Daisy!" But Daisy ignored her, stalking forward to stare down at Rafferty like a queen inspecting a barbarian tribute.

"Arrest me?" she hissed. "For what? Where's your proof? Can you accuse me of *anything* without implicating yourself?" She turned and stared at the rest of them. "Can any of you? I

274

kept this town safe and clean, and you *helped*. Don't pretend you didn't know; don't pretend you don't know what will happen if it all falls apart! Summerton will be a ghost town—all the young people leaving, all the business gone. All the drugs and unemployment and crime! We have to do this now, while they sing and dance on the beach. This is a *necessary* sacrifice."

Her face was all lit up with her belief. She could do anything like this, sure of her righteousness. I remembered what Janna had said about how once you started down the left-hand path, it was easier and easier to keep going. I'd scoffed at her then. I wasn't laughing now.

"Mum, this is important," Emily said, eyeing Mrs. Rackard.

Daisy pointed at Mr. Davidson, who was closest to the office. "Kirk! Bring me the boy!"

Mr. Davidson hesitated, and Daisy tossed her long, curly hair and moved past him. She stopped to brush aside some of the sand with her foot, and then went out of the circle.

When she came back, she was hauling Sione with her.

Aroha made a sharp, pained sound in my ear.

He was walking, feet scraping against the floor, but he didn't seem to know where he was, stumbling along beside her with a look of huge concentration dedicated to just making his legs move. The right side of his face was swollen almost beyond recognition, and his nose was a huge lump on his battered face. There was something dark and sticky matting down his hair, and bloodstains all down the front of his yellow shirt.

Daisy walked him past The Pride of Summerton and let him go. He sagged to the floor, looking toward us. Only I wasn't sure he was really seeing anything.

Concussion, I thought. I had several medical manuals, and they were clear on how dangerous concussions could be. I'd suffered one once after being tackled too hard by an enormous player from Nelson Girls' High. It took a week for the dizzy spells to go away, and mine was a mild case.

At least Sione was close to the edge nearest us. With Rafferty out of the picture and the Maukises guarding him on the other side of the circle, there might be a chance to grab Sione and run.

It was past time to put a last-minute plan together, only I couldn't seem to make one. The situation was too unpredictable, with too many variables, and I wasn't any good at improvising. Working the way Janna did, all instinct and reaction, was nothing but a disaster for me. I'd walked out of the house in my old jeans because it had seemed right at the time, and that had cost me my best weapon, lying discarded in my cargo pants on the laundry room floor.

Without moving, I watched Daisy close the circle with sand and pick the glass crown up again. Scraps of plans whirled through my head like litter in a gusty wind, none of them settling into anything I could use to make me move. I knew, as she came closer to us, closer to Sione, that this would destroy his parents. Both of their children dead in a year? They'd just fall apart.

And if I got myself killed trying to help, that would destroy mine.

The colored glass of the crown cut the light into little patterns, just like Daisy's rings, and she lowered it slowly, so slowly against the quick voice in my head chanting, *Go, Keri, go, Keri, go!*

It was my own voice, and it was furious with me, but I couldn't obey. I was stupid and neurotic, just as Hemi Koroheke had said, and the proof of it was that now, without my careful plans, I couldn't move.

But Aroha could. With a cry like an angry seabird, she jumped to her feet and ran, shoulder lowered as she charged.

There was a rush past me as Takeshi and Janna joined her. I stayed where I was, crouched on the stairs and trembling. All my brave words, cut down to this cowardice.

Aroha hit the edge of the circle and bounced back as though she'd run into a steel wall.

Mrs. Rackard screamed.

"Let them in!" Rafferty shouted. "Gloria, let them in!"

Mrs. Rackard froze, but Daisy looked straight into Aroha's furious face.

"I crown the Summer King," she announced, and, smiling, lowered The Pride of Summerton onto Sione's dark curls.

◢

Aroha was crying and screaming at the same time, yelling a string of curses before she lost the ability to make the words, and just went for short, loud shrieks. Janna was pleading with Mrs. Rackard, trying to get her to interfere, but she had hunched her shoulders and turned away. And Takeshi stalked silently around the circle, hands opening and closing into fists, fury clear on his candlelit face.

All this time, the music from the beach played, and Daisy chanted.

Janna gave up on Mrs. Rackard and turned to her daughter. "Emily, Emily, help us!"

"Why should I?" Emily asked. "You were all horrible to me, all of you! All the popular kids, kids like you and Matthew Felise. You never cared about me."

"What about Jake?" Janna asked, glancing at the dark stairwell where I crouched, petrified in the shadows. "Jake liked *everyone*. He was always nice to you. Come on, Emily, what about Jake?"

Emily's face creased. "What about him?"

There was a pressure building up in the room, singing through my head, like the feeling of diving into deep water. I swallowed, but my ears wouldn't pop. Something very wrong was happening in that circle.

The chanting stopped.

And the dead boys began to appear.

The first drifted out of the crown in a wisp of mist that flattened out and grew, glowing from within, until a boy stood there, tall and blond, frozen at the same age his sister was now.

"Schuyler," Janna said, her voice unstrung with pain, and pressed her hand flat against the invisible barrier of the circle. He looked at her and bowed his head. Then, face solemn and reluctant, he put his hand on Sione's battered head for a brief moment and moved away.

Janna moaned.

The next boy came, and the next—tall, short, dark, fair. I didn't recognize any of them, but they had the same misty appearance, and when they touched Sione, they did it with the same unwilling jerkiness.

I was counting them, and when number ten came, I braced myself. Matthew looked very much like Sione, built on a slightly larger scale, and Janna gasped for him, too. When he saw his brother crumpled on the floor, his face contracted with rage. Daisy was sweating, I saw, her lanky body stiff with the effort of making the dead boys obey. Matthew held out for a long time, maybe as many as ten seconds, before he laid his hand on his brother's head.

Something in that ghostly touch must have been familiar, because Sione's eyes opened again. He was staring directly at me.

Matthew was forced away, back to the edge of the circle nearest the office, where the Maukis brothers stared intently at Sione, and Rafferty flinched from the ghosts surrounding him, face twisted in guilt at the murders he'd helped commit.

Again, I nearly felt pity for him. But he must have suspected something was wrong, and he hadn't done anything until it was too late.

I waited. From the moment Schuyler had appeared I had known it — all the dead boys were trapped in the crown. I was going to see Jake again, one more time.

Daisy grunted in satisfaction and lifted the crown from Sione's head. I gasped and reached out to — I didn't know. Stop her. Make her keep going. But she was finished, and the dead boys had all come. All but one.

There, my hand stretching to grasp the untouchable, the realization washed over me. In the still space between two heartbeats, I understood.

Jake wasn't in the crown.

Jake was not a Summer King.

Jake had not been murdered.

It hurt so much that I thought I was going to die, and, at last, I didn't care if I did. Jake had really done it; he'd left us, for reasons I would never understand, or for no reason at all.

What about him? Emily had asked, and she'd been honestly confused.

This has nothing to do with you, Daisy had told me in the shop, and for once, she'd been telling the truth.

If you want to find out who murdered your brother, come with me, Janna had said in the alley, and I had found out.

Jake had murdered himself.

I had all the facts at last, and I could finally move. I stood up on the top step in the half dark, no longer paralyzed by indecision, no longer afraid of what unpredictable magic could do. I wasn't afraid of anything anymore; how could I be, when the worst thing had already happened?

And Sione, staring dreamily at me through the candlelight, reached out his hand and dragged it through the sand of the circle.

No one saw but me.

Without a plan, without any contemplation of all the untraceable variables, I started running.

I hit the gap as easily as I'd ever twisted between two oncoming opponents on the rugby field, good arm swinging wide as I tackled Daisy. I took her high in the chest, crashing down on top of her as she fell, The Pride of Summerton tumbling from her grip.

For a moment I hoped it was all over, but the crown hit the wooden floor with a solid clunk, refusing to shatter.

I kicked with my legs and wriggled out of her grip, reaching.

The killers were all coming at me now, angry hands trying to hold me down, frantic voices yelling at one another and Daisy's over all of them, screaming, "The crown, get the crown!" Someone heavy landed on me, and for a moment I lost sight of my goal.

Then I heard Janna join the battle with a snarl, Takeshi and Aroha right behind her into the broken circle. Someone tore at the weight on top of me, pulling it away; someone knocked a candle over as he or she tried to hit someone else. Only the dead boys were still, caught in place and staring at me as I scrabbled on the floor. They were all different—different sizes, skin colors, features. But all the faces were luminous with fierce hope as they watched me reach The Pride of Summerton.

There was no time to get up, even if I could have found my feet in all that frenzied action. But I had finally remembered that I had a weapon after all, and Daisy had been the one to give it to me, all her terrible choices spinning back to undo her at last.

I raised my broken arm, heavy in the stained gray cast, and brought it down upon the crown of glass.

CHAPTER THIRTY
Sione

✝

THERE WAS SAND IN HIS HAND, AND IT FELT good against his skin, like a reminder that he was real.

"Sione," Matthew said. "Sione, get up."

Sione rolled over and tried to pull his sheets up to his chin. Matthew was going to try to take him jogging again, or make him cover for another night out with the palagi girlfriend he didn't want Mum and Dad to know about.

But there were no sheets, and he wasn't in bed. And Matthew couldn't be talking to him.

Matthew was dead.

Sione forced his eyes open. There were flickering lights and loud voices, and a lot of pain. It was so much trouble that he nearly closed his eyes again, but Matthew was standing over him. That wasn't right. He could see through him.

"You're dead," Sione said, trying to sit up properly.

Matthew's mouth twisted. "Too right, little bro. But I'm free."

"Free?" Sione wondered, and looked around. The room was full of shifting shapes, some solid and some misty, all struggling in the shadows and smoke. Keri was curled on her side next to him, eyes closed and forehead creased as if she were thinking really hard about something. One arm, pale and bruised, was cradled against her chest, bits of plaster sticking to it. Her face and arm were bleeding from a dozen small cuts; there were pieces of colored glass all over her and all over the floor.

There had been something on his head—a weight—and a call to come and make himself glorious, burn himself up for the good of the world. The call was gone now, and he was sad. For once in his life, he could have been somebody. He could have been a warrior, a hero.

"You got to get out of here," Matthew said. "These guys, they're angry. They're not going to hold back for long."

It didn't seem as if the misty shapes were holding back at all. Two of them were tearing at the Hepwood woman's face as she shrieked, and others were holding Mr. Davidson against the wall, hitting him in the stomach. The Maukis brothers were fighting back, but their blows passed through the angry boys as if they were trying to hit fog, and the hits they were receiving were solid and real.

The smoke was becoming thicker.

Where there's smoke, there's fire, Sione thought, and looked for it. One of the candles had fallen and set fire to a painting on the wall. The flames were licking up the wall and spreading. *Pretty colors. Blue flame.*

Wait. Fire is bad.

"Can you pick me up?" Sione said. They had touched the back of his head, these boys, welcoming him among them as the call to glory came.

Matthew tried, but his hands slipped right through him. "Not now. You didn't do anything to me. I can only touch to hurt them." He looked around, frustrated and scared.

Matthew was never scared.

A new face appeared over his shoulder, and Matthew relaxed a little.

"Up," Takeshi said, his hands under Sione's armpits. He hauled. "Up, up, come."

Sione tried, he really did, because it was important not to embarrass himself in front of Takeshi for reasons he couldn't remember right now. But he couldn't make his legs work. *God, please help me*, he prayed, and found enough strength to make it up to his knees.

He stayed there, swaying, sure that he couldn't possibly get any farther. But it was apparently enough.

"Okay, all right, okay," Takeshi said, all in a rush, and bent to stick his shoulder under Sione's stomach. He was shaking,

Sione realized. Takeshi was frightened, and for a moment he felt superior, because *he* wasn't.

Only because they knocked your brains together, he reminded himself. *Poor Little Felise, did you hear? Lost his mind, and that was the only thing he had going for him.*

He was suddenly upside down over Takeshi's shoulder, head spinning like it was going to fall off. He tried to scream out the pain, but all that came out of his mouth was a thin stream of yellow bile, with red globs of congealing blood from his cut mouth. He'd probably wrecked Takeshi's jacket.

"Hold on," Matthew was saying in his ear. "Shit, Sione, you did so great, you can't stop now. You just keep holding on."

Sione tangled his fingers in Takeshi's jacket to steady himself and nodded. "Okay. You come with me, okay?"

Sione lifted his head, and Aroha and Janna were behind them, faces tight with concentration. It seemed right that they were there, but hadn't he told Aroha to run? It was hard to remember. They were carrying Keri between them, her small, stocky body limp. Janna's feet were in red-and-white-striped pirate socks, and as he watched, the red seemed to brighten and spread. All that pretty broken glass. Why wasn't she in shoes? There was music; Janna should be playing music, bright as any flame.

"Stardust," he mumbled.

"Help me!" someone screamed from the room they were leaving behind. A woman. "Mum! Mum! Help me!"

Janna flinched, but she kept going after Takeshi down the stairs, *bump, bump, bump.* The flickering from upstairs was

285

getting brighter and the smoke darker. Takeshi was coughing, and the coughs were jiggling Sione around. He was going to be sick again soon, if he had anything left to be sick with.

There was a blond boy at the foot of the stairs, waiting as they passed. He smiled sadly at Janna, then nodded at Matthew.

"Okay," Matthew said. "We gotta go."

"No," Sione said. The blond boy wasn't speaking, though Janna had stopped to stare at him before Aroha yelled her on. Maybe Matthew was the only one who could talk. Or maybe you could only hear what your own brother said.

Takeshi kept walking, breath grunting out of him with every step, but Matthew stayed still, waiting by Schuyler at the foot of the stairs.

"Wait," Sione said, reaching.

Matthew ran a ghostly hand through his hair. He was fading. "I can't. The crown kept us here. And now I'm free." He smiled lopsidedly at Sione. "Thanks to you." He turned, and he and Schuyler went slowly up the stairs, into the storm of flames, where the screams were dying away.

Their bodies became fainter as they went, fading into the smoke.

"Thanks for teaching me how to swim," Sione said, but Matthew was gone, and he would never know if his brother had heard him.

◢

There were more lights outside, flashing red-blue-red, and the screaming of sirens, and people shouting about water pressure

286

and steady flow. Other people took him from Takeshi's shoulder and laid him down on something flat, softer than the floor. He could feel the heat on one side of his face.

"What's your name?" a woman asked, taking his wrist in her strong hand.

"Sione Felise."

"What happened, Sione?"

"I hit my head," Sione explained. It was getting harder to talk, with the persistent ache in his mouth.

"Yes, you did," the woman murmured. She shone a thin beam of light into one eye, then the other, and then got him to open his mouth, which hurt a lot, and shone the flashlight down there, too. "Blown pupils, confused affect, probable concussion. Pulse steady, breathing labored but no soot in throat, probable broken nose, fractured cheekbone, broken molars—"

She wasn't talking to him, Sione realized gratefully, and drifted away again. Somewhere, a deep voice was explaining that he'd seen the fire and heard screams and tried to help.

"It's horrible," the man said, his voice shaking. "Are the kids okay? Are they going to be all right?"

"Horrible," Sione echoed.

There was a woman sobbing at the edge of his hearing, moaning "Emily, Emily" over and over.

"Sione, when's your birthday?"

"February twentieth." There was a rumble that was louder than the roar of the flames, and a flash in the sky brighter than their burning, and something wet hit his face. Then lots of little wet things hit him all over.

"Hell," said the ambulance officer. "Okay, Sione, off we go—"

"I'm coming with him," Aroha insisted.

"It's raining," Janna's voice said, sounding stunned. "Raining on New Year's Eve."

"It sure is. Just like the weather girl said. First time in years. Hop in, kids."

Water kissed Sione's face. "Good," he murmured. "Then it's done now. It's really done. Thank you, Jesus." And before anyone could ask further questions, he let himself slide into the warm and welcoming dark.

Two people in white coats were pointing more lights into his eyes.

Janna and Takeshi were talking quietly, holding hands.

Sergeant Rafferty was staring at him, peaked hat twisting in his big hands, two fat tear tracks down his cheeks.

Mum and Dad were there, rosary beads clutched in their hands, smiles trembling in place, and there were cousins in the hall—he could hear them praying.

Keri was sitting by the bed, her arm in a new cast, staring intently at him. Janna was asleep in the chair in the corner.

He blinked.

"Hi," Keri said simply.

"Hi," Sione said, and was shocked by how rusty and dry he sounded. There was something sticking into his arm, and his face hurt, and...Memories flooded back, and he lay there for a while, trying to sort them. Keri waited, green eyes solemn.

"Did anyone survive?" he whispered at last.

"We did. Takeshi and Aroha are fine. And Rafferty got the cuffs off and dragged Mrs. Rackard out. Everyone's calling him a hero." Her face left no doubt as to how she felt about that. "The rest...There weren't even any bodies left. The fire department said it was all the paint and stuff in the gallery. The sprinkler system didn't work—there's going to be an investigation. Do you want a drink?"

Sione nodded and let her hold a straw to his cracked lips. The thing in his arm was an IV drip, and it turned out there was a big hole where two of his back teeth had been. He tongued the gap. "How bad do I look?"

Keri managed a small smile. "Pretty bad. Your parents and half your family are downstairs talking to the doctors. Want me to get them?"

"I thought that was a dream! How long was I asleep?"

"Four days, but you kept coming out and sliding back in again. The doctors said it was pretty normal, with head trauma. Your scans all came back clean. They're not too worried. But if you're really awake this time, you'll have to do a bunch of tests."

Sione stared at her. Four *days*? "What...what are we telling them?"

"Rafferty's mostly telling them. People *listen* to him. He tells everyone we were very brave, to go running in there to save those people. But that you must have fallen and hit your head on the way in." She tried that peculiar half smile again. "I don't know whether your mum wants to yell at you or hug you more. She's kind of scary, your mum."

Great. So even the lies that disguised what really happened made him out to be a dumb kid who fell over his own feet and had to be rescued while rescuing others.

Keri shrugged, and he realized he'd said that out loud.

"But *we* know the truth," Janna said from the corner. She yawned and stretched before padding over to drop a careless kiss on his forehead. One of her feet was bandaged up, and she was wearing a black ballet slipper on the other. She looked a lot smaller without thick soles or high heels. "Sione Felise, hero."

"I was wondering when you'd wake up," Keri said. "Sione, tell her to stop treating the hospital like a hotel."

Janna grinned at her. "Sione, tell her to stop moaning like an old woman."

"Both of you help me sit up," Sione told them, and discovered that smiling hurt when they both moved at once to obey. "You broke the crown, Keri?"

"It exploded everywhere," Janna said, sounding proud. "Knocked Keri out. Aroha and me had to carry her downstairs. Let me tell you, she's heavier than she looks."

Keri looked grim at the mention of the crown but pointed at Janna. "And Stardust saved Takeshi."

Janna shook her head. "I told you, I'm sticking with Janna." She didn't sound angry, but she was firm, and Keri nodded an apology.

Obviously he had missed out on a lot. That was okay. There would be time to catch up on everything after he got out of here; whole long lifetimes for them to be friends.

"And Takeshi saved me," he said, and just sat there for a moment. "Wow. We did it. We really did it."

"Proud of yourselves, aren't you?" came a new voice from the door, and both Keri and Janna stiffened.

The woman was white, dark-haired and middle-aged, and she tugged at something in Sione's memory like a fishhook.

The woman stepped into the room, and Janna stepped around the bed, joining Keri to effectively block the woman from getting to him. Sione didn't feel offended; he was definitely in no state to defend himself from any attack. "You killed her," she said. "You killed my daughter. I hope you're bloody happy."

"You killed my brother," Janna told her. "You taught him English for four years, and you killed him. Are *you* happy?"

Oh, hell. This was the teacher, the other one who'd survived. He'd only seen her through pain and smoke, but the agony in her eyes was familiar to him. He'd seen it in his own parents' faces.

"I didn't know," insisted Mrs. Rackard.

"I don't give a shit whether you knew or not," Keri said. "Those boys are still dead. We didn't kill Emily. She was killed by the ghosts of the boys *you* murdered. If you want someone to blame, think about that."

Mrs. Rackard let out a cry and stepped forward, and the girls braced, but a big figure came through the door and grabbed the woman around the waist, easily hauling her backward. "That's enough, Gloria," Sergeant Rafferty rumbled. "You said you were going to apologize."

"I didn't know! I didn't know what she was doing!"

"Jesus, you really think that lets us off the hook? I'm sorry, kids," he muttered, looking at everything in the room but their eyes. "You won't see either of us again. I'll make sure of it."

"Good," Keri said in a voice that cut like broken glass.

Janna folded her arms and stared.

Rafferty hesitated for a moment and then hustled the sobbing woman out of the room.

The girls went back to their places on either side of him as if nothing had happened, sharing only one glance.

"Bitch," Janna muttered.

But Sione had an urgent question he needed to ask before his parents came in and the privacy ended. "I thought... Were they really there, our brothers? Did they come?"

"I'll go get your mum and dad," Keri said, and abruptly turned away.

Sione blinked at the sound of her firm steps down the hallway and then looked at Janna, trying to ignore the momentary dizziness. Everything hurt, and even that tiny motion had reminded him how exhausted he was.

"Matthew and Schuyler were there," Janna said softly. "But Jake wasn't."

"Oh," Sione said, and felt the last piece of the pattern click into place. *Of course.* Jake had always been anomalous—the second in a year, the second in a single place.

Not a murder at all. "Oh, man. Poor Keri. How's she doing?"

"She'll be okay," Janna said, but she didn't sound too sure.

"She will," Sione insisted. "She's got us now." For a second he was worried—now that his usefulness was over, would either girl want to see him again? Waste her time talking to a loser? Then he pushed the feeling away, sure of the girls, and of himself.

And Janna nodded and brushed his forehead again. "Yes," she agreed, sounding more certain. "She does."

"Sione!" his mother said from the door, and Janna stepped away. Sione hardly noticed her leaving. His mum and dad were there, hugging him as though they were holding him together, and before the yelling started, he relaxed into their arms. This was another place he belonged.

Over his mother's shaking shoulder, he saw a flash of coppery hair and a pale, freckled face.

"Mum," he said, grinning as wide as his broken face could stand. "Have you met my girlfriend, Aroha?"

ONE YEAR LATER
Keri

⚡

THAT WOULD HAVE BEEN A GOOD PLACE TO
end the story.

But the thing about life is that there's only one ending to it.
Mostly, life keeps going, and unless you make the choice Jake
did, you have to keep going, too.

The people who take care of terrible things after they happen patched up Sione and sent him home with his parents.
They investigated the fire and listened to Sergeant Rafferty's
lies and decided it was a tragic accident: careless use of candles,

a faulty sprinkler system, too many accelerants on hand—literally lining the walls. And Summerton summers were so dry and warm. Ideal fire conditions.

It was amazing, they said, that it hadn't happened earlier.

Rafferty and Gloria Rackard left town to who knows and who cares where.

Aroha and Takeshi went back to Auckland, and then Takeshi went back to Japan.

And my life kept going, straight downhill.

My normal sharpness turned into squalls of rage and then into a blankness punctuated by long crying spells that I thought I was hiding. My cast came off, and I didn't bother to go back to my paper route or my training routine. I didn't feel like doing much of anything again, ever. What was the point? Horrible things could happen at any time, and you just couldn't be prepared.

But Mum and Dad, even in the middle of their own grief, saw that mine was getting dangerous. At the inquest, a verdict of suicide was returned, and everything came over me at once, how much what Jake had done had hurt us all. I slept for three days, and then stopped sleeping altogether. That was it. I was sent to Nanny Hinekura with a backpack and my old teddy bear, and she spent a week moving me out of bed and around the house and making me eat even when I couldn't be bothered, like a plump little sparrow scolding a fledgling into flight. I *felt* like a fledgling, all tender and new and unprotected, but it wasn't as bad as I'd expected. With just Nanny Hinekura and Auntie Huria and me, there wasn't the usual holiday bunch of family to remind me of what I'd lost, no conspicuous gap in a crowd of familiar faces.

While I was away, Mum talked to Janna, who talked to Sione, who talked to his mother. Two days later, I had an appointment with one of the suicide counselors I'd rejected talking to right after it'd happened. Then I got, in quick succession, a reference to a psychiatrist, a prescription for antidepressants, and more professional support than I could throw a stick at, which was often a tempting thought. Sione's mother did complicated bureaucratic things and called in favors, and got me the sessions for free after the government-funded ones ran out, but my parents had to drive me to Nelson every two weeks. They did it without complaint. Seven hours there and back—plenty of time to stare out the window and think of how fragile the world was, and how easy it could be to lose everything, unprotected from things that went bump in the night.

It was like the voice that had told me to hate Sione and Janna, except, this time, there was no easy solution, no statue to smash. It was all coming from inside.

It took a long time and a lot of work, but I got better.

I would never be okay with what Jake had done, and I would never stop being angry and sad about his missing out on the rest of his life—and mine, too. I knew there would still be bad grief periods, maybe for the rest of my life, and it was hard talking to my therapist, Ms. Wirihana, when there were some things I couldn't tell her without probably getting mistakenly labeled as delusional. But the pain was less overwhelming, and I was getting better at other things. I still planned for possibilities, but it was easier to recognize the planning as part of the anxiety and not being about real things that might really happen.

And I survived being outed. I managed to tell Mum and Dad after Sione went home, before they could hear it from anyone else. Janna sat beside me on the couch, giving me the support that Jake couldn't.

Mum cried. Dad went quiet.

Then they both hugged me and told me how much they loved me and that they would never stop. It wasn't quite an endorsement of being gay, but it was support for being me.

Not everyone was that okay with it.

One of my dad's sisters is in a church that hates queer people. Her little daughters aren't allowed to play with me anymore, and she says she's praying for me. Imagine being *her* gay daughter. Dad stopped talking to her for three months, until I told him I didn't want him to lose more family. Nanny Hinekura knows I'm gay, but she won't talk about it — around her, we're all just supposed to pretend it's not there.

I caught some minor shit at school, but Mum and Dad were on top of that, too. I don't know what the principal said to everyone while I was away, but it must have been effective. The rugby team closed ranks around me, though some of the girls got changed in the bathrooms now instead of the locker rooms. I tried not to let that bother me; it was their problem, not mine. A few people whispered behind my back, and since Janna and I were friends again, they whispered about her, too. A couple of teachers looked at me funny, and hardly anyone seemed able to stop saying, "That's so *gay*." None of that was good, especially when I was already depressed, but it could have been much worse. Most of the time, I could cope.

Besides, in Summerton, people had other things to worry about.

People lost jobs, people I knew and liked. And Sandra-Claire, too; I don't really hate her anymore, but we're never going to be friends. She moved to Nelson, and Mum said she's training as a hairdresser; I reckon she'll be good at that, after all the crap she's done to her own hair.

The schools got an inspection they hadn't had for ten years, and the number of students didn't match the amount of resources given out. One of the primary schools is going to close, and the one that's left is going to merge with the high school. The hospital was downgraded, in line with reforms that should have taken place half a decade ago. These were all normal misfortunes that hit isolated country towns all the time, but they seemed more tragic in contrast to Summerton's good luck, which we'd all taken for granted for so long.

A lot of people moved out of Summerton over the past year, including Janna's mum, who lost her job at the hospital. She went to Christchurch in August. Janna and her sisters went with her.

I was sorry for everyone affected, and really sorry Janna had to leave, but I couldn't be sorry about the real reason why. I had plenty of happy memories of Summerton in its glory days, but they were all tainted, overlaid with the knowledge of who had paid for its success. Let it become a normal West Coast town, as ordinary and beautiful as any other.

I'll tell you something else, though: The tourists still came this summer. Not nearly as many as usual, and they weren't so keen on the fancy hotels, which worries Mum, but they came. And people are moving *into* town, too—outsiders who want to make a life here, people who are here to stay. What Daisy and that lot did was a stupid waste in so many ways. I don't think the town will die. I don't think it was ever going to.

But if it does, that's ordinary and natural, too.

I am really keen on *natural*.

◢

It took months before Sione and Janna and I were all together again. It was Valentine's Day of the year after, and we were all getting damp. The rain was the sort of warm mizzle that slicked down my hair and turned Sione's into a fuzzy halo lit up with tiny droplets. We wandered down the Summerton beach, poking at the sodden remnants of the New Year's Eve bonfires.

No Beach Bash this year. People made their own entertainment.

Aroha was with us. Takeshi wasn't. I thought you probably couldn't get her off Sione with a crowbar, and he wouldn't let anyone try. They were really cute, in a sickening way. Even Mrs. Felise approved, though that might just have been relief that it wasn't Janna.

Sione was the first to break the silence. He'd grown a lot, and not just in his suddenly lanky body. He was a church youth group leader now, and Aroha said the younger kids adored him.

"I had another dream about the fire," he said.

Aroha squeezed his hand.

"I wish we could have saved more of them," he said.

"I don't," I said. I knew I probably should.

"I remember the sound of the flames," Janna said. "Like a truck going past on the highway, only it went on and on."

"And the smoke," Aroha said. "I washed my hair three times to get the smell out."

I didn't want to talk about the fire. It was dead and done, and the murdered boys were set free. And we had lives, to make as bright as we dared.

"How's Takeshi?" I asked.

Aroha stole a glance at Janna, who was looking deliberately unconcerned. "He's okay," Aroha said. "He thinks he's got a good chance of getting into the University of Tokyo, or maybe Waseda."

"That's good?"

"That's pretty much the best." She hesitated. "He doesn't talk about what happened. I think he's convinced himself it turned out the way the official version said. A lot of noise and confusion."

"He has," Janna said, sounding a bit sad. But not very. I didn't think she was cut out for long-distance relationships anyway. "Still. I bet he makes it into space."

"Me, too," Sione said, but not as if he were paying that much attention. He was digging a scar into the wet sand with his foot, and Aroha was watching him and frowning, obviously aware of what was coming next. "Um. You remember Tarquin?"

After a second, I did. Hard name to forget. "The guy in your therapy group? His brother was one of the victims, right?"

Sione kept his feet on the ground. "Yeah. So. I told him about it. About the magic. And that most of them died, the people who killed his brother. I thought he'd want to know."

I took a panicked breath, ready to yell. We'd all agreed that no one could ever know, that no one would ever believe us, that they'd think we were sick kids playing a sick joke on families who had already suffered too much. And if I was really unlucky, they wouldn't think I was lying. Instead they'd call me crazy, prescribe me antipsychotics, get me committed—Janna's hand clamped down on my arm, and I took a deep breath, forcing calmness back into my body, using the techniques Ms. Wirihana had taught me to slow down the dizzying swirl of dire predictions.

"How'd that go?" Janna asked calmly, and Sione managed to meet her eyes.

"Not that great," he said. "I think...I think I made it worse. He didn't believe me—why should he? I don't have any proof. But I made him doubt, and he hates that. You were right."

"I don't know about that," Janna said, and I hitched in another breath, this one of surprise. "I think...if people can handle it, they have a right to know. I've been wondering. We've still got all those contact details. Maybe we should do some more work, check out the families, find out who could accept the truth."

"Who's going to decide that?" Aroha asked. "Us?"

"Who else is there?" Janna said.

"There's Rafferty," Sione said. "I know you guys hate him.

But I don't, not really. He didn't know, and when he did, he tried. I could find him. He could explain; more people would believe him than us."

"No," I said, unable to believe we were even talking about this. "Just...no. No way."

"We should make sure he knows not to talk to them if it would make the families feel worse," Janna said slowly, hand still on my sleeve. "I can't tell my parents—it's been too long, and they don't believe in magic. But we can't keep it from the families if there's good reason to tell, either. None of those boys left a note. No one who loved them knows why they died. Wasn't that the worst thing, for us?"

She let go of my arm just before I would have yanked it free, and I turned away from their silence, walking a few steps toward the gray sea. The wash of waves onshore felt like the churning in my gut. I stared at it for a long time, thinking about Jake, about Matthew and Schuyler, about Sergeant Rafferty, who had tried, too late, to do the right thing.

"Yeah," I said at last. "Not knowing is the worst. Let's... let's see, okay?"

"Okay," Janna and Sione said in unison. I could feel them at my back and knew that they wouldn't move on this until I was ready. Friends were good like that—they could make you do hard, necessary things and support you while you did them.

The silence stretched, and I hunted down another conversation topic before turning to face them, casually beginning to walk again. "Janna, did you hear that Patrick Tan's moving to Christchurch for uni?"

Janna fell into step beside me. "Yeah, he sent me an e-mail. It said, 'I'm coming to your city, you treacherous bitch.'"

"Nice," Sione said, raising an eyebrow.

"Oh, that's a lot nicer than some of the stuff he said after the Bash," Janna said. "He'll probably forgive me in a decade or two. Anyway, he's giving me a ride back to Christchurch tonight. We're talking about finding a drummer and another guitarist. Maybe putting Vikings back together."

"Anything else getting back together?" I tested.

"Ha bloody ha," she said, but I noted the secret tilt of her smile and stored it away so that I could say "I told you so" later. "How's *your* love life?"

There was a girl who waited in the therapist's office for the appointment after the one after mine who had a rainbow-flag badge stitched onto her bag. So far, I knew her name was Marama, that she was a swimmer, that her parents were divorcing and thought she needed therapy to adjust, and that she had the most gorgeous dark brown eyes I'd ever seen. She'd promised to e-mail me. "Nonexistent," I said, and hoped the water in the air would cool my heated cheeks. The rain obligingly picked up, turning from drizzle to a warm downpour. "Let's go back."

"Race you," Sione offered, and ran, stretching his long legs. I think he let me beat him, but I'll take victory where I can find it. I skidded through the front gate a body's length ahead of him, laughing, and almost crashed into my mother.

She looked at me like I was the sun coming up, her eyes misting over.

"Oh, Mum," I said, and hugged her. "I'm going to miss you so much."

"I was just coming down to get you," she said, and squeezed back. "The Felises want to get away before dark. Now, if you forgot anything, just give me a ring, okay?"

"I will."

"Auckland's so far away." Mum sighed. "Keri, are you *sure*?"

I was sure. Sione was going to the University of Auckland, too, where he'd study Statistics. Aroha had a year of high school left, but she was planning on applying to the School of Engineering. I wanted people around me who knew the truth of what had happened.

The advantages of boarding with the Felises instead of staying in an Auckland uni dorm were many. For one, my parents were much happier about my staying with one of New Zealand's best psychotherapists while I did my first year in Physical Education. For another, I could take much more of my own stuff up.

The disadvantages included having to *pack* all my own stuff, but I'd managed it. The hospital staff had cut my favorite jeans off me when they patched me up; those were truly gone now. But I'd kept the last T-shirt I'd given Jake, the one that had tripped me and broken my arm—the one that had ultimately given me the weapon that had won us victory. It was tucked into the bottom of one bag.

I still couldn't agree that Jake was in a better place. But now I could believe that as long as I lived to remember him, he would be with me.

I looked at the street and the people standing there. Dad

and Mr. Felise were shaking hands in farewell, while Sione's mother asked Aroha something and laughed at her reply. Janna and Sione were loading the last of my boxes into the Felises' massive SUV, bickering over whose city would be the site of our next meeting.

How had my family's getting smaller led to its getting so much bigger?

"I'm sure, Mum," I said, and hugged her again, squeezing extra hard with my twice-broken arm.

I didn't know what my future would hold.

I was ready for it.

Letter to the Reader

Hi,

I'm Karen Healey, the author of the book you've just read. Thank you! I appreciate it, and I appreciate you, and I want to say something really important.

If you feel suicidal or suspect that someone you know might harm himself or herself, please consider getting some help before making an irreversible decision.

In the United States, there are many great resources. The following are just a few.

- The National Suicide Prevention Lifeline
  (www.suicidepreventionlifeline.org)
  1-800-273-TALK (1-800-273-8255)

A free, 24-hour nationwide hotline for anyone who is emotionally distressed or suicidal, or who is concerned about someone else

- The Trevor Project
  (www.thetrevorproject.org)
  1-866-4-U-TREVOR (1-866-488-7386)
  A free, 24-hour nationwide helpline for lesbian, gay, bisexual, transgender, or questioning (LGBTQ) youth

- The American Foundation for Suicide Prevention
  (www.afsp.org)
  Lots and lots of resources for suicide prevention through research, education, and advocacy

Actually, the sites of all three projects have lots of information about suicide and suicide prevention. I recommend them all.

There's also the It Gets Better Project (www.itgetsbetter .org). Prompted by a number of suicides of bullied gay and lesbian teens, this project is dedicated to demonstrating to kids in danger that life gets better, and that the future can be wonderful. Although it's directed at LGBTQ youth (since they are, as a group, more in danger of suicide), the message here is important for anyone who's being bullied or mistreated and can't see the hope of a better tomorrow. It's possible. I promise.

Please look after yourself, and those around you.

Sincerely,
Karen

Glossary

New Zealand has three official languages: English, Māori, and New Zealand Sign Language. Māori is a language for study as a first or second language at many schools and tertiary institutions, but a number of Māori words are commonly understood and are not unusual for even nonspeakers to use in everyday circumstances. Samoan, Cantonese, and Mandarin are the next most common languages.

Māori:

Cape Reinga: The tip of the Aupouri Peninsula, in the far north of the North Island. The traditional spot for spirits of the dead to enter the afterlife.

Kāi Tahu (also Ngāi Tahu): The principal South Island tribe.

Karakia: A sacred chant or prayer.

Koha: A gift, often of money. Mourners at tangi commonly give koha to the immediate family of the dead in order to help cover tangi expenses.

Marae: A meeting place, central to community life and identity. Various protocols surround the proper use of the marae complex.

Mokopuna: Grandchild or grandchildren.

Pākehā: Usually refers to New Zealanders of predominantly white European ancestry. Also sometimes used to refer to non-Māori of any ethnicity.

Tangi (also tangihanga): A grieving method somewhat analogous to the Western funeral. Various tribes have different protocols and ceremonies. Typically, tangi take place over several days, from the person's death until after the burial. Traditionally, they took place in marae, but they are now also common in private homes and funeral parlors.

Wharenui: A meeting house, the central building of the marae complex.

Samoan:

Ie faitaga: Formal wear for men—a long, wraparound skirt with pockets, usually made of a dark suit material.

Lavalava: A more casual wraparound, worn by men and women. Usually made of lighter, more colorful material. Keri misidentifies Sione's ie faitaga as lavalava.

Palagi: Non-Samoan, especially people of primarily white European ancestry.

Fia palagi: A negative term applied to a Samoan who is seen to be favoring a foreign lifestyle, abandoning the Samoan way.

Tofa: Good-bye.

Tofa soifua: Good-bye—a more respectful term, usually used in addressing elders.

Acknowledgments

I want to thank all my first readers and advisers for their able assistance. In particular, Lauana, Willow, and Erica were helpful on ethnicity and cultural matters; Gina was helpful on rugby matters; Erinna was helpful on magical matters; Matt was helpful on musical matters; and Robyn was helpful on mental-health matters. My mother and sister drove me along the West Coast so I could remind myself how gorgeous it was, and Carla overhauled Keri's entire character with one question. All remaining errors are mine alone.

I remain eternally grateful to my lovely agent, Barry Goldblatt, and to the excellent editors, publicists, and designers on both sides of the Pacific: Susannah Chambers, Alvina Ling, Eva Mills, Connie Hsu, Bethany Strout, Christine Ma, Emmeline Goodchild, Ames O'Neill, Abba Renshaw, Bruno Herfst, and Ben Mautner.

A number of more experienced and extremely awesome fellow YA authors gave me great advice on the advent of my first novel and beyond. I am especially indebted to Lili Wilkinson, Sarah Rees Brennan, Penni Russon, and Justine Larbalestier for explanations and encouragement and to Scott Westerfeld for the gin and tonics.

Thanks to the Karen Healey Support Club, who gave up many an hour listening to me babble about my work: Belinda, Claire, Emily, Mary, Deborah, Tessa, and Foz (Melbourne division); Jeff and Matt (Christchurch division); Jameson and Kristen (North American division); and the wonderful ladies in the Interrobangers writing group.

Finally, my thanks go to Dave the osteopath and Melinda the myotherapist, who made it physically possible for me to write, and probably thought I was joking about putting them in the acknowledgments.

Reading Group Guide

1. Keri prided herself on always being prepared for the worst, but she never expected her brother to kill himself. How does she respond to the tragedy? How do her parents? Why would Keri prefer to believe that he was murdered?

2. Take a closer look at the structure of the book. Each chapter is told from the perspective of one of the three main characters, but only Keri's chapters are written in the first person. Why do you think the author chose this approach? How does it affect your understanding of Keri?

3. Do clothes really make the man (or woman)? Why are Keri's old jeans so important to her? What do Janna's outfits say about her personality? Why do fine clothes matter to Sione? What did Sione's older brother think of his interest in fashion?

4. Set in the multiethnic country of New Zealand, the novel features characters of Māori, European, Japanese, and Samoan ancestry. How does each of the main characters observe the distinctive traditions of his or her ethnic

group? What common traditions do they all share as twenty-first-century teens?

5. What is the Summerton Effect? How does it influence the population of the town? What makes Summerton different from its neighbors? Is the town really a paradise? What happens once the effect ends?

6. Janna decides (p. 117), "Ritual worked, if you did it right; putting will into the world, calling on deities or just the energy of the universe got results." How does the novel illustrate her point? Do you agree that rituals can alter the course of events? Why or why not?

7. When Keri and Sione sneak into Sergeant Rafferty's home, what are they looking for? What do they find instead? What do Rafferty's possessions reveal about his character? Are his later actions surprising? Why or why not?

8. Janna is a member of a band. Why does she think of her band mates as family? Why does she abandon them just before their most important gig? What might have happened if she had kept her commitment?

9. Who were the people responsible for the Summerton Effect? What were their individual motivations? What held them together as a group? What pulled them apart?

10. What secret about herself is Keri trying to keep? Why was she afraid to be completely honest? How do friends and family respond once they know the truth?

11. *"This is what evil looks like.... Ordinary people doing terrible things."* Whom is Janna referring to here (page 263)? What terrible things were these people doing? Do you think ordinary people are capable of evil?

12. How did Daisy's coven select its victims? What part of the country did the boys come from? What kind of families did they have? Was Daisy telling her circle the truth about the emotional stability of their victims? What could be her motive for lying?

13. What does Keri ultimately discover about her brother's death? What makes the truth so painful?

14. "How had my family's getting smaller led to its getting so much bigger?" Keri asks herself at the very end of the novel (page 305). What does she mean by this? Do you agree?

Don't miss the new novel from

KAREN HEALEY

Coming in March 2013

CHAPTER ONE
Yesterday

My name is Tegan Oglietti. One of my ancestors was a highway-man, and another was a prince. Two were Olympic medalists, three were journalists, half a dozen were chefs, a whole bunch were soldiers, and a lot were housewives who didn't get a quarter of the credit they deserved.

I've been thinking about inheritance a lot lately, about what we make, about what makes us, about the legacies we give those who come after us. Well, I would, wouldn't I?

We all begin with our past.

That last day, I was running late for the train, and I almost didn't stop to say good-bye. But Mum called me into the kitchen, where she was working on an experiment for her little restaurant.

"Ricotta and beef ravioli," she said, waving a laden fork at me. "Open your mouth."

I did. The pasta was light and silky, and although I prefer

cheeses with more flavor, I had to admit the ricotta added something to the texture.

"Good?" said Mum, quick dark eyes moving over my face.

"Good," I said through my mouthful. "Contributing to global destruction with the production of heat-trapping methane gases, but really very tasty. Tasty destruction! Now can I go?"

"Mm," she said, eyeing the liqueur bottles lined up beside the microwave. With any luck, I'd be coming home to a spectacular dessert. "Oh, wait." She hooked an arm around my neck and hauled me back, kissing my cheek. She smelled like herbs and flour, the warm smell that meant home. "There. Now you can go and save the world."

I laughed, kissed my fingers to the photo of Dad hanging on the kitchen wall, and ran out the door, rubbing the pink lip gloss off my face. Alex would be waiting, and she would want the complete goss report before we met Dalmar at the station.

Smart, intense Dalmar, who cared about the environment and domestic violence and famine. Handsome, talented Dalmar, whose skin was smooth and dark, whose eyes were round and a deep, rich brown, like new-turned soil. Perfect, perfect Dalmar, who'd been my brother's best friend for eighteen years, and my boyfriend for one day. The climate-change protest was going to be our official first date, and I was already planning our wedding.

My name is Tegan Oglietti, and on the last day of my first lifetime, I was so, so happy.

≈ ‡ ∞

I'll tell you the whole story.

You might wonder why I bother; you already know the facts. But one thing I've learned over the past months—maybe even before—is that facts aren't enough. It's not enough to know; you have to *believe*. It has to be personal. So here I am, giving you my memories and my feelings and my words. My soul, if you like. It's the only thing that still belongs to me, and there were some times, bad times, that I doubted even that.

But I know the Father was wrong. No one can take your soul from you. You have to give it away.

Here's my soul. I'm giving it to you.

I hope you're listening.

≋ ‡ ∞

Alex opened the door before I could knock, her grin wide on her narrow face. She was wearing what she called her protest uniform—long red peasant skirt, leggings, heavy boots, and a bright shirt under a sleeveless vest covered with buttons. STRAIGHT NOT NARROW. WOMEN AGAINST WAR. RIGHT IS MIGHT. UP THE UNIONS. I could see placards with more meticulously lettered slogans leaning against the wall and tried not to grimace. Those things were heavy, and I'd been hoping not to lug one around all day. But for once, Alex had concerns other than saving humanity from itself.

"I got your text," she said. "Tell me everything, from the beginning."

"Fourteen billion years ago, the universe expanded," I said, jumping out of Alex's reach. She'd stopped boxing, but she still had a mean right hook, even when it was just for fun. "Okay. Okay. He came around to my place yesterday, and I said, 'Owen already left for Tasmania,' and he said, 'I know. I want to talk to you.'"

"Oh my god, Teeg," Alex breathed. "We're running late, but tell me as we go."

Alex swung her battered satchel over her head. I knew from experience that the bag might contain anything from a couple of muesli bars and a bottle of water to fireworks, a complete set of lock picks, and a collapsible crowbar. She picked up two of the signs and thrust them at me, shouldering the rest herself.

"Do I have to?"

"Yes, lazy," she said, and called a cheerful good-bye to her foster mother.

"It's just that it's so freaking hot."

I already had heat rash, prickly red bumps on the backs of my knees, and it was only September. Mum said that when she was my age, Melbourne's spring had been long and wet and cool, hitting the nineties only in November or even December. The superstorms and bushfires hadn't been so bad, either.

But it was 2027, and things were getting worse—which is why Alex and Dalmar were so keen on this protest. I mean, they were always up for a march or promoting a petition from a stall on Swanston Street, but this time the Prime Minister was attending the rally. I didn't think she'd actually do anything about the climate, but it was an election year, the youth vote was up for grabs, and Dalmar had some cautious hopes.

He had a lot of hope, Dalmar. I think that's why I fell in love with him. It was all those conversations in the garage, where, between practices, he tried to get Owen involved. In anything, really.

"We're going to inherit the world, and everything needs to change," he'd said. "Adults don't care, so we have to make them care, or replace them."

Owen called him obsessed, which was pretty hilarious because Owen was the single most obsessed person I knew. His whole life revolved around music, usually to the exclusion of minor things like environmental collapse, or the horrific state of refugee camps in the Horn of Africa, or his little sister. I started playing the guitar to spend more time with Owen, but I ended up listening to Dalmar. I learned to care.

To be honest, I cared more about Dalmar than things like climate change. One was right there, in the extremely awesome flesh, and the other was slow and terrible and felt far away. I cared, but not like Dalmar and Alex did. Still, it's not like I betrayed myself and my own ideas to get closer to a beautiful boy. I just couldn't resist his hope.

"So he said, 'I want to talk to you,' and *you* said..." Alex prompted.

"And *I* said, 'Oh, really?' like a total idiot."

"Hah!"

"But it doesn't matter, because then he took my hand—"

"Oh my god."

"—and said, 'Tegan, I've been thinking about you a lot, and if you say no, I will understand, and it won't ruin our friendship, but would you like to go out with me?'"

Alex stopped in the street. "Seriously?"

I grinned. "Just like that." Every word he'd said was written on my brain in blazing letters of gold.

"And then what?" she demanded.

"Classified." My whole body was buzzing with the memory.

"Teeg, I will kill you and sink the corpse in the river."

I snorted. "What river?" The Yarra ran through the city, but you couldn't hide a body in that shallow brown flow.

"I will dig a river and fill it with my tears, because I will be weeping from the betrayal of my best friend not giving me every damn detail!"

"We kissed," I said. "Well, I kissed him, and he kissed me back. In the front hallway."

"Oh wow. That is the best."

"Then Mum walked in and said, 'Oops,' and walked back out, and Dalmar said sorry and I said sorry at the same time, and then we went up to my room, and seriously after that is classified."

Alex pursed her lips and nodded. "Acceptable."

"He said I was beautiful," I said softly. I could feel a tingle in my lips, the ghost of Dalmar's kisses. We hadn't done much, just held each other and talked and laughed. The talking and laughing we'd done for years, but after so much waiting, the touch was all new, and it was like a drug, making me giddy and calm at the same time. I didn't want to pick apart something so special with Alex, much as I loved her. Let it be just for us, Dalmar and me.

"You *are* beautiful," Alex said. "I wish I had your boobs."

"You want my backaches?"

"Well, maybe not," she conceded. "Or your red nose."

"I burn so fast," I sighed, and scowled at the tip of said red peeling nose. Dalmar had kissed that spot last night, I remembered, and the frown smoothed out.

"Haaah, look at you. You're so in love!" Alex spun around in the street, signs and all, wide skirt flaring up around her hips. "You and me and Dalmar and Jonno have to do something. A couples dinner. Couples bowling!"

"Um," I said. I didn't like Alex's boyfriend that much. He was one of those pretentious guys who thought conversation was all about being smarter and more important than everyone else in the room. And he talked down to me all the time, just because I was the youngest. But Alex thought Jonno was hotter than summer at the beach, and I had to be supportive. "Can I keep Dalmar to myself for a bit?"

"Of course, yeah. Want me to get lost at the rally?"

I hesitated. I really did, but... "I don't want to be that girl, you know?"

"Please, I know you'd never abandon me for a guy. I'm offering! We go together; I conveniently get lost in the crowd; oh no, where is Alex? Gosh, it's just you and Dalmar, holding hands.... You can make out all you want."

"Gross," I said. "In public?"

"Whatever, lovebird. But tonight, you and me are still up for some exploring, right?"

"Right."

So the satchel was holding the lock picks and the collapsible crowbar, and probably a couple of flashlights, too. Alex's version of exploring meant breaking into abandoned buildings, underground tunnels, and the occasional construction site, ferreting out the secrets of the city. It was a great way to spend a few hours, and not something I thought my mother ever needed to know about.

It was nearly midday, and we were flagging in the heat. Like most 2027 Australians who weren't sun-loving beach bunnies, we tried to avoid the outdoors between eleven and three in the hotter months, when it seemed as if the sun was maliciously beaming right through the hole in the ozone layer and setting us aflame. I was slathered in a thick layer of SPF 70 sunscreen and wearing dark sunnies and a big floppy hat, and with all that, I knew my nose would still be redder by the end of the afternoon.

But the Prime Minister was meeting the petitioners on the steps of Parliament House at noon, so our sun-shunning habits had to adjust to her schedule.

My pocket beeped. My heart jumped.

"Dalmaaaaaaaar," Alex cooed.

"If you do that when he's here," I warned, and fished out my phone. She was right, of course; the message was from him.

TRAIN DELAYED, TEN MINS LATE XXX

It was a perfectly ordinary message that he could have sent the day before yesterday, or any time in the three years we'd been friends instead of my big brother's preachy best friend/ best friend's annoying little sister.

Except for that postscript of kisses.

For once, the flush in my cheeks owed nothing to the sun. I ducked my head under my hat and silently thanked Alex for her mercy as she pretended not to notice a thing.

Not that it mattered. When Dalmar stepped off the train and met us on the platform, I think the whole world could have seen how I felt. But for me, the rest of the world wasn't there. Just Dalmar, with his easy stride and wide smile.

I know Alex was talking, but I can't remember a word. I've tried, I really have, but it's all just buzzing.

He leaned into me, and we touched fingertips. It was a game we'd come up with the night before, finding how little we could touch and still be in contact. We were seeing who could hold out longer, but eventually he gave in and held my hand. He had bass-player calluses. He'd built them up fingering those thick strings, and now they were rough, stroking down the side of my little finger. Nothing in the world had ever felt that good.

"I missed you," he said, relieving me of the placards.

"I missed you, too," I replied, and leaned my head against his free shoulder.

A narrow hand landed in the small of my back and shoved. It was Alex, her other hand on Dalmar's back. "We've got to catch a train, lovebirds," she grunted. "Next platform, move move move."

Dalmar laughed. "You should be a general, Alex."

"No way, man. Make love, not war." She darted up the escalators before us, multicolored curls bouncing on her shoulders.

We made it to the platform in time to catch the train to Parliament Station. The car was full of people dressed in Earth Punk fusion; I felt completely underdressed and sweaty in my shorts jumpsuit with a nonmatching long-sleeved cotton bolero thrown on at the last second to try to stop my arms from burning. Dalmar, with his orange safety vest catching the lights in the car, and Alex, with the badges on her protest uniform, fit right in. The train car was loud with debate.

I caught a glimpse of the golden statue of the goddess Mazu, who watched over the shallow remnants of the Maribyrnong River that dribbled by the Buddhist temple. She might bring us good luck today. Mazu was the protector of the sea, after all, and rising oceans were probably one of her concerns.

But I wasn't Buddhist. Instead, I silently asked the Virgin Mary, Star of the Sea, to intercede on our behalf.

Prayer concluded, I let the train's motion sway me against Dalmar where he stood braced against the yellow pole. "I wrote you a song," I whispered in his ear, resisting the urge to kiss his earlobe.

"Really?" He slipped his hand from mine and draped it over my shoulder, pulling me close.

"I'll play it for you tonight," I promised. "Just so you know, nothing good rhymes with *Dalmar*."

"Far. Car. Tar. Star. Bizarre?"

"Help!" I sang, making up the lyrics as I went along. "I need

Dalmar. Help! He's so bizarre. Help, you know I need Dalmaaaar. Help!"

"You and your Beatles," Alex said.

"Best musicians of their century," I said, as I had many times before. "And ours. And all the centuries to come."

"Let's make sure the species *has* centuries to come," Dalmar said.

As the train jerked to a stop, we stepped out together, into the future.

≈ ‡ ∞

I don't remember if it hurt.

There are questions I get asked a lot, in therapy, at school, and even at the compound, when the girls loosened up enough to talk to me. *What do you remember? What did you see? How did it feel?*

I'll tell you the whole story. Even the embarrassing parts, even the bits where I behave like an enormous loser.

But I can't tell you if there was any pain.

The truth is, it all stops with us pouring out of Parliament Station and up the steep steps, with Dalmar's arm around my shoulders and Alex grinning at how cozy we were together. I was thinking of finding a quiet place to kiss Dalmar, and wondering whether Alex could be talked into letting me do some free-running practice before we broke into whatever abandoned hulk she wanted to explore. I was thinking about whether Owen might bring me something back from Tasmania, and if Mum might be whipping up my favorite raspberry maca-rons, and if Dad would be proud of what I was doing today.

And then it all stops. The final memory of my first life is a freeze-frame of me leaning against Dalmar on the way up the steps.

But when Marie thought I was ready, I saw the same footage everyone else did.

It's awful phone video, not even a real camera. Nothing like the superclear footage you guys have of everything now. But you can still make it out easily enough if you know what to look for.

There's the Prime Minister in a blue skirt suit standing under a shady canopy, speaking to the protesters, saying pretty things that aren't quite promises. There's the dark-haired girl high on the steps, just visible in the corner of the screen. There she is, falling down. There are screams as the crowd starts to realize what's happened, and someone shouts, "It's a sniper!" and then the camera turns to the sidewalk as the unknown vid-eographer runs away.

Memory loss is a perfectly normal trauma reaction, Marie says, but it still feels weird. Watching that footage doesn't spark a thing. It could be a perfect stranger dying on the steps of Par-liament House.

But it was me.

I woke up one hundred years later.

And then things really went to hell.